alone,
together

Other Books by Jack Weyland

alone,
together

Jack Weyland

DESERET
BOOK

SALT LAKE CITY, UTAH

This is a work of fiction. Characters described in this book are the products of the author's imagination or are represented fictitiously.

Library of Congress Cataloging-in-Publication Data

Weyland, Jack, 1940-
  Alone, together / Jack Weyland.
    p.   cm.
  ISBN-10 1-59038-575-6 (pbk.)
  ISBN-13 978-1-59038-575-3 (pbk.)
  1. Mormon missionaries—Fiction. I. Title.
  PS3573.E99A79 2006
  813'.54—dc22   2006001647

Printed in the United States of America
Publishers Printing, Salt Lake City, Utah

10   9   8   7   6   5   4   3   2   1

*To all the young men and women of the Church
who strive to follow the guidelines, principles, and
standards the Lord has provided, even if at times
you may feel isolated and alone*

chapter
one

"Elder Baxter, you know Sister Forsgren, don't you?" Sister Richardson, the mission president's wife, asked.

"Yes, of course! Good to see you again, Sister Forsgren," he said, shaking her hand. He was surprised how firm her handshake was. He also couldn't help noticing her smile. She had the whitest teeth he had ever seen.

He turned to face Sister Richardson. "Sister Forsgren and I served in the same zone for awhile, and I followed her into Wilkes-Barre. The whole time I was there, the members kept telling me how much they missed the sisters and what a great missionary Sister Forsgren was." He grinned. "She was a hard act to follow."

Sister Forsgren smiled. "Wherever I've served, our district leaders always told us we should all try to be more like Elder Baxter."

Elder Josh Baxter stood six-foot-three while Sister Forsgren appeared to be nearly six feet. He had dark brown hair and a dark complexion. Her hair was medium brown, and she had green eyes that fascinated him. He didn't appreciate this sudden awareness of her physical appearance showing up while he was still on his mission. He had prided himself on keeping mission rules, and he was determined to tough it out to the end.

"Any success I've had came from Father in Heaven. He deserves all the credit, not me," he said.

"That's true for all of us," Sister Forsgren said, smiling warmly at him.

Elder Josh Baxter and Sister Madison Forsgren were part of a group of six missionaries who would be flying home the next day. They had each been interviewed by President Richardson, enjoyed an elegant dinner, and had participated together in a testimony meeting.

And now, just after nine o'clock, as the group of two sisters and four elders sat with President and Sister Richardson in the living room of the mission home, all of them avoided talking about going home. The missionaries were painfully aware how much they would miss the people they'd taught and the other missionaries they'd worked with. That's what they were doing, sharing experiences and reminiscing.

After a while, President Richardson excused himself to make some phone calls. A short time later he came and asked for Sister Richardson's assistance.

Elder Baxter was sitting on a chair next to the couch where Sister Forsgren was seated.

"I wonder how long President Richardson will be," she said, glancing at her watch.

"From the look on his face when he came in here to get Sister Richardson, I'd say it might be a long time."

"I was going to ask him for a priesthood blessing," she said.

"Well, even if this does take a long time, I know he'd be happy to give you one whenever he can, no matter how late it is."

"I hope he isn't too long. I'm ready to get some sleep." She looked away, thinking, then turned to him. "What would you think about giving me a priesthood blessing, Elder Baxter?"

The request took him by surprise. "Uh, sure," he said, then added, "I'd be happy to."

"Let me go ask Sister Richardson where we might do it."

"Okay," he said.

As she stood up and walked past him to the door, a thought came into his mind, *She's actually good looking,* but he quickly put it out of his mind. Elders weren't supposed to think of the sister missionaries in that way.

Sister Forsgren returned a short time later.

"Sister Richardson suggested we do the blessing in the dining room."

Josh turned to Elder Nally. "Will you help, Elder?"

A short time later Josh and Elder Nally stood behind the chair that Sister Forsgren had just sat down on.

"Before we start, we should have a prayer," Josh said. "Sister Forsgren, would you offer it?"

"Of course."

In her prayer, she thanked Heavenly Father for the experience of serving a mission and then prayed for an understanding of what she should do with her life after she returned home.

Then Josh leaned forward. "What's your full name?" he asked.

"Madison Elaine Forsgren," she said, and Josh and Elder Nally laid their hands lightly on her head. Her long hair was soft, and in order not to mash it down, Josh placed his hands more on the sides of her head than on top. But Elder Nally put his right on top.

Before he began, Josh paused briefly, saying a silent prayer for help.

During his mission, he had given many priesthood blessings, especially over the past few months, while serving as an assistant to President Richardson. He had learned the importance of listening to promptings of the Spirit. Often he had been surprised at what he said in the blessings he gave.

Perhaps it was because this was the last night of his mission, or because of the inspiring message they had heard from President Richardson that night at dinner, or maybe the testimonies that had been given by the missionaries who were about to leave the mission field but, for whatever reason, Josh strongly felt the Spirit as he began to give Sister Forsgren a blessing.

"Your Father in Heaven accepts the sacrifice you and your family have made for you to serve a mission. He appreciates your dedication to

Him and the love you have shown to all you have met and testified to and taught."

He paused. "As you go home, He will help you know the path you should take in your life."

A sudden impression came to him, spoken in a voice that only his mind could hear: *This is the girl you will marry.*

He felt embarrassed. He offered a silent prayer that Heavenly Father would help him be more in tune with the Spirit.

He felt prompted to say: *Don't worry about who you are going to marry. Even though there are few members of the Church where you live, Heavenly Father will soon make that person known to you.*

He found himself in an argument with some unseen person. *I can't say that,* he thought.

Just say it!

No, I'm not going to say it!

It will help her.

I don't care if it helps her or not! I'm not going to say that to a sister missionary.

He could feel Sister Forsgren move her head a tiny bit. He imagined she might be wondering why he hadn't said anything for a long time.

Say something! the unseen individual said.

Josh blurted out, "Heavenly Father will help you throughout your life, even in regard to employment and . . . uh . . . other things."

He felt his face turning red. He felt ashamed that he might be turning a priesthood blessing into an opportunity to get himself a wife, so he ended the blessing.

She stood up, turned to him, and with something of a puzzled look on her face, shook his hand.

"Thanks."

He was blushing. "Sorry," he said.

"No, it was very helpful." She looked at her watch. "Well, it's late. I'll see you in the morning."

"Yes, of course." He quickly shook her hand again but couldn't look her in the eye.

He couldn't go to sleep, replaying over and over in his mind what had happened during the blessing. He had spent the past two years disciplining himself to listen to the promptings of the Spirit, but now he felt betrayed. What had gone wrong that this random thought would come into his head during a time like that?

He kept going back in his mind, trying to remember everything that had happened since he and his companion had arrived at the mission home.

Was I staring at her during dinner? No, I wasn't. Not at all. Well, maybe a little. This is crazy. Flirting with a sister missionary is not who I am and is not how I've served my mission. How did this happen?

The only comforting thought was that Sister Forsgren had no idea of what had taken place. He promised himself he would never tell her. *All I've got to do is stay away from her tomorrow. We'll part ways, and this will be over and done with. I'm still a good missionary.*

Finally, around one o'clock, he was able to fall asleep.

At six-thirty the next morning, he woke up, showered, and got dressed, and went downstairs. He could hear someone in the kitchen and went in.

He found Sister Richardson there, already preparing breakfast.

"Good morning, Elder Baxter! How did you sleep?"

He didn't want to talk about it. "Good. And you?"

"Just fine."

She was spooning frozen orange juice concentrate into a glass pitcher. As she did so, she said, "We are really going to miss you, Elder Baxter. President Richardson has enjoyed working with you very much. He tells me he's never had a harder-working assistant."

That kind of talk embarrassed Josh. He'd taken pride in just doing his duty, without any thought of earning accolades. At least, that's what he always told himself. He had to admit, though, it was nice to hear the praise.

He didn't acknowledge the compliment, instead he asked, "Can I help?"

"Why, yes, thank you. How about if I put you in charge of toast?"

He smiled. "Right. Toast. I'm very good at toast."

She glanced at him.

"Should I start now?" he asked.

"I think you'd better. You know how the elders like to eat," she said. "Some of you need to get to the airport, and these eggs will be ready in just a minute.

Josh took the twist tie off a loaf of bread and dropped four pieces into the toaster.

As an assistant to the president, Josh had been around Sister Richardson a lot, and although she gave him several opportunities to talk this morning, he confined himself to yes and no answers.

"You seem a little preoccupied," she finally said.

He paused, wondering if he should say anything about what was worrying him. He felt close to Sister Richardson, but he didn't want anyone else to know. He glanced around, grateful none of the others had come into the kitchen yet. He cleared his throat. "Last night I gave Sister Forsgren a blessing."

"Yes, how did that go? President Richardson wanted to spend more time with everyone, but there was a very sticky situation that only he could address."

"Something happened while I was giving the blessing."

"What?"

He felt his face turning hot. "I had the feeling that . . ." He sighed. "And I know this is crazy . . ."

The toast popped up. "Oh, could you butter that, too?" Sister Richardson requested.

"Okay."

Because of his embarrassment at what he was about to say to Sister Richardson, he wasn't thinking and lathered a large quantity of butter onto one piece of toast.

"Not that much, actually," she said, smiling.

"Sorry."

"During the blessing, did you have a prompting?" she asked.

"Yes."

"Did you tell her what the prompting was?"

"No, I could never do that."

She seemed confused. "Isn't that what you're supposed to do?"

"Something went wrong. I must not have had the Spirit. I'm just not sure where it came from. I want you to know I haven't spent more than thirty seconds my entire mission thinking about Sister Forsgren."

"So this thought was about you and Sister Forsgren?"

"Yes." He sighed and lowered his voice. "I might as well tell you. I had the feeling that she's the one for me." He paused. "By that I mean that she's the girl I will marry some day."

"Oh, my! That must have been quite a surprise."

"I couldn't believe it. What was I thinking?"

"Maybe it came from Heavenly Father."

"No, that's not possible."

"Why not?"

"Because I'm still on a mission. There will be plenty of time to think about marriage after I'm home."

"And that will be in how many hours?"

He looked at his watch. "Eight."

"Elder Baxter, you've fulfilled a marvelous mission. If there is any thing you have been known for, it is that you follow mission rules, work hard, and rely on the Spirit."

"Right, and then this happens."

She smiled. "I'm not sure you should dismiss what you felt."

"What do you think I should do?"

"Well, the least you could do is try to see Sister Forsgren after your mission."

"She's from northern Minnesota. I'm from Wyoming."

She smiled. "I understand there are ways to get from Wyoming to Minnesota."

"She'd wonder what I was doing there."

"I'm sure she'd be happy to spend time with you."

He shook his head. "I've tried so hard to be a good missionary."

"Yes, you have, and so has she. Maybe this is Heavenly Father's gift to you both—for being so faithful."

"She asked me to give her a blessing because she respects me. If she knew what I'd been thinking, she would lose all respect for me."

"What if you were inspired?"

He paused. "Okay, maybe I should at least get her e-mail address and write her a couple of times."

"I definitely think you should do something. Would you mind if I told her?"

"You mean at breakfast with everyone listening in? I don't think so."

Sister Richardson laughed. "No, later, if I have a chance to be alone with her. I could even write her."

He nodded. "As long as I don't have to talk to her today." He paused. "And only if you think it would be appropriate. I haven't thought about girls for two years, so I feel a little ashamed to have thought about her that way last night."

She smiled. "Thinking about marriage is nothing to be ashamed of."

Just then, Sister Forsgren and her companion entered the kitchen, and Josh panicked, hoping she hadn't heard what Sister Richardson had said. He dropped the piece of toast he was buttering.

"Sorry, Sister Forsgren, I dropped your toast," he said.

She looked at him strangely. Her eyes were a bewitching shade of green, and he could smell the fragrance of her shampoo.

Once again he felt like an idiot. "Sorry. In my family that's an old joke."

She was still just staring at him.

He thought it was about the toast. "The joke is if you drop some food, you say it was, you know, like your sister's piece of toast."

She looked at him like he was a bug under a microscope. "I see."

He set aside the toast that had dropped. "Actually, this is my toa . . . toa . . . toa . . . toast."

Embarrassed for him, she quickly looked away.

Growing up, Josh had difficulties with stuttering. Especially in high-stress situations, such as talking to a large group. But on his mission, Heavenly Father had helped him overcome it.

But now he felt betrayed. *What is going on here?* he thought.

"Sorry," he said quietly.

"What for?" she asked. "You already took ownership of the toast you dropped, right? I mean, you are going to eat that piece, aren't you?"

He smiled. "Yes. Yes, I am."

"Then that's all I need to know."

He didn't trust himself to say much after that, even during breakfast while everyone else was telling about their families and who would be at the airport to pick them up.

Elder Nally told about a girl who had waited for him his whole mission, and how they had talked about getting married in a few months. Another elder told about his girl and their hopes.

"Do you have anyone waiting for you?" Sister Richardson asked Sister Forsgren.

"No."

Sister Richardson glanced at Josh and smiled.

"Could I have your e-mail address?" Josh asked.

"Sure. In fact, let's all do that. I hope we can all keep in touch through the years," Sister Forsgren said.

He made eye contact with her and then lowered his gaze to his plate again.

The less interaction I have with her the better it will be. This is crazy.

True to his resolve, he stayed away from Sister Forsgren. The last he saw of her was outside the terminal as the missionaries shook hands all around, grabbed their luggage, and scattered to their various airline ticket counters.

An hour later as he sat in his window seat in the plane and watched the farmland slipping past below him, he thought about what had happened, trying to figure out what it meant, if anything.

The guilt he had first felt seemed to be diminishing, but it was still a puzzle.

If this is from Heavenly Father, what is my responsibility? he thought. *I guess I would need to visit her, or at least phone her, or e-mail her. But what would I say?*

Why didn't Sister Richardson scold me after I told her what thoughts had come to mind when I gave Sister Forsgren a blessing? Why didn't she tell me I had broken a mission rule? Why did she encourage me to contact Forsgren?

Josh could not think of any good reason why this would have happened.

chapter

two

Josh at Sixteen

Josh Baxter was the most unlikely sports hero to ever come out of the Ottumwa, Iowa, high school basketball program. As a junior, he had played only a few minutes the entire season. And in the finals of the state high school tournament that year, he sat on the bench until the final forty seconds, when his team's leading scorer got injured.

With just ten seconds left in the game and the Ottumwa team trailing by two points, someone passed him the ball. Since nobody on either team expected Josh to be much of a threat, he got a good look at the basket. With no one to pass the ball to, and with time running out, he threw up a three-point shot that bounced high off the rim and fell cleanly through the net. The clock expired, and students poured onto the floor to celebrate Ottumwa's state championship.

Josh was not prepared for their enthusiastic response. Someone stuck a microphone in his face and asked, "How does it feel to have made the winning shot?"

When Josh was younger, he had a problem with stuttering. A boy in his first grade class made fun of him constantly, calling him, "J . . . J . . . J . . . Josh." Before long everyone was calling him that. When the teacher would call on Josh in class, even if he knew the answer, Josh would usually shake his head. But when he absolutely had to speak, he panicked because he never knew what was going to come out of his mouth.

He had outgrown the stuttering for the most part, but the fear of being teased still terrorized him.

The only time he stuttered now was when he was asked to speak in public. And so now, on TV, he panicked. He felt that all he should give were one-word answers to the reporter's questions. "Great!" he said.

"What was going through your mind just after you received the ball?"

"Help!"

After a few more short answers, he turned away and quickly made his escape to the locker room.

Half an hour later, after all the other players had left, Josh was still in the locker room, hiding from the reporters.

The coach came into the locker room after he finished his interviews. "Josh, what took you so long? A lot of people were asking about you."

"Sorry."

"On Monday we're going to have a victory rally. I want you to say a few words about what it was like to make that shot. You think you can do that?"

"I. . . . don't know . . . if I can, Coach. Sometimes, I have trouble . . . you know, talking to a big group."

"Well, do your best, because I *am* going to call on you."

When Josh finally came out of the locker room, his folks and fourteen-year-old sister, Hannah, were waiting for him.

"Sorry to be so late," he said. He didn't have much trouble talking to his family or one-on-one with his friends. It was only when he was in large crowds that he stammered.

"Oh, Josh, we'd have waited all night for you!" his mom said, giving him a big hug.

His dad hugged him, too. "I guess that basketball hoop and backboard I set up on the garage paid off after all, right?" his dad said, cuffing him on the shoulder. "I don't know if I ever told you, but I got the backboard and basket for free. I was driving past the school one day and saw them throwing it away. Something like that in a store might cost a hundred bucks, but I got it for free. It just shows what you can do if you keep your eyes open, right?"

"We don't care about that now," his mom said. She looped her arm through Josh's and pulled him close to her.

Josh's dad was six-foot-three, mostly bald, and had a big stomach that hung over his belt. He wore an old baseball cap with a farm co-op insignia on the front. Even after work, he preferred to wear work shirts with the name of the company he worked for on the front pocket.

To Josh, his dad didn't seem very smart, especially with managing money. In March a year earlier, he had bought a heavy pickup mounted with a snow-scraping blade to plow out businesses in town, only to find out that everyone had signed for snow removal services in August of the previous year. His dad kept the truck until July and then sold it at a loss.

His mom had once been beautiful, but years of hard times had etched a perpetual look of resigned disappointment in her face, as if no matter what happened it wasn't going to be good. She never spoke negatively about their dad, but neither did she speak glowingly about his accomplishments.

As usual, Hannah was wearing a black T-shirt and ragged jeans with a hole in the knee. She stayed in the background, as if she wished she weren't in the family, but when Josh approached her, she looked up momentarily, smiled, gave him a hug, and then resumed the bored expression she always showed around their parents.

Hannah had lucked out when it came to inheriting genes. She had the dark brown hair, dark complexion, and brown eyes of her mother, combined with being tall for her age. Her height and a lower voice than most girls her age made her seem more mature, and that attracted older boys.

The next morning, a Saturday, Josh's parents needed to drive to Muddy Flats, Wyoming. That's where Josh's grandparents on his mom's side lived; his grandfather was having surgery early on Monday, and they wanted to be there for it.

"You're in charge, Josh," his dad said before they left. "Hannah, try to cooperate with Josh, okay?"

"Yeah, whatever," she said.

Hannah wasn't that rebellious, but her friends were starting to drift into an alternative, punk lifestyle, and she was finding it a challenge to keep her friends and yet live the standards she'd been brought up with.

After their parents left, she spent most of the morning in her room on the phone with friends. Josh stayed in his room, working on what he would say at the rally on Monday. In his room with nobody listening, he managed to get through it with no trouble, but he knew it would be much worse trying to talk in front of the entire school.

For lunch he made sandwiches, then went to Hannah's door and knocked. "Lunch is ready."

She came to the door. "What is it?" she called out.

"Peanut butter sandwiches."

She scowled. "Forget it. I'm not hungry."

"Whatever," he said, returning to the kitchen.

A short time later she sat down at the kitchen table with him. "There's a dance tonight at the high school," she said.

"I'm not going."

"I already knew that, but I want to go. You could come with me and make sure I don't get into trouble."

"I don't want to go."

"You're afraid you'd have to talk to someone, aren't you?"

"No, that's not it."

"Look, Josh, it's not a big deal. Okay, so once in a while, you stutter. So what? Your friends don't care about that."

"They might ask me to talk about making the winning shot."

"So what if they do?" she asked.

"I'm not going."

"Some of my friends are going," she said. "They say it'll be fun."

"You're too young for a high-school dance."

At first she looked as though she was going to argue with him, but then she paused and smiled. "You're right. I am too young. Okay, so I won't go. I'm so lucky to have a brother like you who looks out for me all the time."

"Seriously?"

"Yeah, it's no big deal."

At nine-thirty that night, Hannah came into the living room where Josh was watching a basketball game on TV.

"I'm tired, Josh. I'm going to bed."

"Do you want to have family prayer?" he asked.

She laughed. "What do you think?"

"It won't kill you to pray, will it?"

"And what good have your prayers done you? You sit in your room all day, afraid to come out because of the way you talk. What kind of a life is that? I'm going to bed. Thanks for everything. I had a good time today," she said, then went to her room and closed the door.

An hour later Josh was also ready for bed. On his way down the hall, he passed Hannah's room. Usually she went to sleep listening to her music, but tonight it was quiet in her room. Thinking it strange that she was already asleep, he knocked gently on her door. No answer. He opened the door to see if she was asleep. She wasn't there. He walked in and saw a rope tied to the bed frame and hanging out her window to the ground.

She went to the dance, he thought. He got dressed and jogged to his high school. A few minutes later, as he walked around the dance trying to find Hannah, several people came up to him and congratulated him on the game the night before. To each of them, he said, "Thanks," and then moved on.

Finally he found one of his sister's friends. "I'm looking for Hannah," he said. "Do you know where she is?"

"She was here, but she left with a guy."

"Did she say where they were going?"

"She said something about going to the barn."

The barn was a place known to all the high-school students. It had once been an actual barn, but now kids went there to hang out and use drugs.

The barn was located a couple of miles outside of town, down a seldom-used county road. Because his folks had taken their only car to Wyoming and it was too far to walk, Josh went home and got Hannah's old bicycle from a pile in the back of the garage.

The bike must have been in somebody's garage for years even before his dad picked it up at a garage sale for Hannah's tenth birthday. It was a Schwinn girl's bicycle; it was painted pink and it had big balloon tires. Even at age ten, Hannah had ridden it only until her friends from school started to make fun of it. After that it had stayed in the garage, unused.

The back tire was flat. He pumped up both tires and started on his way. It took him half an hour to get there.

When he entered the barn, the place was crowded. A rock band was playing, and when a girl approached Josh, she had to yell to be heard above the music. "Hi, I'm Jamie! You're Josh, aren't you, the guy who made the winning shot last night?"

"Yeah."

"Oh, Josh, way to go!" She threw her arms around his neck and hung onto him as if they were best friends.

"I'm looking for my sister," he said, pulling away from the enthusiastic girl.

"What's her name?"

"Hannah."

Jamie tapped the shoulder of a girl dancing by herself. "This is Josh. He made the winning basket last night! He's looking for his sister."

The girl was too high to be much help, so they moved on.

"You're the one who never talks, right?" Jamie asked.

No matter how many times people talked about his speech problems, it always hurt.

"Look, don't feel bad, okay?" she said. "Look at me. I used to be really shy, but I'm not now. This place has helped me so much! When I'm here, I just feel so free and happy, and I love everyone! Like I must have talked to about ten guys here tonight. And they all like me. Isn't that great! Wouldn't you like to feel like you weren't afraid of anything or anybody? Well, that's the way it is when you're here." She pulled a small plastic bag from her pocket and shook out a capsule into her hand. "Here, try one of these. It'll free you up!"

He looked at the capsule and shook his head.

"Go ahead, just take one. What have you got to lose? How do you know you don't like it unless you try it once?"

He took the capsule from Jamie and put it in his pocket.

"You just put it in your mouth, okay? I mean, you don't need a glass of water or anything."

"I need to find my sister."

"I'll help you find her," Jamie said, taking his hand.

She led him through the crowd, introducing him as the guy who'd made the winning basket the night before. She also told everyone that he was looking for Hannah.

After checking with almost everyone, she looked at him and smiled. "I've done you a favor, now you do one for me and dance with me."

He wasn't a good dancer, but she didn't seem to mind. She closed her eyes and bobbed in time with the music that was blaring from some huge speakers in the rafters. She seemed to be in her own world, unaware of him. After a minute or two, she opened her eyes and smiled. "You see what this place has done for me? When I'm here, I'm not afraid of anything or anybody. Whatever I want to do, I do it. It's so great! You know what? I really want you to be happy like me. Take what I gave you. It will change your life forever."

Josh wondered what it would be like to be able to talk to anyone without stuttering, to be able to stand up confidently on Monday in front of the entire school and talk for as long as he wanted without fear of messing up. How would it be to always say the right things, and to have people like him and want to be around him?

He might have taken the capsule, but he was afraid if he did he would forget about trying to find Hannah.

"Is there anywhere else my sister might be?" he asked.

"Well, sometimes, people hook up and go out to a car for a while. That's the only other place I can think of."

"Could you go out there with me?"

"You mean . . . to look for your sister, right?" she teased.

"Right. I don't even know you."

"That doesn't matter here. When we're here, we just do whatever."

Outside, they slowly made their way through the rows of parked cars.

"Where's your car?" she asked.

He couldn't admit he'd ridden a bike. "It's over there somewhere."

"We could go to your car and . . . talk," she said, holding onto his arm and resting her head against his shoulder.

"No, that's not why I'm here."

"What's wrong with you? I hook up with guys all the time."

"Do you remember any of their names?"

"I knew their names at the time. That's all that counts, right?"

"Is that what you think?"

She sighed. "You're making me feel bad." She placed another capsule on her tongue.

"Why did you do that?" he asked.

"To keep things happy. When I'm here I always want to be happy, so sometimes I have to take more than one a night. It used to take only one, but now it takes more."

"Jamie, are you sure this is what you really want?" he asked.

"Yes, I'm sure. This is all I want, except I want it all the time. But you can't have it all the time, so sometimes you have to go through some bad times."

"Is there any other place we can look?"

"Sometimes people go into the woods."

He looked at the grove of trees behind where the cars were parked. "It's so dark in there."

"It's not so bad once you get used to it."

She led him along a path into the woods. A short time later she stumbled across something. Josh grabbed her arm to keep her from falling, then knelt down to see what it was. A guy lay on the ground.

She knelt down beside the guy. "Hey, wake up, Sleepyhead!" she called out in a bright cheery voice. "It's time to wake up. Come on." She shook him, but he didn't budge. After shaking him harder, she stood up. "He's okay. Let's just go."

"We can't leave him here."

"He'll be okay. And even if he's not, there's nothing we can do about it."

"We could call 9–1–1."

"No, we can't."

"But what if he's dying?" Josh asked.

"Nobody dies out here. Everyone is happy all the time. He'll be okay. I've been like him lots of times and look at me."

"I've got to find out if he's even alive or not," he said as he stood up. "I need to get somebody who can help me carry him inside."

"Don't worry about him. He's just taking a nap. Look, I'll show you."

She knelt down beside him. "Hey, wake up, okay?" After she shook him a few more times, the boy opened his eyes.

"Are you okay?" Josh asked.

"I ran out."

"Here you go," Jamie said.

He sat up and took the capsule she offered him.

Josh left them and headed back to the barn.

"I hope you find your sister!" Jamie called out.

Inside, Josh began one last walk through the place. A minute later he found one of Hannah's friends, dancing with a guy who looked about twice her age. "Do you know where Hannah is?" he asked.

"She was here for a while, but then she told me she was going home. I think she got a ride."

When Josh got on the bike to leave, he noticed one of the tires was nearly flat. He tried to ride it, but after a few minutes, he gave up and ended up walking the bike the rest of the way home.

When he finally walked up the driveway of their house, he noticed the kitchen light was on. He stormed into the kitchen.

"I can explain everything!" she said, knowing she was in trouble.

"Look, I'm tired of your lies. I can't believe you snuck out of here to go to the dance! But that's not the worst thing! You went to the barn. What were you thinking?"

"I just wanted to see what it was like."

"And what did you find out?"

She paused. "It's not what I thought it would be. Don't say anything to Mom or Dad, okay?"

"Why shouldn't I tell them?"

"Please. Okay, I messed up, but it will never happen again. They don't need to know about this. It would only freak them out."

"The barn is a really bad place." He told her about the guy passed out on the ground, and about Jamie, how she had to keep taking more pills to avoid crashing, and about her invitation for him to spend time with her in a parked car.

"I've learned my lesson, Josh. I won't ever sneak out at night again. Please don't say anything to Mom or Dad."

He sighed. "I'll think about it."

A short time later they each retired to their rooms for the night, but Josh couldn't sleep. *I still have to say something at the rally Monday,* he thought. *So, really, nothing has changed.*

A thought came into his mind. *You know where you can get help.*

He went to his scriptures and read something that he'd discovered a few weeks before in the Book of Mormon: *I give unto men weakness that they may be humble; and my grace is sufficient for all men that humble themselves before me; for if they humble themselves before me, and have faith in me, then will I make weak things become strong unto them.*

He stood and read the verse out loud, as if he were speaking before a large group. When he finished reading, he said to himself, "Maybe if I'm humble and pray for help, Heavenly Father will help me, not only just for Monday, but all my life."

He read the verse out loud again and then thought about Jamie telling him that her drugs had made her free. "I don't need that. This is how someone can really be free."

Hannah called out through the wall. "Josh, who are you talking to?"

"Just to myself."

"You sound good."

"Thanks."

A minute later, she came to the door to his room and knocked.

"Come in."

"I've been thinking about something. How did you get to the barn?"

"I rode your bike."

"No, you didn't."

"I rode it there, but when I started for home, the back tire was so flat that I ended up walking it home."

"Did anyone see you?"

"I don't know. Why?"

"Didn't it bother you that people would make fun of you if they recognized you?"

"I don't care. People have been making fun of me all my life. The important thing was to find you before something bad happened."

"Oh, Josh," she said. "That's the nicest thing anyone has ever done for me. Thank you." She came over to him and gave him a hug.

She stepped back. "You went to so much trouble just to get to the barn. And then to be with all those people. I know it's hard for you to be with people." She paused. "Anyway, thanks. I will always remember what you did for me. And, you know what, you can tell Mom and Dad if you want."

"I won't tell them if you promise never to do this again."

"I promise I won't."

"Okay, then."

"Good night, Josh."

"Good night, Hannah."

After she was gone, he knelt down and began a very long prayer. When he was done, he felt hopeful.

The next morning they got a ride to church with the family of one of their home teachers. After priest quorum meeting, Josh asked the bishop if he could talk to him. Bishop McNamara closed the office door and sat down next to Josh, in front of his desk.

"What can I do for you?" the bishop asked.

Josh hesitated a moment, then said, "I have to give a talk on Monday at a pep rally."

"So you're worried about that?"

"Yes. Sometimes I have trouble talking."

"I don't think people pay as much attention to that as you think. Everyone has something they're self-conscious about. Some people think they're too tall, others not tall enough. Or it could be they worry about how much they weigh or the color of their hair, or the shape of their nose. I think most people carry with them a fear that people are making fun of them."

"People *do* make fun of the way I talk, Bishop."

"But there's nothing wrong with the way you talk."

"There was when I was growing up." He paused. "Maybe they're just remembering how I talked then."

"I bet that's true. Anyone who would be critical of you, well, it's their loss because the things you say are always so worthwhile."

"Thanks. The reason I'm here is to ask for a priesthood blessing. My folks are out of town, so I can't ask my dad."

"All right. I'd be happy to do that."

A short time later his bishop laid his hands on Josh's head and began to give him a blessing.

"I bless you that you will be able to speak without hesitation or worry, that your obedience to your baptismal covenants will someday bring the message of the gospel to those who are prepared to hear it, that you will speak comfort and peace and hope to those around you . . ."

After the blessing, Josh shook his bishop's hand. "Thank you very much. That's just what I needed."

After answering the bishop's questions about where his parents were, Josh thanked him again and then left.

Hannah was waiting for him. As they began their half-mile walk home, she turned to him, "What did you talk to the bishop about?"

"He gave me a blessing."

"Why?"

"For help with tomorrow."

"How was it?"

"Good." He paused. "Real good."

On Monday afternoon, Josh arrived fifteen minutes early to the school gymnasium, where the victory rally was to be held. Two rows of chairs were set up on a raised platform at one end of the floor, behind a podium and microphone. Josh took a seat on the back row, hoping he wouldn't be noticed.

Josh had been up since five o'clock to get ready for early morning seminary. He hadn't had much time to pray or read his scriptures, but there had come a peace of mind about speaking to the entire school. With that peace there also came a realization that he had a responsibility, too. He needed to be kind to others, to avoid bad thoughts, and then afterwards to express gratitude to Father in Heaven.

Gradually, the rest of the team wandered in. They came in groups of five or six, the sophomores, the juniors, and last the seniors.

"Well, look who we have here," Blake, one of the seniors, called out cynically. "It's the star of the game. We're so honored to have you with us today, Josh."

Josh wasn't sure who was more embarrassed, the regular starters like Blake, who each would have predicted they would have been the one to single-handedly win the game, or himself, who never had any expectation he would even play.

Alexis, a girl in the pep band, came up to him. "Josh, this is Mr.

Arnold's last day as band director. Could you say something nice about him?"

"Why is this his last day?"

"He's got cancer. He has to quit. The pain is too much for him."

Blake turned around. "We don't have time for that. This is to honor the team, not some loser band director."

"He's my uncle," Alexis said.

"Well, when he dies," Blake said, "let me know. I'll send a card, but there's no way we're going to take time away from the team."

Alexis looked like she was going to cry. Josh patted her arm. "I'll take care of it."

Blake turned around. "What do you mean, you'll take care of it? Who put you in charge?"

"The coach said he was going to have me say a few words."

Blake turned to the guy sitting next to him. "He makes one lucky shot, and now he thinks he's headed to the NBA."

Josh put his hand on Alexis's arm. "Don't worry. Your uncle will get the send-off he deserves."

"Thank you, Josh. I knew I could count on you." She gave him a hug and then left.

As the bleachers were filling up, Jamie, the girl he'd met at the barn Saturday night, approached him.

"Hi, Josh, do you remember me?"

"I do. You're Jamie."

She seemed pleased. "I didn't know if you would or not. A lot of guys I meet at the barn on the weekend won't talk to me at school on Monday."

"I don't see why. You were a big help to me Saturday night."

"Did you find your sister?"

"Yeah, I did. She'd already gone home."

She looked around at the students as they came into the gym. "You know what?" she said. "Everyone coming in is seeing me talking to you. They probably think we're friends."

"Well, we are, aren't we?"

"I never thought I'd be a friend with, like a sports hero."

Blake turned around. "Look, he made one lucky shot, okay? Don't make such a big deal out of it."

"Whatever. Well, I got to run. See you later." She kissed him on the cheek, stepped back, and to make Blake mad, said, "We're all proud of you, Josh. Without you, we'd have lost the game for sure."

Josh wondered if Jamie had kissed him on the cheek to prove to her friends she knew him. He didn't feel comfortable with that kind of attention.

The coach showed up right before the rally was to begin. He spoke briefly with Mrs. Duvall, the faculty adviser to the cheerleaders and then came over to Josh. "You're going to say a few words, right?" he asked.

"Yes."

"Good." He looked at the clock. "It's time to begin."

Mr. Crockett, the principal, called the students to order and started things out by praising what the team and coaches had accomplished throughout the season. He then introduced Mrs. Duvall. All she needed to do was to introduce each of the cheerleaders and then have them lead some cheers.

In her remarks, Mrs. Duvall continued, "Some people think of the cheerleaders as just some diversion during a game, but what they do is much, much more than that."

Blake and the guy next to him began making crude remarks about the cheerleaders.

Josh overheard what they were saying. Because he felt such a dependence on Heavenly Father to just get through his talk, he leaned forward. "Guys, I don't think it's right to talk like that."

Blake turned around. "Hey, butt out. Who cares what you think? Everyone in school knows you're like the class retard."

The coach turned around and glared at Blake. He and his friend quit talking.

After one more cheer from the cheerleaders, the coach said a few words about the season and the title game, then introduced Josh.

Josh walked to the podium and looked out at all the students. He said a silent prayer for help.

"You might wonder how someone like me could ever make the winning basket. I guess it's because nobody expected much of me. It was great to be able to make that last shot, and I will never forget what it was like watching that ball go through the hoop, but not only that, to be on a team with Blake and all these guys was such a great experience.

"Are any of you like me and have people writing you off all the time, thinking you're not worth much? That's what the other team thought about me. But I never thought that. If that's ever happened to you, remember this—you have a great future as long as you don't believe the negative things people say about you. You have great potential, every one of you, and all you've got to do is to believe in yourself. The reason I'm talking to you here today is because I believed in myself. And, you know what? I believe in you, too, and I always will."

Josh glanced around at individual students. For that brief second, he'd connected with some of them.

He continued. "Today is Mr. Arnold's last day as band director. Mr. Arnold, would you please come up here?"

Mr. Arnold was frail and thin, and it took him a moment to step up onto the platform and walk to the podium.

Josh waited for him, then continued. "Mr. Arnold, all of us here just want to thank you for all you've done for this school."

The band members stood up and, with Alexis leading them, played "Stars and Stripes Forever."

As they played, Mr. Arnold wiped away his tears. When they finished, after struggling to gain his composure, he said, "Thank you very much. I have loved working here. I will miss all of you." He feebly waved to the students and walked slowly back to his seat.

While he waited for the students to quiet down, Josh looked around the gym. "You know what? I was just thinking, these are the only high school years we've got. For the rest of our lives we'll look back to this time. We need to be good to each other, and treat each other with respect." He paused. "That's what I was thinking just now, looking at you guys. Well, anyway, thanks again." He sat down.

For a few seconds, there was silence, and then a few started applauding, and then it grew into a groundswell of noise with students stomping their feet on the bleachers.

The coach went to the mike and held up his hand for quiet. When he could be heard, he said, "Josh has reminded us that this isn't about a basketball game. It's about never giving up on yourself. And being good to each other. That is what he's shown us this season. I expect big things from him next season. With his leadership, I'm sure we'll have a good chance to make it to state again next year."

The rally ended with everyone standing and singing the school song.

Afterwards many of the students came up to talk with Josh. There were the usual sports fans, but also those who were somehow moved by what he'd said.

As the crowd was thinning, Jamie came up and hugged him. "That was so good what you said," she said.

"Thanks."

She looked at him closely. "What makes you so different from any guy I've ever known?"

"What do you mean?"

"I mean, you don't take. You give. What's up with that?"

"I don't know, I guess it's the way I was raised. The church I belong to teaches us to think about others."

"You go to church?"

"Yeah, The Church of Jesus Christ of Latter-day Saints. I'm a Mormon." Josh had never made a point of telling others about his religion, but he had a strong impression. He looked at Jamie and said, "Would you like to know more about what I believe?"

She laughed. "Religion? I don't know. But maybe I should. The way I'm going now isn't working."

"I can pick you up for church next Sunday . . . if you'd like."

"I don't know. Is it really okay if I come?"

"Yeah, sure."

She thought about it. "You know what? Maybe I will. What time?"

"It starts at nine o'clock. I could drop by about eight-thirty. Okay?"

She grinned. "What do you do there? Pray and all that?"

He laughed. "Well, sure. But there is some singing and some talks. It's pretty interesting."

"Do I, like, have to get all dressed up?"

"Not all that much. Most girls wear a skirt or a dress. Whatever you've got."

"I'm pretty much a jeans and sweatshirt kind of girl. But maybe I can find something to wear. Eight-thirty? That's pretty early."

"What do you say?" he asked.

She hesitated for a moment, then said, "I'll stay away from the barn this week so I'll be able to get up."

"That'd be great."

She wrote down her address and phone number and gave it to him.

Long after everyone else had left, Josh stayed in the gym, sitting on the raised platform and thinking about the rally. He was grateful that he'd been able to speak without stuttering, and that he had felt the Spirit. But most of all he was excited that Jamie wanted to learn about the Church. He shook his head. It wasn't like him to invite a nonmember to church. But it felt good, and he hoped she'd really end up going with him. *You know,* he thought, *this is probably the happiest day of my life.*

All that changed, though, when he got home later that day. His folks had returned from their trip, and they were packing up and loading things into a U-haul truck. Hannah, with tears in her eyes, was trying to argue with her dad. "Why can't I stay here?"

"What's going on?" Josh asked his dad.

"We have to move," his dad said.

"Where?"

"Muddy Gap. Your grandfather's operation went okay, but it's going to take a while before he's able to work. We need to run his gas station while he's recuperating."

"When are we going?" Josh asked.

"Tomorrow, at the latest."

"What about school?" Josh asked.

"They have schools in Wyoming. You'll make new friends."

"This isn't fair," Hannah complained.

"Life isn't always fair," their dad said. "I can't stand by and watch everything your grandfather has built up over the years be lost. Moving isn't my choice, either, but we're all going to have to pitch in and work together, because that's what families do."

As their dad started back into the house for another load, he turned to them. "I could use some help here."

Hannah stood there and sobbed.

Josh put his arms around her and hugged her. "It's going to work out, okay?"

"No, it isn't. It's going to be awful. I just know it is."

He held her in his arms and let her cry.

Their dad came out with another box and glared at them. "You two, I can't do this all by myself."

Josh nodded and whispered to Hannah. "Maybe we'd better help."

She pulled away. "Not me. I'm never going to help."

Josh, feeling as though his entire life had suddenly been erased, went inside and began carrying boxes out to the truck.

chapter
three

Madison at Fourteen

are you coming Friday night?" Nicole asked during lunch at school.

"I'm not sure," Madison Forsgren said.

"You should come. It'll be a lot of fun. Everyone will be there."

"Everyone will be drinking though, won't they?" Madison asked.

"Not everyone. There might be some who aren't. But you don't have to drink if you don't want to."

"Will you be drinking?" Madison asked.

"Maybe, but just a little. Please come. I'll watch out for you."

"I'll think about it."

Madison spent much of the evening that night in her room, trying to decide what to do. She looked through a photo album that Nicole had given her for her birthday. In it were pictures of them since they became friends in the sixth grade, just after Madison and her family had moved in across the street from where Nicole lived. Those first few days in a new school had been hard for Madison. Everyone else had friends, but she had nobody to even eat lunch with.

And then one Saturday, Nicole had come to Madison's house. "You're the new kid, right?"

"I guess so."

"You want to help me clean my room?"

"What?"

"My mom says I have to clean my room, so do you want to help?"

Madison thought about it. "Why not?" she said.

"Great. Let's go. I hope you're a hard worker because that's what I need right now."

It took them all afternoon to clean the room. During that time they also made popcorn, watched a movie, and sang their favorite songs.

"Nice job on the room," Nicole said when they were done. "I might keep you."

"Keep me?"

"You know, as a friend. You okay with that?"

Since then, Madison and Nicole had been best friends. Even though Nicole was not LDS, she was active in her church, and so they were in total agreement about how to live.

But now, three years later, things were changing, and Madison had a choice to make.

That night her mom told Madison that Mr. Scoville, their next-door neighbor, had died. He had retired a few months earlier, and he and his wife had moved from their home in Thunder Bay Falls in Canada to Duluth, Minnesota, because they didn't want to be so isolated during the cold winter months.

When the Scovilles first moved in, Madison had gone with her mom to take them a plate of cookies, but other than that, she didn't really know them. Nor did anyone else in the neighborhood. They were older and pretty much stayed to themselves.

The next day at school Nicole asked Madison, "So, are you going with me Friday night?"

"I still can't decide."

"It's just a stupid party, that's all. It's no big deal."

"I want to go, not because of the party, but because you're going."

Nicole nodded. "Everything is more fun when we're together, right?"

"It's true. And I want it to be the way it's always been with us, but . . ."

"But *what?*" Nicole asked.

"This isn't just about one party, is it? If I don't go with you Friday night, then next week you'll go to another party. And that'll happen week after week, so we'll end up never doing anything together."

"That's why you need to come with me Friday night."

"What if both of us don't go? We could stay home and watch movies."

"We could do that, but, for me, it's time to move on to something more interesting," Nicole said with a silly grin.

"You mean boys, right?"

"Maybe, but other things, too. Like not being bored all the time, and doing things we've never done before."

That night Madison thought and prayed about it, and in the end decided not to go to the party.

The next day she told her mom about the party and what she'd decided.

"I'm glad you decided not to go," her mom said.

"But, the thing is, I really feel bad because Nicole is my best friend and I'm losing her and I don't know what to do."

"Maybe she'll see your good example and come back to you."

"I don't think so."

Madison's dad was a successful attorney in Duluth. People came to him and sought his advice. His advice for Madison was that she'd find other friends. That wasn't what she wanted to hear.

On Friday night Madison stayed in her room and listened to her music. She felt more alone than she'd ever felt before. She thought back to all the private jokes she and Nicole had between them, and all the times they'd turned to each other for help. Nicole was more like a sister than a friend.

And now we'll never be as close, she thought. *It's not fair. All I want is for it to be the same as it used to be.*

There was a knock at the door. Madison wiped her tears and called out, "Come in."

Her mom opened the door. "I need you to help me. Mr. Scoville's funeral is tomorrow, and their two sons are coming, so I'm making a casserole to take over to them."

"Mom, they're not even members of the Church."

"What has that got to do with anything? I feel so sorry for Mrs. Scoville, and bringing in food is something I can do. Please, come help me. It will take your mind off your own problems."

Madison sighed and stood up. "How long will it take?"

"Not long if we work together."

Madison's job was to peel potatoes and slice them into little wedges. She did the work but she wasn't in the mood to talk.

"I went over and talked to Mrs. Scoville today," her mom said. "She's taking it pretty hard. She and her husband had worked and saved all their life so they could enjoy their retirement, and then this happened. Now she wishes they hadn't moved here and bought a home. They had good friends where they used to live, but not many here."

Madison didn't really care about Mrs. Scoville and her problems. She had enough of her own to worry about.

Her mom continued. "Without her husband, she's not sure if she even wants to stay here, but if she sells her house now, with the market down like it is, she'd probably lose money. And if she does move, should she move back to Thunder Bay or try to locate closer to her sons? I don't know what she'll decide. It's going to be so hard for her without her husband."

"Why are we doing this? Maybe they don't even like casseroles."

"Maybe they don't, but at least it's something we can do for them. And it's better than doing nothing. A casserole says we know you're going through a difficult time. This is not about casseroles. This is about show-ing love for a neighbor."

Madison rolled her eyes. She looked at all the potatoes she'd peeled. "Is this enough?"

"Yes, that's great. You've done a good job. Oh, also, if you could do one other thing for me. I thought we could bring them a vegetable tray. Could you get started on that?"

Madison gave a frustrated sigh. All she wanted to do was to go back to her room.

"Please, Madison," her mom said.

Madison shrugged and went to the refrigerator, pulled out the vegetables, and began to cut them up.

"It's hard for you, not being with Nicole tonight, isn't it?"

Madison nodded. "It's not fair that our friendship should be totally decided on whether or not I go to some stupid party. I thought that living the way the Church teaches is supposed to make us happy. Well, I'm not very happy right now."

"Would you rather be with Nicole at the party?"

"I just know that I hate being alone like this."

"What would you do if you were at the party and someone offered you a beer?" her mom asked.

"I wouldn't drink it."

"People generally do what their friends are doing. Maybe not the first time, but eventually."

"Look, Mom, you don't have to lecture me, okay? I didn't go to the party, did I? In fact you wouldn't have even known about it if I hadn't told you."

"I know. I'm very proud of you for deciding not to go."

"But don't you see? I'm losing all my friends over this."

"I'm sorry if that happens," her mom said.

"Sorry? How can you be sorry? You have no idea what this is like for me. Nobody knows what I'm going through. I'm all alone now!"

"In time you'll see that—"

"Mom, let's just not talk about it, okay?" Madison said. "I'll do the work you want me to do, but right now I just want you to leave me alone."

Madison worked hard until she'd finished preparing the vegetable tray and then she went to her room. She sat on her bed and looked at pictures of her and Nicole together.

An hour later she heard a car pull into the driveway next door. She

looked out and saw a bald man get out of the car. Mrs. Scoville ran outside and threw her arms around him. "How was your flight?" she asked.

"No problem. Oh, David text-messaged me just before we took off.
He won't be able to make it to the funeral. Something came up at work.
A big emergency actually. He'll come in a few weeks though."

After a long pause, Mrs. Scoville asked, "David won't be coming?"

"No. Sorry, Mom. He'll call you tonight and tell you all about it."

She sighed. "I see. Well, we'll just have to make the best of it without him. Are you hungry?"

"A little. They didn't feed us much on the plane."

"My neighbor just brought over a casserole. It's pretty good. I think
you'll like it."

Madison returned to her bed and continued looking at pictures of
her and Nicole.

On Monday, because Nicole and Madison had a class together, they
had a chance to talk.

"You should have been there Friday night!" Nicole said with a big
grin on her face. "We had so much fun! Oh, and I met this guy. He just
graduated from high school. I told him I was a junior and he believed me.
He's having a big party this weekend. His folks are going to be out of
town all weekend, and he's invited me to go with him. You should come
too."

"He's kind of old for you, isn't he?"

Nicole laughed. "I'm very mature for my age."

"This isn't right, Nicole."

"I think I'm probably the best judge of what's right for me, don't
you?"

"I'm worried about you."

"Don't worry! I can take care of myself. But what about you? You're
still such a little girl. When are you ever going to grow up?"

That hurt. And the next few days passed very slowly. Nicole had the
looks and personality that whenever she entered a room, everyone turned
and smiled. That was great when Madison was with her because she

shared in the attention. But now that Nicole wasn't a part of Madison's life anymore, she began to feel like she was invisible.

On Friday afternoon, Madison came home from school, went to her room, closed the door, and knelt beside her bed and began to pray. "Father in Heaven, do you even care that I've lost my best friend? What am I going to do now?"

As she prayed, the grief was still there, but she also felt the comforting influence of the Holy Ghost, but when she opened her eyes, everything was the same.

She went to her window and looked out. Next door she saw Mrs. Scoville in her backyard sitting at the edge of her flower garden. A few weeds lay on the grass next to her, but the old lady wasn't working. She was just sitting there.

Madison wondered what she was doing until she saw Mrs. Scoville pull out a tissue and wipe her eyes. And then Madison knew what she was doing.

In her mind, she heard her own voice in her prayer asking, *Do you even care that I've lost my best friend? What am I going to do now?*

A short time later, Madison, in her work clothes, opened the gate to the Scovilles' backyard, and walked slowly to where Mrs. Scoville was.

The older woman looked up. Her old eyes were shiny with tears. "Can I help you?" she asked.

"I've come to help."

"I can do it myself."

"I know, but I don't have anything else to do."

"Are you sure?"

"Yeah, really."

Mrs. Scoville wiped at her eyes with the tissue and cleared her throat. "All right then. I've been weeding. Why don't you start over there?"

Madison made her way to the middle of the garden and began pulling weeds.

After a while Mrs. Scoville began talking about her husband, how they met, when she knew she was in love, and highlights of their life together.

"He was not just my husband. He was my best friend. That makes his going so hard for me."

"It is hard to lose a best friend," Madison said. "I'm losing my best friend right now."

"Oh, that's so sad. Tell me about it."

"Her name is Nicole, and she lives across the street. We've known each other for a long time. We used to have so much fun together, but now she's going to parties and drinking and being with guys. I just can't do that. It's not right. So now we don't even talk to each other much."

"You're doing the right thing, but, still, I am sorry about Nicole," Mrs. Scoville said.

"Thank you. And I'm sorry your husband died."

"It was very kind of you to come and help me. I was doing all right and then I came across a rosebush he'd given me for my birthday. We'd planted it together. It's that one over there," she said, pointing it out.

"It's very beautiful."

"Thank you." Mrs. Scoville sighed and stood up. "We'll get through this, won't we?" she said, smiling sadly.

Madison smiled. "Yes, I think we will. If you wouldn't mind, I'd like to come over and help out every Friday. Would that be all right with you?"

"Oh, you blessed child. That would be the best gift you could ever give me."

Madison smiled. "This is not about pulling weeds. This is about showing love for a neighbor."

And so every Friday afternoon, until Mrs. Scoville moved to Michigan to live with her son, Madison spent an hour or two helping next door, not just pulling weeds but doing whatever needed to be done.

Working for Mrs. Scoville didn't solve all of Madison's problems, but it did give her something to do until she had friends her own age—true friends who would honor her standards and encourage her to be good.

But that dream would still be a long time coming.

chapter
four

Josh at Sixteen

nobody chooses Muddy Gap, Wyoming, as a destination. Tourists stop to get gas or grab a hamburger before continuing. Or if it's late at night, they might hole up in a motel for a few hours, but as soon as they wake up and shower, they get out of there.

Two days after leaving Iowa, Josh and his family pulled into the driveway of his grandparents' house in Muddy Gap. Josh was driving the rental truck with Hannah beside him while his mom and dad drove the family car. They'd tried other combinations, but this one worked best because it allowed Hannah to complain without their dad getting mad and saying, "Look, there's nothing we can do about that. You're just going to have to live with it."

Josh was aware that for over a year his dad had had a hard time finding a permanent job. He could get seasonal jobs in farming or construction in the spring and summer, but for the past two winters they had been on welfare.

Hannah had nothing but complaints when they finally entered Muddy Gap, and who could blame her? The town itself consisted of a couple of motels, a café, and two gas stations—one in town and the other farther down I-90, which belonged to their grandparents. Their grandfather called it a full-service station because he did a few minor repairs.

Their grandparents' house was a small, three-bedroom, wood-frame house a mile from town. Two rusted-out tractors belonging to a previous owner sat in a field twenty yards from the house. The house badly needed a paint job; there were several places where chunks of paint were missing, revealing bare wood.

What had once been the front lawn was now mostly weeds. Someone had put a clear polyethylene sheet over each window to cut down on heat loss during the winter, but the sheets on the two front windows had torn loose and were flapping in the breeze.

"I can't stay here," Hannah declared.

"It's probably not so bad inside," Josh said. "Let's go in and take a look."

Under ordinary circumstances, visitors to the house would have been overwhelmed by the combined clutter of too many years packed into such a small area. Cheap plastic souvenirs from long-ago trips were propped up on every surface, along with newspapers and magazines going back at least fifteen years.

But even the clutter could have been forgiven were it not for the odor that permeated the place. It was the smell of bedpans too long neglected, spit-up food caked to bedding, and of two cats marking their territories.

To Hannah and Josh the smell was sickening.

Grandma gave them all hugs, then escorted them into the bedroom where Grandpa was resting. "He's sleeping now, but maybe he'll wake up for you."

"Delbert, Josh and Hannah are here to see you."

He opened his eyes, nodded, and fell back asleep.

"He's usually better in the morning," she said, after they left the room.

"He doesn't look very good," Hannah muttered.

"I know, but he's already better than when we first brought him home from the hospital. I think it's been good for him to be here."

Their dad looked at his watch. "Well, that's all well and good, but we need to get unloaded today so we don't have to pay another day's rent on the truck. Josh and Hannah, I need you to help out."

The three of them went outside. "Let's put everything in here," their dad said, opening the garage door. It was already full of boxes and plastic bags.

"What do we do with all this stuff?" Josh asked.

"Let's just give up and go home," Hannah said.

"No, this is our home now," their father said.

"This will never be my home," Hannah complained.

"I don't need that kind of attitude from you now, Hannah," their dad snapped. "We need to get the truck back so we don't have to pay for another day. Let's take everything out of the garage and dump it in the yard. I'm sure there's a tarp somewhere in there that we can put over it in case it rains. Then we'll move our things in, and I'll take the truck back."

The garage, besides being neglected for years, had also become home for generations of mice. Hannah freaked out when the first one ran past her as she moved boxes.

"I hate this!"

"Don't worry about the mice," Dad said. "Tomorrow we'll put the cats in here and shut the door. That will take care of it. Until then, just keep working. They're not going to hurt you."

One of the trash bags was so old it ripped apart when Hannah lifted it, spilling its contents onto the floor of the garage.

"Can you clean that up?" Dad asked.

"How?" Hannah asked.

"Go inside and ask Grandma if she has any trash bags."

"Why are we doing this, anyway?" she complained.

"Why is it always so hard for you to do what I tell you?"

"All right! I'll get the stupid trash bags!" she raged, heading toward the house.

Dad looked at his watch. "You can take things out of the garage later," he said to Josh. "Right now let's just empty the truck so I can take it back. You two can finish up after Mom and I leave."

Twenty minutes later, Dad left in the truck with Mom driving the car, leaving Josh and Hannah to do all the work.

Josh continued to drag things out of the garage and pile them in the yard, but Hannah refused to do anything.

"I hate this stupid town and this ghetto house," Hannah complained.

"I know. Me, too." He stopped to look at her. "I could use some help here."

She muttered something then slowly got up and pulled a trash bag from the garage.

Eventually they got everything out, staked out a tarp to go over it, and then began packing their belongings into the garage.

Mom and Dad returned two hours later.

"Looks like you two are doing a good job," Mom said. "We're going inside to figure out sleeping arrangements."

After they left, Hannah said sarcastically, "Thanks for helping us!"

They didn't finish for another hour. By then, all Josh wanted was to get some sleep.

Inside they found out there was no room for them. Grandpa was in one room, Grandma in another. Mom and Dad would be in the third bedroom.

The only place left for Josh and Hannah to sleep was on the living room couches, one next to the front window, and the other on an inside wall.

On that first night they learned a lesson. Sleeping on a couch in the living room might be bearable in some houses but not in one where several times through the night the sound of their grandfather's hacking cough rang through the house.

When he needed help, he would call out, "Mabel, are you there?" He repeated this every few seconds until Grandma and Mom went to his room.

"What do you need?" Grandma asked.

"Is it time for my pills?"

"Not yet."

"I really need them. I'm hurting so much."

"You've got another hour."

"The pain is killing me."

"I don't know what to tell you."

"Please, just give me my pills."

"Well, all right, but not for at least half an hour. Would you like some water?"

"I just hurt so much."

Grandma and Mom went into the kitchen. "It's like this every night," Grandma explained. "If I give him the pills early, then it throws off the schedule for the rest of the day."

"Josh, are you awake?" Hannah called out from her couch.

"Yeah."

"I can't stand this."

"I know. Me, either."

One of the cats came into the living room and climbed up on Hannah's couch. She picked it up, carried it to the door, and put it outside.

"I think these cats are inside cats," Josh said.

"Not anymore," Hannah said.

She found the other cat and picked it up. "Go catch mice," she said, putting it outside too. The last thing she did was put the litter box outside the door, trying to get rid of that smell. Then she came back inside and plopped back on the couch.

By this time Grandma and Mom had returned to Grandpa's bedroom.

"Delbert, we cut the pill in two. We'll give you half now and half in an hour."

"Okay."

"Do you want me to mix it with applesauce so it won't make you sick?"

"Yes."

"All right, that's what I did anyway. Can you sit up?"

One of the cats started to meow at the door, wanting to come in. Hannah threw a shoe at the door, scaring the cat away.

The pill-giving procedure was repeated an hour later. The cats kept meowing at the door. After a few minutes Hannah gave up and let them in.

Around two in the morning Josh and Hannah were finally able to get to sleep. They slept until seven, when their dad, about to leave for the gas station, got them up so they could get ready for school.

"Josh, I'll need you to help out at the station after school. I'll work until six. All you have to do is work until ten, and then you can close up and make the deposit. I'll show you how to do that."

"Okay," Josh said sleepily.

That morning Hannah and Josh enrolled in school—Josh in high school and Hannah in junior high.

The high school was small compared to what Josh was used to. Everyone seemed to already have friends, and no one went out of his way to meet him. The one guy who did talk to Josh bragged about all the drinking they did on the weekends.

"I don't drink," Josh told him.

"Why not?"

"I'm a Mormon."

"What's that?" the guy asked.

"My church. Its actual name is The Church of Jesus Christ of Latter-day Saints."

"Whatever," he said, continuing on his way down the hall.

For a few minutes after school Josh stopped by to watch the basketball team practice. They had one more game left before the end of their season. They weren't very good. *I guess I'll put basketball on hold until after we move back home,* he thought.

One good thing about living with his grandparents was that he got to use Grandpa's car. It was a twenty-year-old Buick that had seen better days, but at least it ran.

After school, Josh drove the Buick to the station. Dad filled him in on all the details of working there. "I'll go home and get your dinner and bring it back for you, and then you're on your own. If you have any questions during the night, just give me a call."

"What about Hannah?"

"She's too young to work here. And I sure wouldn't want to leave her all alone at night."

"Dad, I'm worried about her."

"She'll be fine, once she gets used to the way things are here."

Josh's first night of work wasn't hard. There were about four customers an hour. Some of the locals got their gas there just out of loyalty to his grandfather. Also, a few tourists heading west took their exit instead of the one that sold cheaper gas.

Just like Grandpa, the service station was old and run down. The chairs were rickety, upholstered in oil-smudged, cracked, orange vinyl. The place smelled of old grease and rubber. Piles of receipts going back years lay just to the right of the cash register, itself an antique.

Josh couldn't imagine anyone ever coming back after using one of the restrooms. Decades of rust had put their mark on the sink, and the toilet paper dispenser hung precariously at an angle. A steady but slow leak from the toilet tank left the floor always a little damp.

On Saturday night, just after seven, as Josh finished with a customer, he looked down the street and saw Hannah riding her pink bike toward the station. She was wearing one of his sweatshirts with the hood over her face so nobody would recognize her.

She rode up next to where he was standing by one of the gas pumps.

"Why did you come here?" he asked.

"I had to get away." She walked the bike to the side of the station and let it fall to the ground. "The back tire is flat but I rode it anyway."

They stepped inside. "I'm glad you came," he said.

"Let's head back to Iowa tonight."

"In what?" he asked.

"You've got a car."

"It's not my car. Besides, I don't have enough money to even get us there."

"Okay, we'll save up and go as soon as we have enough," Hannah said.

"How could we live back there with no money?" he asked.

"Somebody would let us stay with them."

"That'd be great," he said.

She studied his face. "You'd never do it, though, would you?"

He thought about it. "Probably not. Dad needs our help."

"He doesn't need my help," she said.

"I do, though. How about if I hire you to help me here?"

"Doing what?" she asked.

"Cleaning up this place. It's such a mess. Some of those flyers on the wall are like ten years old."

"And you'll pay me?"

"I will. I'll pay you half of what I get."

At first tentatively, and then with greater enthusiasm, Hannah began to straighten up the place. Because Josh praised her for everything she did, she seemed to lighten up a little.

At about nine o'clock, Josh said, "You'd better get home," he said. "I'll drive you."

"How can you do that?"

"I'll close up for a few minutes. It's no big deal."

"Are you sure? Dad might not like you closing up."

"He also doesn't want you riding a bicycle in the dark. Let's go."

"This is looking so much better now," he said as they walked to the car.

"Yeah. Things don't have to stay the same, do they? Things can change, can't they?"

"They can," he said. "I think what you're doing will bring more business to the station."

"There's so much more we could do," she said. "Like when it warms up a little, we could plant some flowers."

"Great idea. That way it won't be so depressing to come here."

"I'd rather be here than in the house. It smells so bad, and all anyone

45

talks about is how Grandpa is doing. If he's taken his pills, if they should put applesauce with his pills, if they should get him up. I feel like I'm really in the way. And the TV only gets two stations, and neither of them comes in very clear."

On Sunday they went to church at the Muddy Gap Branch. They met in a small rented building at the edge of town. There were only about thirty people in attendance.

The good thing for Hannah was that one of the sacrament speakers didn't show up, so they got out early.

Monday after school, Josh went home to eat dinner before going to work at the station.

"I'm going to go with Josh, too," Hannah told Mom as she sat down at the kitchen table to eat with Josh. "He and I talked about it Saturday night. I'm going to clean up the place."

"You should stay here and do some cleaning," their mom said.

"I can't. It's too depressing here."

"I'm not sure your father will like the idea of you working at the station at night."

"I'll be with Josh the whole time."

"Don't expect Dad to pay you for your work," her mother said. "Things are tight enough as it is."

"I know."

"It'll be good," Josh said. "Hannah has a lot of good ideas on how we can fix up the place."

"All right, then, if Dad says it's okay, I guess it's all right with me."

At the station they found their dad in a good mood. "Guess what? I did two oil changes and a tune-up today! That's pretty good, isn't it, for somebody who's not a mechanic."

"That's really good, Dad," Josh said.

"You know what?" Dad said. "This is the only full-service gas station in town. I'm sure that with a few changes it could bring in enough to make a living on."

"Did you notice how I cleaned up the place?" Hannah asked.

"Oh, yeah, good job! It does look a lot better in here."

"I want to keep working on it every night with Josh," she said.

"Are you sure? I couldn't pay you," their dad said.

"That's all right. It'll give me something to do."

"Well, if you want to, go ahead. I'm going home and get something to eat. Have you guys eaten?"

"Yeah, we did, just before we came here," Josh said.

"Okay, then. One more thing, I'm not sure it's such a good idea for us to close the station on Sundays."

"How would we keep it open?" Josh asked.

"Well, one of us would have to miss church. Or we could take turns. All I'm saying is, think about it."

"Dad, we're just filling in here until Grandpa gets better, right?" Josh asked.

"That's true, but it will help him if we can build up the business."

"I'm okay with missing church," Hannah said.

"I'm not leaving you here alone," her dad said. "Well, I really need to get something to eat."

They watched him drive off.

Hannah plopped down in one of the chairs where customers usually sat while they waited for their cars to be done. "So, we're stuck here until Grandpa can run the place, right?"

"Looks that way."

"I'm not sure I can stand it," she said.

"What choice do we have?"

"We could just get in the car and drive away."

"That wouldn't solve our problems."

"It would solve one. Being here is my biggest problem."

"I know."

"I just want to get away."

A car pulled in for gas. "Come out with me. I'll fill the gas and you wash their windshield."

"Why should I?"

"It'll make the time go faster."

"I'm not the kind of person who works in a gas station."

"C'mon, it'll be fun. Make them think the biggest thrill of your life is washing windshields."

She smiled slightly. "You're so weird."

They hurried out to the car. "Yes, sir, what can I do for you?" Josh asked.

"I can do this myself," the driver said.

"No need to, though."

"I said I'll do it myself." He noticed Hannah about to wash his windshield. "Get away from my car!"

Hannah gave him a dirty look and swore at him and went back inside.

"Are you going to let her talk to me that way? If this was my place, I'd fire her on the spot."

"Well, she's my sister, so I really can't fire her. Besides, she's not getting paid anyway, so it wouldn't make any difference if I did fire her."

"Next time I'm taking my business elsewhere," the man said.

"Whatever you want, sir. It's a free country."

After he filled his car, the man came into the station with Josh to pay. Hannah was using a razor blade to get rid of some crusty old Scotch tape on the window that had held up the flyers she'd already thrown away.

"Do you have something to say to me, young lady?" the man asked.

She looked up at him. "Have a nice day, sir."

"I was thinking of an apology."

"Thank you, sir. I accept your apology."

The man grabbed his change, mumbled under his breath, stormed out to his car, and drove away.

"What a jerk!" Hannah said.

"Yeah, he was. He'll be back, though."

"Why do you say that?"

"Because he's going to be offended at whatever place he goes to get gas. So, after he runs out of places to go, he'll be back."

While they worked to clean up the place, Josh asked Hannah about school.

"It's actually worse than I first thought," she said.

"How's that?"

"The first day I thought that the reason why nobody was paying any attention to me was because they had their own friends, or maybe that they were kind of shy and backwards and didn't know how to meet new people. Well, today I figured out it's because almost every guy is tied to a girl. So the guys aren't going to make friends with me because of what their girl will say. And the girls hate me because I look better than any of them."

"You are so conceited!" he teased.

"Hey, it's the truth, what can I say? So the only ones left for me are the guys who only want to make it with me so they can brag to their buddies. And they're so obvious, I don't even talk to them. So that's why I don't have any friends and won't as long as I'm here. Do you ever talk to anyone?" she asked.

"Not really."

"Do you answer any questions in class?"

"No, do you?"

"Of course not, but you should."

"Why?"

"So you can get over your fear of talking to people," she said.

"I only freeze up when I'm nervous."

"But if you don't talk in class, you'll always be nervous. You can't go through your life being afraid to talk. You've got too much to offer for that to happen."

He shook his head. "I don't have anything to offer."

"That's not true, Josh. You're like my hero."

"You need to pick better heroes."

"Look, all I'm saying is you should either ask or answer one question a day. I'll be checking up on you every night, so you'd better do it."

"I'll think about it," Josh said reluctantly.

"Don't think about it. Just do it."

"Who made you my boss?" he asked.

She laughed. "I did."

"Well, okay, I just wanted to know."

She borrowed some change from him so she could get a candy bar from the machine.

"You want part of this?" she asked.

"If you give me some, I still expect you to pay me back what you borrowed."

"Even if you eat half? That's not fair. I should only have to pay back half."

He laughed. "I'll never win against you, will I?"

"Not likely."

After they finished the candy bar, she asked, "How about loaning me some more money so we can have another one?"

"No way. One is enough."

"I knew you'd say that."

"How?" he asked.

"Because you're always in control." She slumped down and rested her head on the back of the chair. "Where did you come from, Josh? You're not like Dad." She hesitated. "Do you ever think about him? I mean, let's face it, he's pretty much a loser, right? He can't keep a job. And I don't think he has a clue what we're really like."

"He's our dad. He always tries to provide for us."

"Yeah, but face it, he fails at everything he tries."

"Maybe he's like me, just waiting for the big game where he can make the winning basket."

"Well, I just hope it comes soon. And another thing, he never talks to me. Yeah, he tells me what to do, but we never talk. It's like he doesn't even want to know me. Why?"

"I don't know. I guess maybe because he's just always busy."

"That's not it, and you know it."

"I don't know, Hannah. Maybe you'd better talk to him about that."

"That's never going to happen."

A week later, a beat-up old car pulled into the station. It was in bad shape, with duct tape holding one door shut. A guy about Josh's age got out and nervously looked around, saw Hannah, and headed toward them.

"Oh, no, it's Billy Garff!" Hannah groaned.

"Who's Billy Garff?" he asked.

"We have a class together. He's so pathetic. I'm serious. He has no friends. He's flunked two grades, so he's older. He came up to me today and just stood there, staring at me. I made the mistake of talking to him. Now everyone thinks I'm a complete loser because nobody else in the entire school will talk to him."

Billy was tall and chubby and awkward. His modified duck-walk alone, with his feet pointed out to the side, invited laughter, and his high nasal voice made one think of a cartoon character.

He came inside the station, stared at Hannah, and then pulled some loose change from his pocket and tossed it on the counter in front of her.

"What's this for? Are you giving me money?" Hannah asked.

He shook his head. "I want gas."

Josh counted out the money. "I'll go put it in," he said, walking out the door.

"I'll help!" Hannah cried, hurrying after him.

"I can help, too," Billy called out, following after them.

"No, that's okay! Stay there! We can get it," she said.

Billy went back inside. After they had put a dollar's worth of gas in Billy's car, a woman in a nearly new Corvette pulled in for gas. She stayed in her car and paid with a credit card.

While Josh and Hannah were working on the Corvette, Billy, inside, stood in front of the candy machine, trying to decide on something to eat.

"How long do you think he'll stay?" Hannah asked.

"I have no idea. Do you want me to get rid of him?"

"I can't decide. He's the only one in school who will even talk to me."

"Tough choice, isn't it?" he said with a smile.

51

"Yeah. Oh, well, he's harmless. Let him stay, I guess."

As they walked through the door, Billy pointed to two Snickers bars on the counter. "I got you guys something."

"That's really nice of you, Billy," Hannah said.

"Yeah, so go ahead and eat it."

Hannah picked up one of the Snickers. "I think I'll wait and have it tomorrow, if that's okay."

"Sure, you can eat it anytime you want. That's the good thing about junk food."

Billy finished his Snickers and then used his sleeve to wipe his mouth. "Did I get it all?" he asked.

"You did. Good job," Hannah said.

"How do you like my car?" he asked.

"It's a very interesting car. Josh, what do you think about Billy's car?"

"I've never seen duct tape used in so many ways."

"I did that," Billy said proudly. "In fact, it didn't even used to work, but now it does. So that's something, right?"

"That is definitely something to be proud of," Josh said.

"You want to take a ride around the block?" Billy asked Hannah.

She laughed. "This is Muddy Gap. There are no blocks, okay? Okay, there might be one block."

"You know what I mean. We'll go into town, turn around, and then come back."

"That's all we'll do, right?"

"Yes, that's all."

"So you'll be driving the entire time, and we won't even stop?"

"Well, there is a stop sign."

"You can stop at the stop sign, but what I meant is you're not going to pull over at any time, right?"

"That's right. You'll be back in, like, five minutes."

She turned to Josh. "What do you think?"

"Do you have a driver's license, Billy?"

"Yeah, I do. It's right here." He pulled out his wallet and showed his license to Josh.

"Well, I guess that'd be okay," Josh said. "But if you're not back here in ten minutes, I'm coming looking for you."

"You can trust me. I'm not like other guys."

"Anyone can see that," she said with a slight grin in Josh's direction.

"Are you going to open the door for my sister when she gets in your car?"

"Well, her door won't open, but I can open my door and let her slide in."

"I guess that will have to do. Are you a safe driver, Billy?"

"Very safe. My car won't go much over thirty-five."

Josh looked at his watch. "You guys have five minutes."

The car was burning so much oil that Josh was sure that if they didn't come back right away he could just follow their smoke trail.

Five minutes later they returned.

"This is the best day of my life!" Billy said as he and Hannah came inside the station.

"Why's that?" Josh asked.

"I had a pretty girl ride in my car! I never thought anything like that would ever happen to me."

"Well, I bet there will be plenty more girls riding with you in the future," Hannah said. "Especially as soon as you fix the passenger door so it's not held shut with a rope to the steering column."

"I'm going to work on that right away! You just see if I don't." He stood up and headed for the door. "In fact, when I get it fixed, I'll come back and let you ride with me again! Will you do that, Hannah?"

"I guess so."

"Wow! That would be awesome! Some day I hope I could buy us ice cream cones, and we could eat them in the car. That would be so cool! Well, I'm not going to be able to sleep tonight, that's for sure!"

"Uh, just one thing," Hannah said. "We're not dating, okay? I'm not your girlfriend."

"But you're my friend, though, aren't you?"

She paused. "Well, maybe a little."

"Whoo! I'm going to go fix that door! See you guys."

"Yeah, see you, Billy," she said.

As soon as he pulled away, she turned to Josh. "Is it a mistake for me to be nice to him?"

"I don't see how being nice could be a mistake."

"I feel sorry for him. But I keep thinking, what if we can never get rid of him?"

"That could happen."

"Tell me if you think I should stop letting him come around, okay?"

"I will."

Fifteen minutes went by without any customers. "I'm bored. Entertain me, Josh."

"Why should I?"

"Because you're my older brother. You're supposed to keep me happy. Stand up and give me a speech."

"No."

"C'mon, you've got to start talking more. I get worried when I see you just sitting there without saying anything."

"I don't have anything to say."

"Well, you should. Stand up, I say."

He stood up but didn't say anything.

"Go ahead."

"I don't have any trouble talking to you. It's just when there's a lot of people around."

"But you did it at school after the state basketball championship game."

"I had help from God for that."

"You think God wants you to not say anything the rest of your life?"

"I don't think he cares one way or the other."

"How can you say that? Don't you know how amazing you are?"

He shook his head. "I'm nothing, Hannah."

"Are you kidding? You're the only reason I can stand it here. Every day I think about how we're living now. You should be playing high school sports, but you're not. You should be one of the most popular kids in school, but you're not because in this school all anyone can think about is getting drunk on the weekends. You should be the student body president because if you were you'd do your best to make things better. You're the one I'll hope my kids are like."

"It's not that bad here."

"Not that bad? Are you serious? You're sleeping on a couch, for crying out loud. You work every night in a dumpy gas station that people stay away from because they're not sure if we're open or not and they've heard about our bathrooms. And yet you never seem to get discouraged. It helps me because I say, 'If my brother, Josh, can do this, as good as he is, then I can do it, too.'"

"Thanks."

"So get up and give me a speech."

"About what?"

"I don't care. Anything."

He stood up and cleared his throat. "Ladies and gentlemen, today I want to tell you about my sister, Hannah."

"No! Not that!"

"I'm so glad Heavenly Father gave me Hannah. She's really a good sister. Through the years she's made me laugh so many times. I can always go to her and talk when I've had a bad day. Right now she's not only my sister, she's my best friend, too. She's trying to help me so I won't be afraid to talk in public, and that's why I'm giving this talk. I don't know what I'd do if she wasn't here with me every night. The End."

Hannah stood up and whistled, stomped, shouted, and clapped. "Wow, that was the best speech I've ever heard in my life!"

Josh took a bow.

"Okay, every night a different speech. You hear me? Every night."

"Why?"

"For when you're on your mission," she said. "You're going to have to give a lot of talks on your mission."

"No, I'll just go door to door."

"God doesn't want you hung up on things you think you can't do."

"Since when do you know what God wants?" Josh asked.

"You know I'm right."

"I don't know that. I don't know anything."

"Please, Josh. Work with me, okay? That's all I'm asking."

He thought about it. "Okay."

She nodded. "Good." She looked at the clock on the wall. "Let's close up and go home."

When they got home, everyone was asleep. They went into the kitchen to see if there was anything to eat. There were two pieces of cake on the counter with a note telling them that somebody from the church had brought it over and to help themselves.

They sat down at the table, cluttered with pill bottles, and had milk and cake. Josh finished his first, but Hannah was taking her time with hers.

"So from what you said to me at the station, I'm pretty much the best brother you've got."

"You're the only brother I've got."

"Same thing. So if you care about me so much, then you probably wouldn't mind giving me a tiny piece of your cake, right?"

She shook her head. "No, get away."

He tried to stab a piece of her cake with his fork, but missed. She picked up the plate, turned away from him, stuffed it all in her mouth, and then turned back with a huge grin on her chocolate coated teeth. "Nice try, loser."

He let her get ready for bed first. By the time he was ready, she was already under the covers on the couch across the room. "You want to have a prayer?" he asked.

"No, I'm already asleep," she said.

"Whatever." He knelt down at the side of his couch. By the time he finished, she was by his side. Right after he said amen, she ran back to her couch, pulled a blanket over her, and turned away from him.

"Thanks for praying with me," he said quietly.

"I don't know what you're talking about. I've been here all the time."

"Hannah?" he said.

"Yeah?"

"Thanks for trying to help me."

"Yeah, sure. Thanks for being such a good big brother."

◆　　◆　　◆

"I'm not having my kids work Sundays," their mother said.

"If we close the station, we'll lose business," Dad said.

"I don't care. If you want to spend your Sundays working, then that's one thing, but Josh and Hannah will not be working."

As a compromise, their dad closed the station in the morning for church but opened it in the afternoons. And he was the one who worked on Sundays.

A couple of weeks later, on a Sunday, Grandpa had had a good day. He seemed to be feeling better.

"Josh, Hannah, Grandpa wants to talk to you both," Grandma said to them as they sat on the porch.

"Josh, you're so in trouble," Hannah teased. "What did you do now?"

"Nothing. It must be you."

"Not me. I'm perfect," she said, batting her eyes innocently.

They went into their grandfather's bedroom. "What do you need, Grandpa?" Hannah asked.

"Drag some chairs into the room. I want to talk to you both."

They brought in some chairs from the kitchen and put them near the foot of the bed.

"No, get closer, so I can get a good look at you both," Grandpa said.

They moved the chairs closer and sat down.

He must have noticed Hannah sniffing the air. "Does it smell bad in here?" he asked.

"No, it's okay," she said.

"Josh, open the windows to let in a little fresh air," their grandfather said.

As Josh started to open the windows, Grandma came to the door. "What are you doing, Josh?"

"Opening the windows."

"You can't do that. The screen is broken, and I don't want flies in here."

"There aren't any flies," Josh said. "It's too cold now."

"I told them to open the windows," Grandpa said.

"Why?"

"Because it smells bad in here. Right, Hannah?"

She smiled faintly. "Just a little."

"Don't blame me if flies come in here, then," Grandma said.

"We won't. Mabel, I want to talk to Josh and Hannah privately."

She left.

"There, we got a little breeze in here, so how's that, Hannah?"

"Better."

"I wanted to talk to you both, because . . ." He stopped. " . . . well, because I'm not going to be around much longer, and I just wanted you both to know that except for Mabel, I'm going to miss you two most of all."

"You are? Why?" Hannah asked.

"All grandparents are like that. Even Lehi, when he was about to die, he called his grandchildren together to give them each a blessing. I'm sorry I haven't been much good to you since you've been here. I'm sure it's going to get worse, but today is a good day, and so while I'm feeling good, I want to give you each a blessing. Josh, you're the oldest. Let's do you first."

Josh moved his chair closer to the bed and sat down. Grandpa scooted over to the edge of the bed. "Hannah, can you put some pillows behind me so I can get where I need to be?"

A minute later he was propped up so he could put his hands on Josh's head.

"Joshua Dean Baxter, by the authority of the Melchizedek Priesthood, and in the name of Jesus Christ, I lay my hands on your head . . ." he began.

He started out barely able to speak the words, but near the end of the blessing, his voice became strong and clear. "You were chosen before you came to the Earth to be a leader for good. Your influence will bless the lives of many as you learn to speak with authority and conviction. Begin now to prepare for your mission because much will be asked of you that now you would not be ready for."

Grandpa began coughing; he couldn't seem to stop. Finally, he closed the blessing and asked for a drink of water. Hannah ran into the kitchen and brought him back some water.

He drank the water but continued to cough.

"I'm okay. It'll pass. Don't worry. I'm fine," he said.

"We can do my blessing later when you're feeling better," Hannah said.

"No, we'll do it now. Just give me a minute to catch my breath."

A few minutes later he gave her a blessing. It was a short blessing, but in it he promised her that someday she would be married in the temple to a worthy young man and have children who would honor and respect her.

When he finished, she gave him a hug. "Thank you, Grandpa! That was so awesome."

With tears in his eyes, he smiled. "It was awesome for me, too."

"What can we do for you?" Hannah asked.

"Just you two being here has been a wonderful gift."

"There must be something we can do."

"Let me think about it."

"Think of something for Josh to do, too."

Josh glanced at her with raised eyebrows, and she made a funny face back at him. "Something hard that will take a lot of his time."

Grandpa sighed. "Well, actually, I can think of one thing. I'm not sure either of you will want to do it, though."

"What is it?"

"My feet are so dry, and sometimes they itch so bad I can't get to sleep. Maybe you could put some lotion on them once in a while."

"Sure, Grandpa, I can do that. Let me go talk to Mom about what kind of lotion would be best."

After conferring with Mom and Grandma, Hannah returned with a big jar of hand cream.

Josh stood at the door and watched as Hannah carefully set aside the bottom of the sheet so she could work on Grandpa's feet.

"Now you tell me if I hurt you, okay?" she asked.

"I will."

She dabbed two fingers into the jar to get some. "Now this might be a little cold at first, okay?"

"That's all right."

"Here we go."

At first, she didn't say much, but after a few minutes she became more comfortable with what she was doing, and began to talk.

"Grandpa, you'd be so happy with the changes me and Josh have made to the station. We're fixing it up real nice. I work every night with Josh. He's in charge of the customers, but my job is to clean things up. We got rid of all those old posters on the windows, and I dusted all the shelves, and we're going to paint the bathrooms so they look a little better."

"I can hardly wait to see it."

"Working with Josh is the best part of my day."

Josh stood in the doorway, watching as Hannah worked on Grandpa's feet, chattering to him about every aspect of her life. Grandpa seemed happy to be thinking about something other than his pain. And sometimes Hannah made him laugh.

Half an hour later, Grandma came into the room. "It's time for your pills."

"Already?"

"Yes."

"Isn't that something? I've been having such a good talk with Hannah that I didn't even think about my pain. Hannah, you sweet child, it is such a blessing to have you here with us. How did we ever get to have someone so wonderful as you in our family?"

Hannah beamed. "Thank you for letting me do this for you."

"I can't think of anything better than spending a few minutes with you and Josh."

That night at work, Hannah asked Josh. "What are you going to do for Grandpa?"

"I can't think of anything."

"Well, I can. You can start tomorrow by fixing the screens in his room."

From then on, the first thing Hannah did after coming home from school was to put lotion on Grandpa's feet while she filled him in on how her day had gone.

She kept Josh busy, too. He fixed the screens so they could open the windows and get a little breeze into the room. She also had him make the night stand taller, so Grandpa could retrieve his things without having to bend over so much.

A few days later, at the station, near closing time, with little or no business, Josh asked Hannah a question.

"How can you stand to work in Grandpa's room when it smells so bad?"

She shrugged her shoulders. "I just say to myself, 'That's my Grandpa. He won't be around forever, so I'd better enjoy my time with him while I can.'"

"How did you become so good?"

"This is not about being good, Josh. This is about caring about people. You're good, in fact you're way better than I am, but your problem is you don't care about others very much. That needs to change, hopefully before your mission. But don't worry about it, okay? I'll be here to help you."

"If you really cared about people, you'd give me some of your cake when I ask you," Josh teased.

She laughed. "Don't expect that to happen any time soon."

"That's what I thought."

"Look, instead of going around school like you're a zombie, why not look around for somebody you can help. Maybe that way you'll make some friends."

A few days later, Josh got a chance to apply Hannah's new goal for him to help others at school. As he was leaving the cafeteria on his way to his locker, he saw Colby and Colby's girlfriend, Savannah, in an argument. Colby was the school tough guy. On weekends, when he drank, he picked fights for fun.

Josh wasn't sure what they were arguing about, and he didn't care, but just before he reached them, Colby shoved Savannah, sending her against one of the lockers.

Normally Josh would have kept walking, but for some reason he stopped.

"Savannah, excuse me, you okay?"

They both turned to stare at Josh.

"This is none of your business," Colby said. "Move on."

"Is he bothering you?" Josh persisted.

Colby swore at him. "I said, 'move on.'"

"Do you want me to go with you to the principal's office so you can report him?"

"No, it's okay, really," she said. "You'd better do what Colby says. He can really get angry."

"If he's got such a bad temper, why do you stay with him?" Josh asked.

Colby punched the locker with his fist, then turned to face Josh. "If you don't get out of here right now, I'm going to kill you."

"Colby, let me give you some friendly advice. I think you should consider taking an anger management class."

Colby would have thrown a punch if it weren't for Mrs. Drummond walking by. She stood only five feet tall and weighed less than a hundred pounds, but she made up for her lack of size by her shrill voice and mental toughness.

"Colby," she warned, "you listen to me. If you start a fight, I'll throw you out of school for good. And don't think I won't."

Colby glared at Josh, but then turned and walked away. He yelled at Savannah, "Let's go, come on, I don't have all day."

"You don't have to go with him," Josh said.

"You don't know how he can get."

"Is he really worth giving up your freedom for?"

She studied Josh's face as she thought about what he'd said, then turned and caught up with Colby.

A few days later, Savannah unexpectedly left town to live with her aunt in California. Colby swore to make Josh pay for putting crazy thoughts into her head.

On Friday night, while Josh and Hannah were at work, a car pulled into the station filled with four guys from high school. The driver began honking for service.

Hannah noticed Josh tensing up. "Is that Colby?" she asked.

"Yeah, it is."

"What are you going to do?" she asked.

"Put gas in his car. Lock the door, okay?"

"Be careful."

"I will," Josh said.

Josh approached Colby in his car. "Can I help you?"

Colby accused him of talking Savannah into leaving and told him he'd pay for it.

"Actually, this is a gas station, not a drive-in counseling center. Do you need any gas?"

"Yeah, give me a dollar's worth. And check the oil, water, and tires while you're at it."

While Josh was checking the oil, Colby honked his horn. Josh flinched and hit his head on the raised hood.

"Hey, you're paying for that damage! You dented my hood!" Colby shouted out for the benefit of his drunken friends, who laughed hilariously.

Josh came around to the driver's side. "Sir, I'm going to ask you to not honk the horn when I'm working on your car."

"And what are you going to do if I honk the horn?"

Josh went to the front of the car and slammed the hood shut, then came around to Colby. "If you want your oil and water checked, I'd suggest you go some place else. That will be a dollar and six cents."

"Six cents? I said I wanted a dollar's worth. I'm not paying six cents extra."

"It's really hard to put in exactly one dollar's worth of gas."

Colby got out of the car. "You trying to rip me off? Is that what this is about?" He shoved Josh.

His friends quickly piled out of the car, eager to watch the fight, or if things didn't go well for Colby, to join in.

Hannah came out with a tire iron in her hand. "Hi, guys, how's it going? Guess what? I just called the sheriff. He'll be here any minute. We'll press charges. I figure you'll all get six months. Have a nice day." She turned and went back inside.

Off in the distance they could hear a siren. Colby shoved Josh again, and then he and his friends jumped into the car and drove off.

Josh went inside to talk to Hannah. "Thanks for teaching me what a great idea it is to try to help people," he said sarcastically.

"Hey, did I say to start a fight in school? No, I did not. It's not my fault you cause trouble wherever you go, is it?"

"The next time we have cake, I get all of yours."

She sighed. "Well, okay, maybe one time."

He turned to face her. "It wasn't looking good out there. So, what I want to say is . . . well, thanks."

"No problem. You help me, I help you. It's what we do."

"I guess so. Anyway, thanks."

When the sheriff arrived, Hannah told him what had happened, and then added, "And then they drove off without paying for their gas."

The sheriff laughed. "They didn't pay for their gas? Well, isn't that convenient? Thank you very much. My nephew is one of Colby's friends. You know what? I believe I will put the fear of God in those boys."

Later that night, Colby and his friends were arrested. They spent two days in jail. Rumor had it the sheriff had threatened them with time in the county jail if they ever messed up again.

Colby and his friends soon found other enemies to harass.

One night at the station, Hannah started talking about Grandpa. "It's all very sad, isn't it? He's going to die, and then we won't have him any-more. Just when we were both starting to like him. It doesn't seem fair, does it?"

"People die."

"I know. But it sucks. How do we handle this?"

"I don't know," Josh said.

"How can you say you don't know? You're supposed to know."

"Why?"

"Because you're older than me."

"Look, I'm doing the best I can, okay? Let's go home."

At home, by the time Josh came from the bathroom into the living room, she was on the other couch, with her back to him.

He sat on his couch. "Hannah?"

"What?"

"I'm sorry I don't know everything."

"That's okay."

"I don't know how anyone deals with someone dying," he said quietly.

"Me, either. It's not fair if Grandpa dies just when I'm starting to love him."

"I know." He paused. "Do you want to pray?"

"No, I'm mad at God if he's going to take my grandpa."

"Well, I'm going to pray now."

"Be my guest."

He said his prayers and then lay down to sleep.

A few minutes later Hannah slipped out of her blanket and knelt beside her couch.

To Josh it looked like she was saying her prayers, but he didn't dare say anything because he knew it would make her mad.

But it did make him happy.

chapter
five

Madison at Sixteen

as Madison waited after church for an interview with her bishop, she wondered if she'd finally have the courage to talk to him about something that was troubling her.

Her problem was that she felt invisible.

Being the only member of the Church in her school, she felt that nobody really understood her and that she couldn't open up to anyone. For her, high school was a series of tasks to complete without having any close friends. When she walked down the hall, few if any students even said hello.

Nicole, the girl who had been her best friend when she was fourteen, had left town in December with a guitar player from Chicago she'd met at a concert, and now nobody in school knew where she was living.

Madison's best friend now was Emma Jean, a girl from one of her classes. Emma Jean was, if possible, even more ignored by everyone in school. She wore no makeup, never did much with her hair, and dressed in clothes that could have only come from a thrift shop. Emma Jean's younger brother was Toby. He was shy and didn't ever say much. The three of them usually ate lunch together.

Madison wasn't talented in music, drama, or dance, so she hadn't made friends through those activities. She had to work hard just to get good grades, and that kept her busy.

The biggest social activity at her school was partying on the weekends. Since Madison didn't drink, she had no social life. For the most part at school she felt ignored, overlooked, and unimportant.

There was a close-knit group of kids from another church who didn't drink, but they didn't want to have anything to do with her because she was LDS.

The only activity she did that brought her into contact with others was writing for the school paper. Here again, she was dependable and thorough, but nobody except the faculty adviser for the paper seemed to notice.

Because she had nothing to do on the weekends, except homework, she would often bake a cake or some cookies. With some ice cream and a movie, life was almost enjoyable. Her dad was on a low-carb diet, and her mom only ate dessert at dinner. So, sometimes, on Friday or Saturday nights, Madison would end up eating the whole cake, all the cookies, and at least a half gallon of ice cream.

She knew she'd started gaining weight, but she couldn't face spending Friday and Saturday nights alone, munching on carrots.

Madison and her mom often went shopping to pick out her clothes. "It would be wonderful if when you're about to be married in the temple, you don't have to throw out anything that is inappropriate," her mother would often say.

Madison didn't object to being modest, but when they went shopping, her mom picked out clothes that made Madison look hopelessly out of style.

The only place Madison felt acceptance and respect was at church. She was the Laurel class president in her ward. Before that she'd been the Mia Maid class president, and before that the Beehive class president.

Bishop Anderson left the clerk's office and approached her in his usual fast pace, radiating enthusiasm and energy. Although he was in his early forties, he had a full head of gray hair that made him look very distinguished. He taught economics at the University of Minnesota at Duluth, and he sometimes used terms from his profession in talks at church as if they were in the scriptures somewhere. Madison couldn't count the number of times he had said, "This is just like the law of sup-ply and demand" when talking about missionary work, family history, food storage, and even the need for strict chastity in one's life.

"Madison, I'm sorry I made you wait. Brother Adams is out of town today, and we needed two people to handle the money, so I had no other choice."

"It's okay. I haven't been waiting that long."

"Please come in," he said, leading the way into his office. "Oh, I read in the paper that the high school baseball team won the state title Friday night. Did you go to the game?"

"No. I'm not that interested in sports."

"Well, from the newspaper account, it must have been an exciting game."

"I'll read about it when I get home." She handed him the application papers for the Young Womanhood Recognition Medallion, which was the official purpose of her appointment. "You're supposed to interview me for this."

"Great. Let me look at it for a minute."

I'll talk to him after he interviews me, she thought. *But what will I say? That sometimes I wish I weren't LDS, because then at least I'd have a few friends? No, I can't say that.*

The bishop finished glancing over the form she'd brought and set it aside. "Nicely done, Madison. But of course everything you do, you do to perfection."

He leaned back in his chair and put his hands behind his head. "I was talking to Sister Jensen last week. She told me she'd never met a girl who so fully exemplifies the ideals of the Young Women program—your wholehearted participation in every activity, the leadership you give in every calling and assignment you receive, and your adherence to gospel principles. We are all so proud of you. It has been such an honor for me to work with you these past few years. You've been the heart of our youth program, and we will miss you tremendously when you graduate next year."

His praise overwhelmed her, making it even more difficult for Madison to have the courage to tell him what was bothering her. "Thanks, Bishop."

He grabbed a pen to sign the form. "I assume you're still living the gospel standards. Is that right?"

"Yes . . . except that I eat too much."

He laughed. "Tell me about it!" He signed the papers and handed them back. "I hope you know what to do with these."

"I do."

"Is there anything else?" he asked.

I should tell him now, she thought. She couldn't do it. "No, that's all."

As she left the bishop's office, she felt disappointed she hadn't told him what was bothering her, but then she realized that even if he'd asked, she still might not have been able to open up to him. She felt that since she was a leader, she wasn't supposed to have any problems.

Her dad served in the stake presidency and was usually gone on Sundays. Her mom was a counselor in the ward Relief Society. Because they were all so busy, many of their family home evening lessons consisted of planning out the upcoming week. But, of course, they did talk about living the commandments, and because of her dad's involvement in missionary work in the stake, how important it was to be friendly. She had tried to be friendly, but it didn't seem to make any difference.

Usually after church she ate lunch and then went to her room to read her scriptures or write in her journal, while her mom worked on Relief Society business. They ate dinner later in the day, after her father got home from his meetings.

On that Sunday, after reading the scriptures, she went to the mirror on her wall and stared at her reflection. She wondered what improvements she would have to make in herself before a boy at school would even notice she existed.

She was taller than most of the girls in her high school, had shoulder length, medium-brown hair, and green eyes. Those eyes were her most distinguishing feature, but because they were so different, she had always been more embarrassed by them than proud of them.

She looked carefully at her teeth. They were not perfectly straight, and when she was little, she developed the habit of holding her hand over her mouth to hide them when she talked or laughed. Her mom continually reminded her that she had a good smile and was always on her to use it to good advantage. But Madison doubted if the most popular kids in school noticed or cared about her smile.

I wish I could do something about my nose, she thought. Once in seventh grade, a girl in one of her classes had told her she had a witch's nose.

"I'm not a witch," she had said.

"Maybe not, but you sure look like one," the girl insisted.

That night she told her parents what the girl had said. "You have a wonderful nose," her father said. "It's just like my nose, and, not only that, it's been in our family for hundreds of years."

"I don't like it," Madison said. "Is there something I can have done to make it better?"

"No, not really," her dad said. "You'll just have to get used to it. Don't let what people say bother you. You're a pretty girl."

And so she'd given up on her nose.

She knew she was eating too much, and most of the time she felt fat. Her mom told her she wasn't, but her mom was also overweight, so Madison wasn't sure she could believe anything she said.

I need to lose some weight, and I need to do something different with my hair, she thought. *And I need to get a job so I can get some new clothes.*

She tried to think of various inexpensive ways of doing her hair and makeup, but after a few minutes she gave up. *None of it would make any difference,* she finally concluded. *If I really wanted to be popular, all I'd need to do is start drinking on the weekends.*

It's not fair. I will be so glad when I graduate and can go to BYU.

She heard the phone ring. With her dad in the stake presidency and her mom in the ward Relief Society presidency, and with nobody her age she could call a friend, the phone was seldom for her.

But this time it was. Her mom knocked on her door. "Madison, it's for you."

Madison opened the door and took the phone from her mother. "Hello?"

"Madison, this is David Wheeler's mother. He asked me to call you. He's come down with the flu and won't be in class on Monday. He needs you to interview . . . let me see, I wrote it down . . . oh, yes, Kenny Dikstra. Do you know who he is?"

"Yes. Everyone knows him. He was the quarterback for the football team."

Mrs. Wheeler seemed to be consulting her notes. "David says Kenny also pitches for the baseball team. And that they won the state championship this weekend. David wants you to ask him what it was like for him, and any other questions that come to your mind. He said he'll work on the rest of the article at home, so all you need to do is e-mail a transcript of your interview to him and he'll do the rest. Do you have any questions?"

"Hold on a minute." Madison quickly wrote down the information she needed to gather. "Okay, I've got it. Can you give me David's e-mail address?"

David's mom gave her the address and then added, "Oh, and David asked me to warn you about Kenny. I'm not sure how your generation says it, but from what David says, Kenny is quite the ladies' man."

"I'm not sure I know what that means."

"David says that Kenny made a bet a few months ago that he could kiss every girl in the cheerleading squad in a week. Apparently he not only accomplished that, but also, as a bonus, kissed all the girls on the drill team. David says that girls have a hard time resisting Kenny's charm, so he just wants you to be careful."

"I won't have any problem with that." She hesitated to reveal how she felt in school, but then she added, "I'm pretty much ignored in school, so I'm sure he won't pay any attention to me. Tell David I'll e-mail my interview by Monday at noon."

"Thank you very much."

After saying good-bye and giving the phone back to her mom, Madison wrote out several other questions she might ask Kenny. And then she took a nap.

Her mother woke her two hours later and asked her to help her set the table for dinner.

"Is Dad home?" she asked.

"Yes, he is, but not for long. He has a fireside to speak at tonight."

During dinner her father asked, "How was your Sunday School class, Madison?" One of his responsibilities in the stake presidency was overseeing the Sunday School, and so he was always interested in improving teaching.

"It was okay."

"What was your lesson about?"

Because Madison couldn't remember, she decided to be vague. "It was about how we should all work harder."

Her dad was a successful lawyer, a member of the school board, and was on the board of directors of two corporations. To him working harder seemed a worthwhile lesson topic. "That's true. We can always work harder," he said.

What for? she thought. *I'm sick and tired of trying to be a good example when nobody cares or notices. I want guys to notice me. What is the point in going through life ignored and overlooked?*

◆   ◆   ◆

On Monday morning, Madison got to school early and waited next to Kenny Dikstra's locker so she could interview him. She watched as he entered the building and sauntered down the hall with a cocky grin on his face. He was wearing his letterman's jacket.

One of his friends saw him pass by. "Great game, Kenny!"

"Actually it was a team effort," Kenny said, no doubt trying to sound modest.

"That's not the way it looked to me. How many did you strike out?"

"Twelve. I was very lucky."

He stopped at his locker, glanced at Madison and then decided he had more important things to do than say hello to her. He turned and started to work the combination.

"Kenny, I'm with the school paper. I'm supposed to do an interview with you. Just a couple of questions. Can you do it now?"

He glanced over his shoulder at her. "I guess so. I know I've seen you around."

"We were in a class together last spring."

"Oh, sure." He tried to act like he remembered her.

"Do you know what class it was?" she asked.

Kenny paused, then replied, "Not really."

"American History."

"Well, it was a big class," he said.

"I sat behind you."

"You've changed your hair, right?"

"Not really. Look, it's okay if you don't remember me."

"I remember you, sort of."

"Don't worry about it. Everyone knows you, but you can't know all of us."

"Tell me your name."

"Madison."

"Oh, yeah."

"So, can we do the interview? I know you'll be busy later on, especially with the victory rally. This is a big day for you, isn't it?"

"Actually, it's a big day for the whole school."

She pulled a notebook from her backpack and looked at her notes. "For you personally, what was it like to win the state baseball title?"

"We were trailing as we entered the bottom of the ninth inning. There are some important lessons about life you can learn from a situation like that."

"Like what?"

"Like never giving up."

She stopped him so she could write down what he'd said. "Sorry, I'm a little slow . . . 'Never give up.' Okay, I got it."

She pulled out the sports section of the local newspaper. "Have you read what they said about you in Saturday's paper?" She read the head-lines, "'Dikstra's Clutch Pitching and Homerun Clinches Title Game.'"

"It was a team effort."

Brittany Riley, one of the cheerleaders, approached. She glared at Madison. "Who's she?"

"Nobody."

"Then why are you talking to her?" Brittany asked.

"I work for the school paper," Madison said. "We're doing a piece about the state baseball tournament."

The girl rolled her eyes, then asked Kenny, "How long is this going to take?"

"We're done," Madison said. "Kenny, if you want, I'll save out a few extra copies for your family."

Kenny nodded.

Madison watched them walk away. Because of the victory rally that afternoon, Brittany had chosen to wear her cheerleading outfit to school, even though most girls wore school clothes to class and changed just before a pep rally. In terms of modesty, Madison didn't respect Brittany for her choice but noticed boys watching Brittany as she passed by.

One time during a pep rally, Madison had watched the boys near her as they checked out the cheerleaders. She noticed that most guys were watching Brittany. When she jumped up in the air with her arms lifted high in the air, several inches of her waist were revealed. Brittany had amazing abs, with a flat stomach that would be the envy of any girl in school. And she was always tan, even in the dead of winter.

The one thing Madison felt the most self-conscious about was her stomach. It wasn't flat like Brittany's was. In fact, it protruded.

Madison wondered what it would be like to have good abs. She could imagine if she had that, she wouldn't mind showing them off to the school.

It's not just that I need to lose a few pounds, Madison thought. *It's everything else. My stupid nose. And my eyes, too. The way Brittany does her eyes make it so every emotion—excitement, sadness, happiness—is magnified. I look like a blank page.* She shook her head. *The truth is I am a blank page.*

Even on days when Brittany didn't need to wear her cheerleading outfit to school, she always seemed to come up with clothes that were okay when she stood perfectly erect, but if she leaned forward even the slightest bit, much more was revealed than Madison would ever have felt comfortable with. But when a boy said something about it, Brittany always acted like the problem was that he had a dirty mind but she was innocent. And yet day after day, Brittany wore the same style of immodest clothes.

She knows what she's doing, Brittany thought. *Maybe if I looked like her, I'd do the same thing. I guess I'll never know though.*

Just as she'd promised, Madison e-mailed her interview to David Wheeler shortly before noon. He sent her a return e-mail thanking her and asking if she could ask Kenny one more question.

She went to the school cafeteria to find Kenny.

The cheerleaders and the jocks ate in the same area. To be invited to eat in that section was considered a great honor, one which Madison had never experienced. She quickly ate lunch with a girl from one of her classes and then, notebook in hand, approached Kenny.

He was telling a story about the last game of the state baseball tournament.

When he finished, everyone laughed, and he hugged the girl sitting next to him at the table. Madison stood there, feeling stupid and wondering how to get his attention.

"Kenny, excuse me, but I need to ask you something."

He didn't recognize her. "What for?"

"I did an interview with you for the school paper this morning . . . I have one more question. Can I ask it now?"

"Yeah, sure, go ahead."

"Have you decided if you're going to play baseball or football in college?"

"It depends on the offers I get."

"Really?"

"Who's your little friend?" one of the girls asked.

"She's nobody," Kenny answered, then turned to Madison. "Do you have any other questions?"

"No."

He didn't even say good-bye. Instead, he simply turned back to his friends.

As Madison walked away, she heard one of the girls say, "Did you see what she was wearing? What's her *problem?*"

"She's either in a church choir or else she's planning on becoming a reference librarian," someone else joked.

Madison could hear them laughing at her.

She felt like crying and wanted to be alone, so she went to the school library. She sat there for awhile, trying to get over the humiliation. She hated the way they had sneered at her, and she kept picturing how she must have looked as she walked away. Compared to them and their perfect little bodies, she *was* fat, and she knew her clothes weren't in style. But then she thought, *What difference does it make what I wear? Nothing looks good on someone like me anyway.*

After crying for a while, Madison wiped her eyes and picked up a teen fashion magazine and began leafing through it.

A full-page advertisement caught her attention. Under a headline that read: "How Will You Spend Your Summer Vacation?" was a before-and-after photograph of a girl her age. Madison read about the Teen Mega-Makeover Contest. Each of the ten winners would spend eight weeks at a luxury spa in California where Eduardo Sanzabar and Marianna DeSoto, stylists of the stars, along with Dr. Evan Salinger, plastic surgeon under contract with several of the major movie studios, would oversee their complete makeover. "Look and Act like a Star!" the ad read. It also promised that as a part of the eight-week program each girl would be given a screen test by a movie studio.

She studied the before-and-after photos of the girl in the ad. In the before shot, she was wearing a loose fitting, dark sweatshirt over what was obviously a gross body, and she didn't look happy. In the after-shot, the same girl was wearing a tight-fitting pair of spandex exercise shorts and a halter top. She was tanned and her bare stomach had well-defined abs. Her hair and makeup were perfect, and she was smiling happily.

That's what I want, that's what I need, Madison thought.

Even though she knew there was little chance of being selected, she skipped her next class and took the time to fill out the application—fantasizing what it would be like to look different. She was required to give her measurements and include a photo. She decided she would send one of her yearbook pictures. At first she thought about not being honest on her measurements but then decided against it. Then she wrote the required essay on why she should be picked as one of the ten winners.

My high school is run by thick-necked football, baseball, or basketball stars, and cheerleaders. The rest of us are put in the role of the admiring underlings. I'm tired of hearing every Monday how the Chosen Few spent their stupid weekends.

If you pick me, I'll take what I learn and teach it to other girls, so they will have a chance to feel good about themselves too. So if you pick me, it will be like picking many girls just like me from my school.

All I want is for girls like me to be treated like they're worth something. And if that isn't good enough for this contest, then that's just too bad.

Because she wanted to make sure she had enough postage on the envelope, she walked to the post office after school and sent it registered mail so she'd know it had arrived.

Four weeks later she received a letter in the mail informing her that she had been chosen as one of the ten winners and advising that a packet of materials was on its way.

Madison was stunned. She couldn't believe it. She read the letter over and over again. *This is the answer to my prayers!* she thought.

alone, together

The next day Madison got home from school to find a Fed-Ex package from Teen Radiance, sponsors of the Teen Mega-Makeover Contest. It contained a brochure from the Paradise Falls Health and Fitness Resort in San Clemente, California. It was clear from the photos that the resort catered to the rich and famous.

There were also four permission forms that needed to be signed. One of them gave permission to Teen Radiance for the chosen girls to appear in TV commercials for the Teen Radiance Makeover Program and also to allow their before-and-after images to be used in promotional materials.

Madison hadn't told anyone about entering the contest. Now it suddenly hit her that it might be difficult to persuade her parents to let her participate.

She decided to tell them about the contest after they had eaten dinner on Monday night. That was the one evening when her parents insisted that they all be home together.

As she was clearing away the dirty dishes, Madison took a deep breath and said, "Mom, Dad, I've got some good news."

Her mother immediately looked interested, but her father acted as though he hadn't heard what she said.

"What is it?" her mother asked, smiling expectantly.

"Well, I entered this contest a few weeks ago, and I was one of the winners. I just got news in the mail."

"What kind of contest?" her mother asked, still smiling. Now her father was also paying attention.

"I won a chance to have a makeover—"

"A makeover? What exactly does that mean?" her father asked.

"It's a trip to California, where they will teach me how to do my hair and use makeup. It's also a way to lose some weight and get into better shape."

Her dad was looking at her like he always did when she wanted to do something that wasn't his idea.

"Who are *they?*" he asked sternly.

"The sponsors of the contest. I'll show you what they sent me." She hurried out of the dining room and came back with the brochure, instructions, and permission forms.

"Look," she said, unfolding the brochure advertising the spa, "it's a beautiful resort, and everything is free."

"Humph," her father snorted, picking up the permission forms and examining them. "There's no such thing as *free*. There has to be some angle. People don't just give things away, unless they are going to get something in return."

Her dad looked at the form and shook his head. "I am not giving blanket permission for them to do whatever they want to do. This means they could put your picture on every billboard in the country."

"Dad, they're not going to do that."

"How do you know what they're going to do? Maybe you trust them, but I certainly do not." He moved the piece of paper to the side. "I will not sign this the way it stands now."

Madison's mom was looking at the brochure. "Andrew," she said, "this is a great honor for Madison to have been chosen."

"How do you figure that?" he asked. "If I understand it, she was chosen as one of the most needful of a makeover. How is that an honor?"

"Maybe if you talked to someone who works at Teen Radiance, they could put your mind at ease."

"All right, I will do that tomorrow."

He picked up the next form. If signed, it would give permission for any and all cosmetic surgeries deemed necessary by the staff of professionals.

He read it, shook his head emphatically, and set it on top of the first permission form. "Absolutely not!"

Madison felt like telling her dad to stop being a lawyer for once and to just be her dad.

"I am not giving permission for them to carve you up any way they want," her father continued. "If they want to do anything, I want to know what it is, and what the risks are."

"But whatever they do will be free," Madison argued.

"What if we give you permission for an operation and something goes wrong and one of their procedures turns you into a freak of nature?" her dad asked.

"Dad, I already *am* a freak of nature. They're just going to try and fix me."

"You're not a freak of nature. You're my daughter, and I care about you too much to let somebody slice and dice you like some potato."

"Andrew, I really think you're overreacting," her mom said.

"Overreacting? How am I overreacting? Okay, I could understand if they want to show Madison how to do her hair and makeup better, or if they're going to teach her more about fashion and what clothes look good on her, but I don't feel good about agreeing to their performing cosmetic surgeries on a sixteen-year-old girl," her dad said.

"I'll be seventeen in a few weeks," Madison said.

"Well, of course, in that case, let them hack away!" her dad said sarcastically. "I mean, we're just the parents, right? These people obviously know more about you than we do."

Madison actually did believe the Teen Radiance staff would know more of what would be good for her than her out-of-touch, conservative parents.

Her dad read some of the possible procedures. "Breast augmentation? That is ridiculous! No daughter of mine is having that!"

"In some cases I can see where it might be a good thing," her mother said, "but not for you, Madison."

"What *will* you let them do?" Madison asked.

"I don't want them to do *anything* to you," her dad said. "I think you're fine just the way you are."

"So it's okay with you that I don't have any friends at school?" Madison asked.

"To be perfectly honest, not having friends in high school is not the worst thing in the world," her dad said. "I never had any friends in high school."

"But that wasn't important to you because you were always studying. I'm not like that."

"To tell you the truth, I'm not at all comfortable with any of this," her dad said.

"What?" Madison complained. "How can you say that? I can't believe this."

"Madison, why don't you let your father and me discuss this for a few minutes," her mother said.

Madison could feel tears of frustration coming. The more her parents talked against it, the more she wanted to go through with it. She glared at her father. "I'll be in my room," she said and hurried upstairs.

She sat on her bed and waited. She could hear scattered snatches of conversation, mainly from her dad. Being a lawyer, he had developed a commanding presence that worked to his advantage before a jury, but to her mom's credit, it didn't seem to get him anywhere when he tried to use it at home.

"You have to consider this from Madison's point of view," her mom said.

"Are you so naive as to believe these people are doing this out of the goodness of their hearts?" her dad asked. "One thing I can almost guarantee—Teen Radiance will exploit these girls. There can be no doubt about that."

"I can't believe anyone would exploit Madison with you around. Instead of thinking about legal issues, maybe you should think about what this could do for Madison."

After that the conversation dropped to a level that didn't carry through the walls.

Half an hour later, her mom knocked on the door.

"Yes?"

Her mom opened the door. "Your father and I would like to talk to you."

"Is it bad?" Madison asked.

"It's not as bad as it could be."

Madison met with her parents around the dining room table.

"Your father has agreed to let you be involved in the program, if I go with you to California for a few days to check things out and to hear what kind of cosmetic surgery, if any, they will be wanting to perform on you."

Madison cringed. "You have to go with me?"

"Just for a few days."

"It's either that or nothing," her dad declared. "Your choice. Personally, I think it is a very reasonable offer."

"Yes, you would think that. That's because it's your offer, and I have no choice except to go along with it."

"That's the way it goes when you're a parent."

"Fine!" she snapped, heading for her room.

"You have until tomorrow at noon to tell us what you decide," he said.

"Andrew, I hardly think it necessary for you to give your daughter unreasonable deadlines."

He thought about it and then called out, "Okay, you can have until five o'clock!" he called out to Madison just before she slammed her bedroom door shut.

One week later, after school got out for the summer, Madison and her mom flew to California.

After reaching the West Coast, they had to circle for twenty minutes before their flight received clearance to land.

"I know how excited you must be about all this!" her mom said.

"Yeah, I am."

"I'm excited for you, too. I hope it will be everything you want it to be."

She patted Madison's hand. "At the same time, I wonder what you will be losing."

"What do you mean?"

"Have you ever asked yourself the question, 'What is better, to *look* good or to *be* good?'"

"I think you can do both," Madison said.

"I'm sure that's true. Oh, you have been such a joy to us, Madison. Your father and I are so proud of you."

"Is he proud of the B grade I got in math last term?"

"I'm not talking about achievements. I'm talking about that you're so kind to others. Like the way you were with Mrs. Scoville after her husband died. She often told me how much you lifted her up every time you came to work with her in her garden. You're not going to lose that, are you?"

"No."

"Good. I would be very sad to see you turn into a vain, self-centered young woman who only thinks about herself."

A few minutes later her mom said. "Can I confess something to you?"

"Okay."

"As soon as I knew I would be coming here, I started to worry what the staff at Teen Radiance might think of me. I didn't want to be thought of as some dowdy old mom." She started laughing. "So I decided to go on a diet. Now if that isn't vain and shallow, what is?"

"Did you lose anything?"

"Well, yes, of course. I'm sure I lost weight. My only problem is that my bathroom scale doesn't read in hundredths of an ounce."

They both laughed, and that made Madison feel like her mom was on her side.

Just before they landed, her mother said, "Madison, look, I know you're not thrilled at having me here. But don't worry. I'll meet the staff today, and then go back to my hotel. Tomorrow I'll do some sightseeing. When the Teen Radiance staff has their recommendations about cosmetic surgery, we'll talk with them, then we'll phone your father and discuss with him what he and I both feel comfortable with. And then when that's taken care of, I'll go home."

"Okay, that sounds good. I guess I should be glad you came. I never could have come here without you talking Dad into it."

"I just want what's best for you, that's all. That's all I've ever wanted."

"I know, Mom."

Half an hour later as Madison and her mother entered the baggage claim area, Madison noticed a smiling woman in her late twenties holding a sign with Madison's name on it.

"I'm Madison Forsgren," she said. "And this is my mom."

"Welcome to Southern California! I'm Mariana DeSoto, one of Eduardo Sanzabar's assistants." Mariana was wearing a silky dress with a scalloped hem, spiked high-heeled shoes, and some long, dangly earrings. Her nails were long and red. With her short, spiked black hair, she looked stunning, unlike anyone Madison had ever been around before.

Madison couldn't remember who Eduardo Sanzabar was, but figured he must be important.

"Mrs. Forsgren, we're so pleased to have you here with us. You're quite welcome to stay in Madison's room."

"Oh, no, I don't want to be in the way. I have already booked a room in a Best Western a few miles away."

"Well, if you need transportation, please let me know. I'd be happy to arrange that for you. We don't get that many mothers here with us, and I think that's a shame. For us in Teen Radiance, moms are always welcome. In fact, if you'd like to sit in on the classes and workout sessions, you're more than welcome."

Madison cringed.

"No, I'll just do a little sightseeing. Actually, this is the first time I've ever been to California. Hard to believe, isn't it?"

"Well, I've never been to, what is it, Duluth, Minnesota, either." She turned to Madison. "We're all so thrilled to have you with us. This is going to be a life-changing event for you. Congratulations!" Mariana seemed to be on turbo speed. She talked enthusiastically from the time they left the airport until they arrived at the resort, describing what the program was designed to do for a young woman.

The resort *was* magnificent. It had been built seventy years earlier when it had been a private residence for some movie star who Madison had never heard of. The grounds were beautifully landscaped, with a huge fountain set in gardens of flowering shrubbery, palm trees, and velvety lawns. From the front porch, Madison could see what Mariana pointed out was a private beach, with the Pacific Ocean beyond. Inside the tiled entryway, framed, autographed photos of famous movie stars along with original paintings hung on the walls. She stood in awe at the mahogany staircase, thick plum-colored carpeting, a massive, crystal chandelier, and a friendly and eager staff.

For Madison, raised in the austerity and harsh climate of Duluth, Minnesota, it was a dream setting.

Mariana picked up Madison's key at the desk and escorted her and her mother up to her room. "This is it," she said as she unlocked the door.

Madison walked in and gasped. "Oh, my gosh! I can't believe this is where I'll be staying." The room was furnished with a huge bed, chairs and a couch upholstered in a flowered print, and had its own lavishly appointed bathroom.

Mariana opened a set of double doors that opened onto a private balcony. "If there's anything you need, don't hesitate to ask. We want to make your stay here very enjoyable."

Madison set her bag down and went to the balcony, overlooking the beach and the ocean. She looked down at the water, the beach, the palm trees, the sparkling swimming pool, tennis courts, and exercise areas, and shook her head.

"This is too good for me."

"No, that's not true. All we'll do here is just for you. Just think of yourself as Cinderella, and all of us on staff as your collective fairy god-mother, and that will pretty much help you to know what to expect."

Mariana glanced at her watch. "Well, I'll get out of here and let you rest up. At five-thirty we'd like you to show up for a reception in the Windsor Conference Room so you can meet the other girls. We'll be eating at six, followed by an orientation where you'll get to meet the staff." She opened Madison's closet, revealing a rack of expensive-looking clothes. "We'd like you to wear this tonight," she said, pointing to gray pants and a creamy white shirt. "Don't tuck in the shirt. It's supposed to be big and flowing. I'll see you at five-thirty." And with that, Mariana swept out the door.

"I'll be going, too," her mom said a few minutes later. "Call me tomorrow when they have some recommendations for what they would like to do for you."

"Mom?" Madison said, suddenly feeling alone and vulnerable.

"Yes?"

"I'm not sure if this was such a good idea or not."

Her mom came over and gave her a hug. "It'll be fine. Don't worry. Everything will turn out just fine." And then she left.

Madison took a shower and then worked on getting ready. She couldn't decide how to do her hair. She tried two or three ways but no matter what she did, it always ended up looking awful. Especially when she compared herself with the way Marianna did her hair. *I have mousy hair and a big nose and I'm fat and I don't have a tan because nobody in Duluth has a tan, unless they go to a tanning salon, and my dad would never let that happen. So why am I here? And why did I ever think I could look better?*

She wanted to stay in her room and never come out. She gave up on her hair and sat on her bed and read the brochures and tried to believe Teen Radiance could do something for her.

She wondered if any of the other girls would be LDS. There was no way of knowing. *What if they ask me to do something I can't do, like smoke or drink? What if, after they improve my looks, I discover that the only reason I've lived my religion is because I didn't have anything else going for me? What if this makes me feel like I've outgrown what the Church teaches? Do I really want to give up my beliefs?*

She had no answers to any of her questions.

chapter

SIX

Later, after Madison had gotten enough courage to go to the convention room, she found that meeting the other girls helped her feel more relaxed. They also seemed a little uneasy about being chosen because someone thought they didn't quite measure up to what they should be.

Madison couldn't help but compare herself to some of the other girls. *I already look better than she does,* she thought. And then she realized the other girls were probably doing the same thing with her.

One of the girls had a receding chin and another a severe overbite. Several were more overweight than Madison.

A cheerful girl with long red hair and freckles approached her with a big smile on her face. "Hi, you've got like the worst nose in the universe," she said.

"What?"

"You heard me. Hey, guess what's wrong with me?"

Madison looked at the girl and shrugged. "I don't know."

"It's my ears, but you can't tell because my hair is so long. Here, I'll show you." The girl pulled her hair back so Madison could see her ears. "They're like alien ears, right? Like from another planet. One of my uncles said they remind him of Dr. Spock, like from *Star Trek*. But then, so I wouldn't feel bad, he goes, 'But Dr. Spock was always very smart.' So I watched a bunch of *Star Trek* movies, and guess what? My uncle was right. I look like I could be Dr. Spock's kid, except I'm not very smart, at least not in school. In life I'm smart, though, and that's what really counts, right?"

Madison wasn't exactly sure what the girl was talking about. "I guess so."

"Oh, let's do names! I'm Alli. I'm from Cleveland, Ohio. When I was little, kids in school called me Dumbo because of my ears. So I definitely want them to fix that. What about you? What are you hoping for?"

"Well, my nose, of course."

"Oh, yeah, totally. And your hair. Did you make it look that bad on purpose tonight, or is it always that bad?"

Madison smiled. "It's pretty much always this way."

"Wow, hard to believe." Alli said. She leaned down to read her name tag. "So, Madison, you think we'll become best friends?"

"Maybe so."

"No, we won't. We'll be comparing ourselves with everyone else the whole time. Look around and tell me who you think will end up looking the best?"

"Why you, for sure," Madison said with a smile.

"Good answer! I like you already!" Alli said. "You know what this reminds me of? A bunch of caterpillars trying to guess who's going to be the hottest butterfly. From now on I'm going to call you Pillar."

The half hour get-together dragged on for an hour. Each girl was introduced, and then there was a group photo-shoot, and then they had a chance to meet the staff. The medical members of the team wore white lab coats and gray pants, while the others wore gray pants and a pale blue, short-sleeved shirt with the Teen Radiance logo on the pocket. It was like a reception line that never ended.

"I'm Dr. Salinger. I'm a plastic surgeon."

"I'm David Caterez. I'm an anesthesiologist."

"Hi, there, I'm William. I'm a cosmetic dentist."

"Hello, I'm Daniella Mahoney. I'm a dermatologist."

"Good evening. I'm Robert Tatyana. I do LASIK eye surgery."

"Hello. I'm Robert McKay. I'm an endodontist."

"Hi, there, Madison. I'm Lydia Dodge. I'm a periodontist."

"Hi, Sweet Cakes. I'm Al. I'm a fashion stylist."

"Madison? I'm Lydia Stratton. I'm a nutritionist."

"I'm Michael. I'm a personal trainer, specializing in body sculpting."

"I'm Alejandra McClellan. I'm a hairstylist."

"Hi, honey, I'm Tammy. I do jewelry."

"Madison, is that right? How's it going? I'm David Squires. I do shoes."

"Hey, Girl, I'm Trina. I'll be your aerobics instructor."

"Hi, Sweetie. I'm Bethany. I'm a makeup artist."

The last one in line took himself the most seriously. "Madison, it is a great honor to meet you. I'm Eduardo Sanzabar. I'm in charge of Teen Radiance. It is so good to meet you! We'll talk tomorrow."

A few minutes later, they were led to the Palisades Room for dinner.

They began with a tossed salad, and then they were each brought a plate containing green beans, coleslaw, a tiny piece of grilled chicken, and an entire baked yam served with no butter.

"This is a great appetizer," Alli whispered to Madison, "but when are they bringing the rest?"

That was all there was. For dessert they each got a small dish, containing, at most, three teaspoons of yogurt.

"We're doomed," Alli groaned.

After dinner, they moved into what had been the mansion's ballroom. Eduardo Sanzabar stood up and adjusted the microphone. He could have spoken without it, but he seemed to like the sound of his own voice reverberating through the high-ceilinged room.

"How many of you are still hungry?" he asked.

Alli was the only girl who raised her hand.

Eduardo frowned at Alli. "If you're still hungry, then I would submit to you that you have been eating more than is necessary to be healthy."

He loved dramatic pauses, and he took one now, before continuing. "Chances are that everything you all currently believe about nutrition is wrong. Not only wrong but in some cases seriously damaging to your health and well-being."

Eduardo's next dramatic pause seemed to last forever.

"My gosh, somebody help the poor guy out. He's totally forgotten what he's supposed to say," Alli whispered to Madison.

Finally, Eduardo continued. "Part of our mission here is to teach you the fundamentals of good nutrition so that when you leave us, you will be able to maintain a healthy, vigorous lifestyle for the rest of your life."

Alli raised her hand. "Eduardo, can you give us an example of what we believe about nutrition that's wrong?"

He glared at her. "I would appreciate it if you didn't call me Eduardo."

"Sorry. That's your name though, isn't it?"

"Call me Mr. Sanzabar."

"Okay, Mr. Sanzabar. Can you answer my question?"

"Yes, briefly. You probably believe that if you want to lose weight, you should go as long as you can without eating, but just the opposite is true. To lose weight, you need to eat five times a day."

"I can live with that," Alli said. "So when do we eat again?"

"There will be a snack at nine P.M. Now, I would like to continue, if that meets with your approval."

"You go, Mr. Sanzabar! What you've said so far is fascinating."

He droned on for another forty-five minutes about how if they would put their trust in the program, their life would be changed forever. By then, Alli had fallen asleep.

Sanzabar was on a roll. "You think it was easy, being born in poverty in Puerto Rico, and then finally making it to America? It wasn't, but I did it, and always with just one thought in mind—to make the world a more beautiful place, by helping women change the way they present themselves to others."

Madison wished she had fallen asleep, too. She poked Alli. "Wake up," she hissed.

"Why?"

"Mr. Sanzabar is staring at you," she said out of the side of her mouth.

Alli, with her eyes still shut, broke into a smile. "Maybe in some unexplainable way he's entranced by my ears."

The last thing Eduardo did was to announce the next day's schedule. "Any questions?"

"Yeah. Where's the nearest vending machine?" Alli whispered to Madison.

Eduardo noticed her whispering. "Did you have another question?"

"I was just talking to my friend."

"What did you say to her?"

"I told her I was wondering where the vending machines are."

"There are no vending machines here. We had them taken away. Do you know why that is?"

"So we'll all starve to death?"

"No. So we know exactly what each of you is eating."

"Well, okay, it's your deal, Mr. Sanzabar, but all I can say is bring on the snacks."

Some of the other girls laughed, but most of them stared irritably at Alli. Madison smiled weakly but didn't want to get on Mr. Sanzabar's bad list.

"You are all dismissed," Eduardo said. "I would suggest you get a good night's sleep because you'll have a busy day tomorrow, and it starts at six-thirty."

The snack at nine consisted of half a banana. Madison went to bed hungry and dreamed of large desserts.

Breakfast was a small serving of hot whole wheat cereal with blueberries scattered in, no sugar, half a slice of dry, whole wheat toast, orange juice, and two or three cubes of sliced cantaloupe.

During the night the ballroom had been reconfigured into small portable offices. After breakfast each girl met with staff members for an evaluation.

Marianna let Madison know that Mr. Sanzabar would like to meet with her and her mother at two-thirty that afternoon.

At eleven that morning, every girl went to aerobics, and then they ate lunch.

Madison was shocked when her mother showed up. Sometime that morning her mom had her hair done. In addition, she was wearing a mauve colored pant and shirt combination with what looked like a purple cape draped over her shoulders. It was clearly something that could only have come from Hollywood. To Madison, her mom looked like the worst possible combination of Martha Stewart and Superman.

Madison started laughing. "Oh, my gosh, Mom, what have you done?"

Her mother was blushing. "Oh, well, I had a little time this morning, and . . ."

"Are you actually taking that back to Duluth?" Madison asked.

"Well, that's not something I've thought of yet. If I had, I probably wouldn't have bought it. But that's not the point. The point is that I'm ready to meet with Mr. Eduardo Sanzabar. I kept picturing him thinking of me as a frumpy woman from Minnesota. I figured Minnesota deserved better than that."

Mr. Sanzabar stood up as Madison and her mother entered his office.

"Well, look what we have here!" he exclaimed. "Mrs. Forsgren, it is such a pleasure to meet you." He vigorously shook her hand. "And let me say, I love the cape! It makes the whole outfit . . . pop!"

"Why, thank you!"

Eduardo seemed to be on charm turbo-drive. "We are so pleased to have you here with Madison." He gestured to the two chairs in front of his desk. "Please, sit down. Can I get you anything?"

"No, we're fine, thank you."

He picked up the piece of paper on his otherwise empty desk. "I have the staff's recommendations for you, Madison. Let me look them over to see if I concur."

He opened a center drawer and pulled out a pair of reading glasses and put them on. He appeared a little embarrassed that he needed to wear them.

As soon as he finished, he took off his glasses and placed them back in the drawer. "Yes, yes, this looks very promising," he said, speaking mainly to her mother. "These are the interventions recommended by the Teen Radiance team: liposuction on Madison's stomach, breast augmentation, rhinoplasty, and cosmetic dentistry. In addition to these more intrusive interventions, we will, of course, also provide her with hair and makeup training, as well as having her work every day with our fitness trainers. In addition, we will help her pick out a wardrobe that will take advantage of the improvements we make."

"What exactly is rhinoplasty?" Madison asked.

"Nose reshaping. Most people just call it a nose job. Mrs. Forsgren, if you were to pay for these procedures yourself for Madison, it would run well over seventy-five thousand dollars. But of course, as a recipient of our Teen Radiance promotion, Madison will receive these procedures at no cost."

"That is extremely generous. However, my husband is fond of saying there's no such thing as a free lunch. He is worried Madison and the other girls will somehow be exploited because of this experience."

Eduardo nodded his head. "Oh, yes. I remember now. Your husband called and talked to Marianna, didn't he?"

"Yes."

"I hope she put his mind at ease."

"Well, yes, to some extent, but he's still not comfortable with the use that will be made of the photos that will be taken of these girls."

"Well, I can assure you that will be done in such a way as to protect them. After a while, I begin to think of them as if they were my daughters."

"I'm glad to hear that."

"But in some ways your husband is correct. There is a price to be paid for all this." He focused his attention on Madison. "The price, Madison, is that for the rest of your life, you will have to live up to the ideals we teach you here. If you let yourself go, if you don't eat right, if you quit exercising, if you go back to the drab clothes you walked in with when you came here, then all our work will have been in vain."

He stood, went to the window, and looked out, as if in deep thought. When he turned back to them, he gushed, "People ask me what drives me to do this. Do you know what I tell them?"

"No, what?" Madison asked.

"I tell them that, as foolish as it may seem, I truly believe that I can make the world a more beautiful place—one person at a time." He turned to gaze out the window again.

"Well, I'm sure you're very dedicated to this . . . well, cause . . . but . . ." her mother said.

Sanzabar turned back to them. "Yes, please, go ahead with your questions."

"Madison is just sixteen—"

"Seventeen," Madison corrected.

"Oh, yes, seventeen. Both her father and I do not approve of breast augmentation for her, although for some I can see it might be helpful."

He looked at Madison, evaluating her. "I think it could be very helpful to Madison's self-esteem."

Madison had never been more embarrassed in her life.

"I'm sure she will continue to mature as she grows older," her mom said.

"I see." Eduardo sighed, sat back down in his chair, and looked heavenward. Madison imagined he was asking himself why he had to deal with such uninformed parents. Finally, he turned to Madison's mom, smiled, and said. "Well, of course, that's up to you and your husband. But, Madison, what do you think?"

Madison could see that Eduardo fully expected her to plead for the procedure and eventually win her mother over to the idea. The thought came into her mind, *Who do I trust? Mom and Dad, or Eduardo?*

It was an easy choice. "You know what? I think I'll go along with what my parents say."

His thick eyebrows raised. "Really? Well, good for you. It's settled then."

"Thank you for respecting our wishes," her mom said.

Eduardo pursed his lips. "Yes, of course. Now, let me ask you a question. You do agree that something simply must be done about Madison's nose, don't you? I mean, it's such a distraction, stuck there as it is on her face."

Madison cringed.

"Yes, I can see that giving her a new nose might be good. I'm not sure if her dad would agree though. He's a little protective of Madison." She smiled. "In fact, he was apprehensive about her even getting her ears pierced."

Eduardo smiled tightly. "Oh, I see. Madison is Daddy's little girl, then, correct?"

"That's right," her mom said.

He consulted Madison's evaluation sheet, then came around the desk. He lifted Madison's chin with his hand. "Let me see your teeth," and when Madison showed them, he shook his head sadly. "Yes, we will definitely need to do some dental work."

He returned to his chair behind the desk. "Well, let me see if I can put these in priority. The nose certainly must be done, and then I would recommend liposuction, and then some cosmetic dental work."

"Why liposuction?" her mom asked.

"Madison could go on a diet for six months and knock herself out and still never lose that role of flab around her middle. Or she can walk in, have liposuction, and walk out less than an hour later, fit and trim. Think about it, Madison—a flat tummy with no love handles. People pay thousands for this procedure, but you'll be getting it for free. It's up to you and your mom, though."

Losing weight and developing a more shapely figure was Madison's main concern, and she had thought about the liposuction as a way to jump-start her exercise regimen. But the girls had talked about how gross the procedure is and how painful it would be to have the fat sucked out of your body.

"I suppose when most people get liposuction, it's only temporary because they don't change their eating habits," her mother said. "So after a while they have to have it done again."

"That is precisely why we spend so much time teaching our girls about proper nutrition."

Madison was looking at Eduardo as he spoke. He had a pompous way about him that she found irritating. And the way he was evaluating her, as though she were a piece of faulty merchandise, made her dislike him even more. She wondered how he could speak of what she needed, as though she wasn't even there to hear it.

"I see. Well, let me talk to my husband and see what we can agree to."

With Madison still feeling humiliated by the terse evaluation, she and her mother went to her room and called her dad at work. Madison listened in on the second phone in the bathroom.

"Andrew, have you got a minute? I have the list of procedures they are recommending for Madison. Madison is on the other phone."

"Hi, Daddy."

"Hello, sweetheart. I miss you."

"I miss you, too."

"Here it is, Andrew," her mother said. "A nose job, liposuction around her stomach, and cosmetic dental work. Let's start with the nose job."

"Madison, you've got my family's nose, and I don't see how that could possibly be a problem."

"Actually, I could see how a nose job might improve her appearance," her mom said. "I've thought several times about suggesting we get it done."

"Everyone in my family has this nose."

"I understand that, but to be quite honest, it's not that attractive for a woman to have it."

Of all the things that bothered Madison about her appearance, her nose was one of the least of her concerns. When she looked at herself head-on in the mirror, it looked fine. From the side, it did have a little knob on the bridge, but it had never been an issue with her. Even when Alli had greeted her with that comment about her nose, Madison had taken it as a joke. And when she thought about the pain that might be involved in "fixing" it, it was a no-brainer.

Her father was asking, "You don't like my nose, is that what you're saying?"

"It's a fine nose for you, but maybe not as good for Madison. I think it would be okay to have it done."

"You know what?" Madison interjected. "I don't think I want my nose done. It's not that important to me."

Her father didn't say anything for a moment or two, then he replied, "Well, good. That seems sensible. What was the next one on the list?"

"Liposuction."

"She doesn't need that," her dad said.

Madison had already decided not to have the procedure. She would simply work harder on the exercises and keep to the diet and see how that went. Before either of her parents could say anything else, Madison said, "Actually, I've decided not to do that, either."

"Good," her dad said, obviously relieved not to have to fight that battle.

Madison leaned around the corner of the bathroom at her mother in the bedroom and by the smile on her mom's face could see she was relieved also.

"Is there anything else, Catherine?" her father asked.

"Well, they've recommended some cosmetic work on her teeth. They'll do a little straightening and whiten them. What would you think about that?"

"Madison doesn't need braces. She's got a nice smile."

"They're not suggesting getting braces. They have a dental procedure where they build some kind of caps on the front teeth. I think it might be helpful," her mother said. "Besides, it's free."

After a little grumbling, her father agreed to that, then asked, "Is there anything else?"

"Except for the diet and exercise and grooming, I think that's it," her mom said.

Her dad sighed, and Madison could imagine the look on his face. After a moment he said, "All right then. I'll go along with your recommendations."

Later that day, Madison and her mother gave Marianna the list of procedures they approved of. Her mother signed the consent forms. And then Madison and her mom took a walk along the beach.

"It is so beautiful here," her mother said. "I'll miss this place."

"When are you going back?"

"Tomorrow. Oh, guess what? I'm going on a sight-seeing cruise tonight."

Madison laughed. "Will you be wearing your Superman cape on the cruise?"

"Madison, we need to come to an understanding. You are never to mention the cape to your father, do you understand? I still can't believe I got it."

"What are you going to do with it?"

Her mom blushed. "I have plans for it."

"Like what?"

"I'm thinking of cutting it up and making dinner napkins."

The next morning, on her way to the airport, Madison's mom dropped by the resort to say good-bye. With her taxi waiting, they gave each other a big hug.

"Mom, thanks for coming out with me. At first I didn't want you to come, but now I'm glad you did."

"It definitely was an adventure. I'll have to see if I can get your dad out here with me sometime."

Madison started to laugh. "So, Mom, are you actually going to take a plane, or just strap on the old cape and use your super-powers to fly home?"

They both laughed. "You're not going to forget this, are you?" her mom said.

"Not likely."

The taxi driver opened his window and called out, "Lady, how long are you going to be?"

"I'm coming now." As she hugged Madison for the last time, she said softly, "Not that I've thought you needed to change anything, but I suppose the next time I see you, it will be the new and improved Madison."

"I guess so."

Her mom got into the taxi. "Let me know how things are going," her mom said through the open window. "And if you ever want to come home early, just let us know."

"Mom, thanks again. I love you."

"I love you, too. More than you'll ever know."

Madison had tears in her eyes as her mother drove off.

She was on her own in a world she had never known before.

◆　　◆　　◆

Over the next several days, all the other girls in the program underwent a series of surgical procedures. While they were recovering, Madison had her teeth capped and whitened and also got a head start on her aerobics and exercise regimen.

The personal trainer assigned to her was a man, and even though he said they were going to start out slowly, he put her through a workout that left her exhausted and sore. She was glad when he finally let her go take a shower.

That night around ten, Alli came to visit. Her ears were bandaged, she had a blanket draped around her, and had in her hand a half gallon of ice cream and two spoons.

"Want some?" Alli asked.

"Where'd you get this?"

"I bribed the maid." She handed Madison a spoon. "We deserve this, right?"

Madison took a spoonful of ice cream and put it in her mouth. "Oh, my gosh, that is sooo good!"

"I know. Are you hurting?" Alli said.

"Yeah. But probably not as much as you."

"Yeah. Whatever they did, it was worth it." Alli took another big bite. "You know what I'm going to do as soon as I heal up?"

"What?"

"Get my hair cut. I want to say to the world, 'These are my ears! Take a good look. Aren't they awesome?'"

They finished the ice cream and then went out on the balcony to look out at the beach.

"Why do we do this? For each other or for guys?" Alli asked.

"Guys, I guess," Madison said.

"Okay, if we do it for guys, then I want to know what do they do for us? Do they have their fat vacuumed out? No? Do they do surgeries so they can have bigger biceps? No. So what do they do for us? Nothing. If we're lucky, they take a shower and run a comb through their hair. That's it. So why do we do this? Are we really that insecure?"

"Yeah, pretty much."

"I hate guys," Alli said.

"Yeah, me, too. At least right now I do." Madison smiled. "That might change at any moment though."

◆　　◆　　◆

Three days after the first batch of surgeries, Eduardo called a meeting with all the girls after dinner. Some of them came in the white robes the resort provided in each room.

He appeared in a crisp white suit, maroon tie, and blue shirt. Alli said

101

he looked like somebody who'd be in a commercial for toilet-bowl cleaners.

Eduardo began his oration. "In times of war, it is the foot soldiers who make or break the outcome of a battle. For example, during the battle of Waterloo . . ."

Alli whispered to Madison. "Water Who? What's that about?"

"I don't know."

"I can still hear, even though the bandages muffle it a little. In Eduardo's case, I wish they muffled it a little more."

Eduardo continued. "So also, my young friends, you are the foot soldiers of beauty, fighting valiantly to rise above the ashes and take your rightful place as a leader among women who were, like you, born with flaws that needed a little work."

"That man is such an inspiration, isn't he?" Alli whispered with a big grin. "I just want to say what a privilege it is to be surrounded by losers like you."

"You want me to box your ears?" Madison teased.

She laughed. "They're so small now, I doubt you could find 'em."

"Look at the other girls," Madison whispered. "They're buying into what Eduardo is saying."

"I know. It's a little scary, isn't it?"

Eduardo continued. "Within a few days most of you will complete the surgical procedures. To give you time to heal, we will curtail any aerobic or strength training exercises for the upcoming week, but we will be meeting together to teach you about nutrition and makeup secrets of the stars. We will have some big names come in as guest lecturers. These are people who work in Hollywood. I'm sure you will benefit from what they have to say."

He took the time to look at each of the girls. "I know it hasn't been easy for you the past few days, but you've made it through the worst, and now it will only get better. I have asked Marianna to say a few words of encouragement to you. Marianna?"

Marianna walked quickly to the front of the room and turned to face the girls. She looked elegant and chic in an off-white suit and a pair of large, silver loop earrings. Her short, black hair was brushed up into spikes, and her makeup was perfect.

"I just want to say how proud I am of you girls. I just want you to know that it's all going to be worth it. To prove that point, I have some pictures of me growing up."

The lights went down, and Marianna began her Power Point presentation. "This is me in sixth grade."

The girls burst out laughing. The girl on the screen wore thick glasses. Her hair looked like it hadn't been brushed in a month, and she was staring at the floor. She wore a red Scottish plaid skirt, a yellow shirt, and long blue socks.

"I can laugh about it now, but at that time I felt pretty bad about myself. My mom was out of the picture, my grandmother took care of me, and the clothes I wore were what my mom had worn, plus Grandma did pick up a few things at garage sales.

"This next picture was taken on the night of the big prom in my high school. I was sixteen." The image was that of a girl sitting on a couch in her pajamas, eating ice cream.

"I didn't go to the prom. Nobody asked me. Nobody asked me out to that particular dance, or anything else in high school. In fact I didn't have any friends who were guys."

The next image was that of Marianna standing in a cemetery. "When I was eighteen, my mom died. A year later my grandmother died. She left me a little money."

"Grammie always told me I could do whatever I really wanted to do. Well, I decided I wanted to be someone people paid attention to. So I moved to Hollywood and got a job on a movie set. Nothing glamorous. Basically, I was a stock clerk, checking things in and out. But I met a few people, and learned a few things, and eventually worked my way into makeup and hair. I did that for six years, when Eduardo gave me a chance to work for Teen Radiance. I've loved it here ever since because I get the opportunity to do for other girls what I wish somebody had done for me when I was your age."

She paused. "I am you, or I was. And you are me, or you will be. Keep that in mind when you're hurting, when you're discouraged, when you wish you'd never come here. It's going to get better. I promise you that." She paused. "I guess that's it, unless there are any questions."

Alli stood up.

"Alli?"

"Did the things you did to change your appearance make any difference in your love life?"

The girls howled their approval.

Marianna smiled and tossed her head. "Well, without going into any details, let me just say I had to upgrade my phone mail system."

"Hey, we don't mind if you go into detail," Alli joked.

The girls again laughed.

"I don't think so, but nice try, Alli."

"Are you with someone now?" Alli asked.

"Yes, I am."

"How long have you been with him?"

She smiled. "Long enough to let the lease on my apartment expire."

"Tell us some more about him."

"Well, he's an actor. Actually, you girls might have even seen him in some of the movies he's done. Right now he's in a TV series. Have any of you ever seen *Street Smart?*"

"Are you serious!" one of the girls cried out. "I watch it all the time. Who is it?"

Marianna smiled. "Devin Corbett. He plays the part of Detective Matthews."

"Oh, my gosh!" the girl called out. "Can you get me his autograph?"

Marianna smiled. "I think I can do better than that. Let me ask him if he'd be willing to come and talk to you girls."

"I can't believe this! Just that makes this all worth it," the girl exclaimed.

"But," Marianna added, "I'll only have him come if you all work hard the next couple of weeks, and if you quit going around like the walking dead and being such whiners. Look, I know you're healing up and there's a lot of pain, but if you'll have faith in us—that we know what we're doing, and that this will work out if you'll just stay with us and do your best. That's all I need from you girls. And if you give me that, then I'll get Devin here for you."

The girl spoke for them all. "We'll do it!"

"Everyone who will be a team player so Andrea here and some of you others who love watching *Street Smart* can have some time with Devin, please raise your hands. . . . Any opposed. . . . Okay, it's unanimous. So that means I expect total cooperation."

"You've got it!" Devin Corbett's greatest fan called out.

"All, right . . ." Marianna paused and looked at each of the girls. "This happens every time. I get attached. And I start feeling like a big sister to each of you. And that's the way I feel now. I admire you for not being satisfied with who you are, for striving to be better, to look better, to take your place with the winners of this world, not with the losers. And to never be satisfied. To just keep pushing and trying and never giving up."

She began walking through the group, talking to each of the girls, calling them by name, asking each of them how they were doing.

When she had talked to everyone, she returned to where she had been standing. "Just one thing. When you go back home, things are going to be different. People will treat you differently. Especially all the guys who used to ignore you. So go easy at first. Don't rush into anything, okay? Also, you need to know that some girls will be jealous, and they'll talk about you. They may say some cruel things. There's nothing you can do about that." She sighed. "You may even lose some friends—those who can't take how much you've changed. But you can't worry about that. In some ways you came here a loser, but you're going back a definite winner. You deserve the best. If it means losing a few friends who don't match up to where you are now, then that's what has to happen. As much as I'd like to, I can't change everyone, and neither can you. So what you need to do is just move on. That's just the way life is. Just be grateful that when you leave here you will be one of the beautiful people of the world. I hope you will enjoy that for the rest of your life. Speaking for both Eduardo and myself, it is our gift to you."

When Madison returned to her room, she had time to think. Even though she had been moved by Marianna's comments, she couldn't help but compare it to the attitude of the apostate Zoramites in the Book of Mormon. She read Alma 31 and was especially interested in verse 17: "And thou hast elected us that we shall be saved, whilst all around us are elected to be cast by thy wrath down to hell; for the which holiness, O God, we thank thee . . ."

Maybe because of her dad, she didn't totally trust Eduardo. Even so, she did feel a sense of loyalty to the other girls in the program. Because they all were far away from home and because they were going through difficult times together, she felt that these girls were now like a family. She wanted to be true to them no matter what.

Two weeks later the girls were recovered enough to begin a rigorous program of body sculpting. After listening to the moans of those who had undergone cosmetic surgery, Madison was grateful she hadn't submitted to any of the recommended procedures. She was also glad for the head start she had gotten in the gym. By the time the others began their concentrated workouts, she had gotten beyond the feeling that the exercises were going to kill her and had developed a little more endurance.

For three hours in the morning and three hours in the afternoon, under the careful guidance of fitness trainers, they did an endless series of aerobics and weight training. "Make it burn," seemed to be their trainers' favorite saying.

Every night Madison went to bed exhausted, her muscles aching, only to wake up and start the entire process all over again the next day.

The girls weren't allowed to weigh themselves, but with the limited amount she was eating and all the exercise she was getting, Madison could tell she had lost some weight and some inches as well. For the first time since she was a young girl, she was beginning to feel fit and healthy and spent a lot of time admiring her changing shape in the mirror and getting used to her new teeth and brighter smile. She had also had her hair cut and highlighted and was learning how to apply her makeup more effectively, to emphasize her eyes and her new smile.

At first the routine seemed like torture, but the girls' attitudes gradually began to change, as evidenced by Alli's surprise, late-night visit to Madison's room.

"Want a snack?" Alli asked.

Madison nodded, fully expecting ice cream to be in the sack as usual. "What flavor did you have the maid get for us?"

Alli pulled out a bag of baby carrots. "Help yourself."

"Carrots?"

"Yeah, I got to thinking, why am I knocking myself out every day if I'm only going to replace what I've lost with half a gallon of ice cream every night? From now on, we get carrots."

"Sure, why not?"

Alli sprawled on the sofa. "Have you noticed some changes in yourself lately?"

"Like what?"

"I've discovered muscles I never knew I had. My stomach is mostly flat. Me, can you believe it? We're becoming what we once could only dream about."

"I've noticed that, too," Madison said.

"It's working. This whole thing is actually working. I can't believe it. You know what? I'm not going to make fun of Eduardo anymore. You know what else? I can hardly wait to go home and show off what I've become. How about you?"

Madison thought about it. "I'm not sure. How will I know who my real friends are now?"

Alli tossed a baby carrot at her. "Who cares? If they're friendly, then they're your friends. You'll pick up a few new friends, and you'll lose some others. It's not that hard, okay?"

"But what if my new friends are shallow and only like me because of the way I look?"

"Hey, if they like you, that's all that counts."

"Maybe so," Madison said, at the same time wondering what the girls in her ward would think about the way she looked now. She worried they would think she had given up her standards just to be popular.

Later that night, as she did one last set of ab exercises before going to bed, she decided she hadn't given up anything, and that no matter what she would always be the same inside, and it didn't matter what changes she'd made on the outside.

Devin Corbett, one of the stars on the hit TV show *Street Smart,* did visit with the girls a few days later. Madison, who was not a fan of the show, and in fact had never seen it because in Duluth it was shown on Sunday night, was surprised at the enthusiasm generated by his visit.

He and Marianna entered the room in quick strides, holding hands.

"Well, girls, this is my show-and-tell for this week," Marianna said proudly.

"Hello, Ladies," Devin said in a deep, modulated voice. "What can I do for you?"

"Never leave us!" one of the girls squealed.

"Or take us with you," another girl said.

"Hold on. He's mine, girls, all mine," Marianna said with a grin.

Devin seemed to have made no effort to impress anyone. He was wearing faded jeans and a T-shirt, and his hair was uncombed, sticking up in all directions. He hadn't shaved, either, but his face and arms were very tanned.

Madison watched him closely, trying to figure out what the others found so irresistible in him. The more he flirted with the girls, the less impressed she was with him, especially as he began answering their questions.

"Do you think you and Marianna will ever get married?" one girl asked.

Devin glanced at Marianna. "Well, of course we've talked about it, but right now we're not ready for that kind of commitment. We're both very busy. My career has really taken off recently. I'll be starting a movie in Hong Kong in two months. If all goes according to schedule, that will take seventy-five days. And Marianna has some other irons in the fire. If we get married, we want it to be at a time when life is not so hectic. Right now we just want to enjoy our time together."

"Tell us about the movie," one of the girls said.

"Well, it's a romantic thriller."

"Who's the female lead?" a girl asked.

Devin paused, glancing at Marianna. "Well, actually, that hasn't been announced yet."

"You know who it is, though, don't you? You just don't want Marianna to know."

"Well, I understand they're talking to Angelina Jolie."

Alli stood up to ask her question. "Marianna, would you be jealous if Devin spends two months in Hong Kong with Angelina Jolie?"

Marianna smiled, but to Madison, it didn't look like a happy smile. "No, not at all. We trust each other."

"That's right," Devin said. "And if the two-month separation is too hard on us, then we'll acknowledge the fact we've both moved on, and we'll part good friends. That's just the way life is."

Madison saw the hurt in Marianna's eyes after Devin said this, but almost as a reflex, Marianna masked it and carried on.

Three more weeks of body sculpting and learning makeup, hair styling, and poise followed.

Three days before the program was to end, the girls were bussed to Hollywood for a screen test and a tour of a major studio.

On the ride in, Marianna stood up and grabbed the bus microphone to talk to the girls. "Okay, how many of you think you're going to do this one screen test and immediately be offered a starring role in a movie?"

All the girls cheered.

Marianna laughed. "Wow! Looks like I've got my work cut out for me, right? The chances you'll be a movie star are like one in a million.

Thousands of girls just like you come to Hollywood every year with stars in their eyes. Most of them end up going home a few months later with nothing to show for all their hard work.

"But let me tell you girls something. You're absolutely gorgeous, and, as far as I'm concerned, I'd take any one of you over the young women who are making successful careers in the movies. But the reality is that most likely nothing will come from this."

"So why are we doing it?" Alli asked.

"Good question. Why are we doing it?" She glanced out the window to gather her thoughts and then turned her attention back to the girls.

"We're having each of you do a screen test so that when you go back home you don't fall back into the same rut you were in before you came here."

With a silly grin on her face, she imitated them. "Oh, yeah, I did a screen test for a major studio, and I'm just waiting for them to call me up and offer me a part."

She paused. "I want you to remember one thing from what happens today. You are in the class of people who do take screen tests. Some of you grew up thinking you weren't worth much. When you go home, I don't care if you forget to do your ab exercises or occasionally eat too much or slip up on something we've taught you here. But I do care about one thing—that you never again think of yourself as just ordinary, because I want to tell you, you're not. You are amazing, each one of you. I feel that so strongly about each of you. So if you let everything else slide, don't let that feeling of pride of who you are ever go away because that's what will make all the difference in your lives."

The girls stood up and cheered Marianna.

She wiped her eyes. "You've ruined my big chance. Now if Steven Spielberg sees me with my red eyes today, he'll just keep going."

"Don't worry. He'd never want you anyway," one of the girls teased.

Marianna threw back her head and laughed. "That's just my point! Who ever knows what a director wants? Okay, let's move on. You're going to have a screen test. Let me give you some advice. First of all, enjoy the experience and have fun. There's no reason to be nervous. Just keep telling yourself nothing is going to come from it, except you're going to have a good time. You'll each take back with you a DVD of your screen test and hopefully you'll show it to your friends and family and they'll all be very impressed and tell you that you definitely should be a movie star, but you'll know that the odds are against that happening. So have fun! I want you to watch this at home when you feel discouraged or when you want to impress a guy you've just met. That's what it's for. It's for you and it's for your friends back home."

The first thing they did upon arriving in Hollywood was to take the Warner Brothers Studio V.I.P. tour, including a visit to the Warner Brothers Museum. And then they boarded a fleet of golf carts and visited the back lots of the studio.

After a sack lunch, they boarded their bus and made their way to an office building a few minutes away where a company claiming connections to movie directors would do the screen tests.

Each girl was assigned an aspiring young actor and two pages of a script.

"You have half an hour, and then we shoot the scene," the woman in charge announced to the girls. "There are some rooms down the hall where you can meet to work out how you will play the scene. Good luck to you all!"

"Let's go outside," the guy assigned to Madison said. "There's a park across the street."

At the park they each sat on a swing.

"What's your name?" she asked.

He shook his head. "There's no time for that."

"How can there not be enough time for me to learn your name?"

"It doesn't matter what my name is." He glanced at the script. "This is supposed to be a comedy. Maybe we could do it with each of us having a different accent."

"It matters to me what your name is."

"Fine, then. I'm Ben."

"Good to meet you, Ben. I'm Madison."

He looked at his watch. "Great. Can you do any kind of an accent?"

"Well, I am from Minnesota, so I could do that."

He nodded his head. "Good. I'll do . . . a Brooklyn accent."

"Are you from Brooklyn?"

"Look, you're wasting my time. I want us to be first in line so I can get out of here." He paused. "Nothing personal, okay? I treat all the girls I work with here the same way."

"I understand. Okay, let's go over it a few times and then we'll walk back and tell them we're ready."

They were the first ones done.

Madison was surprised that once the cameras were rolling, Ben became animated and funny. That helped her open up more, too.

They shot the same scene twice. By the second time, she was almost his equal in their dialogue, and once she made him smile.

"That's a wrap," the director called out.

Ben gave her a parting hug. "Actually, that was good!" he said. "You did a great job. Nice to work with you. Well, I've got to be going."

"I'll be watching for you in the movies," she said.

"Thanks. Keep in touch, okay?" he gave her a card with his Web site. "There's contact information here if you want to send me an e-mail. 'Bye."

And then he was gone.

After all the girls had completed their screen tests, they boarded their bus for their ride back to San Clemente.

As they were pulling onto the street, Marianna stood up to address them. "Girls, we have a big surprise! Right now we're going to a fashion boutique in a famous Hollywood mall. We're giving each of you three hundred dollars to buy some clothes to wear the first week of school, something that will say to the world, 'Here I am, look at me now!'"

The girls cheered.

It was as exciting as Christmas for all the girls as they picked out what they wanted to buy.

alone, together

The process took over two hours. Before getting back on the bus, Marianna treated them to a stop at the mall's food court.

"This is so great, just being here with everyone," Alli said to Madison. She stood up to make an announcement. "Hey, you guys, I'm going to make a speech now."

They laughed.

"No, this time I'm serious. I was just thinking, this is going to be one of the last times we're together. I just wanted to say, well, I really think I'm the most beautiful girl in the group, but, hey, don't feel bad. You're all first runners-up."

The girls laughed.

Alli continued. "Seriously, though, I love you guys. And I hope we'll stay close. We've gone through so much together. You're the best thing that's ever happened to me. And, Marianna, we couldn't have done it without you."

"Thank you, Alli. This has been the best group we've ever had."

They stayed in the food court a long time. Madison felt so close to every girl there. The only thing that bothered her a little was how the girls criticized shoppers their age who passed by.

"Oh, nice outfit," one girl said sarcastically.

"Look at the way that one walks. It's like she's looking for a lost penny."

As they criticized one girl after another, the words of the Young Women's theme came into her mind. "We are daughters of our Heavenly Father, who loves us, and we love him . . ." She wanted to say something, but these were the best friends she'd ever had, and she couldn't bring herself to criticize them.

The next day they were videotaped to get their reaction to the experience they'd had. That interview, along with footage taken throughout their stay, would be used to market and promote Teen Radiance makeovers.

For her part, Madison ended her taped interview with Marianna by saying, "This has changed my life. I will never be the same. I am so grateful for the experience I've had here."

"How do you expect this to affect your life when you return to school?" Marianna asked.

"I'm not sure. I just know I don't have to feel sorry for myself anymore. I have become what I could only dream about before. If you work hard enough, you can reach your goals. That's what this has taught me. From now on I will always know that I can be what I want to be."

After the interview was over, Marianna asked to talk to Madison privately. They went to her office. "Sit down. Why do you suppose you got picked for this?" Marianna asked as she began looking through files on her desk.

"Because I needed it the most?"

"No, that's not it. Eduardo didn't have any interest in you coming, but you were my top pick. Want to know why?" She pulled out the letter Madison had sent with her application and began to read. "'If you pick me, I'll take what I learn and teach it to other girls so they will have a chance to feel good about themselves too. So if you pick me, it will be like picking many girls just like me from my school. All I want is for girls like me to be treated like they're worth something. And if that isn't good enough for this contest, then that's just too bad.'"

Marianna placed the letter back in her file. "That's why you were selected. Because in some way I was hoping you could replicate what we do here, for girls in Duluth, Minnesota. I can't reach them all, you know. So I was hoping then and I'm still hoping you can reach girls I'll never be able to reach."

Marianna stood up. "Let's go. I need to get back to work. But remember one thing. I'll be watching you. Well, not really. But I'll always want to know what you've done with what we've given you here. If it's only about you, then somehow, especially with you, I think we will have failed."

"Thank you so much for everything, Marianna. I won't let you down." She gave Marianna a big hug.

The next morning, thinner than she'd ever been and feeling confident about her appearance, Madison flew home.

chapter
seven

Josh

grandpa's condition continued to worsen, but even so, some days were good for him.

Because Josh and Hannah worked nights, the only time they saw him was after school. Grandpa began to insist that his pain pills be timed so he'd have the best chance of being alert and pain-free when they arrived home.

He enjoyed having them sit with him in his bedroom. Sometimes he would tell stories about his life and what lessons he had learned.

"When I was a little boy, there was one song my mother loved to hear me sing. It's called, 'Jesus Wants Me for a Sunbeam.' And now I'm going to sing it for you."

His voice was scratchy and uneven, clear tones randomly combined with the throaty gruffness that sounded like a controlled cough.

> *Jesus wants me for a sunbeam,*
> *To shine for him each day;*
> *In ev'ry way try to please him,*
> *At home, at school, at play.*

He sang the chorus more lustily.

> *A sunbeam, a sunbeam,*
> *Jesus wants me for a sunbeam.*

A sunbeam, a sunbeam,
I'll be a sunbeam for him.

It was a song Hannah remembered from going to Primary. She hooted her approval. "Way to go, Grandpa! Good job!"

"Yeah, that was really good," Josh said in a much more restrained response. He remembered the song, too, but only vaguely.

"I want you two to learn the song and sing it for me."

"We'll do it, Grandpa. Won't we, Josh?"

Josh cringed.

"Josh?" Hannah warned.

Josh nodded. "Yeah, sure, whatever."

That night at work, Hannah insisted they practice.

"Is that the best you can do?" she asked after they had gone through it once.

"Yeah, pretty much."

"It's pretty bad."

"You sing it for Grandpa then, and I'll just hum along."

"Maybe you just need to hear it a few more times. I'll practice while you work on the night deposit."

With her only a couple of feet from him, as he tried to make the numbers from the day's receipts reconcile, she belted out the song.

"I can't concentrate with you making so much noise."

"What are you talking about? That's beautiful music, you moron."

"Really? Well, do it in the shop then."

"Fine, no problem," she said. She went into the shop and started singing, then stopped and returned.

"Josh, you've got to come in here. There's like an echo. I think even you will sound better."

"I'm busy."

"C'mon, it won't take long. Sing with me."

"In a minute."

"The things I put up with for you."

"I'm almost done."

"I'll sing it at different starting notes. Maybe it's just the pitch that throws you, like it's too high or too low."

"Whatever."

That night he'd somehow lost track of a dime and couldn't get the totals to balance.

She sang the song maybe ten times in ten different pitches, some so low it sounded like she was clearing her throat, some so high she sounded like she was three years old.

One time as she was singing, "A sunbeam, a sunbeam," she stopped to say something. "That's like us, right?"

"What?"

"A sunbeam, a sunbeam, that's like us."

"So, you think you're a sunbeam? Have you quit taking your medication?"

She burst out laughing. "That's very funny, Josh! You're usually not very funny. In fact, most of the time you're boring. But that was funny."

"Good for me," he mumbled, barely following anything she said.

"What I meant was you and I, we're like sunbeams. We're like two sunbeams for the price of one. You know why? Of course you don't. Well, it's because Jesus said to let your light shine before men, that they would see your good works and glorify Father in Heaven. That's what we're supposed to do."

"Right now my problem is I've lost a stupid dime."

She walked over, pulled a dime from her pocket, and tossed it on the counter.

"Here, use my dime."

He nodded and shoved the money and the deposit slip into a bank envelope. "Let's go home. I'm tired."

"Not yet. We've got to sing in the shop. C'mon, it'll only take a minute. Come on. You'll be surprised how good we'll sound in the shop."

She made him stand in the middle of the shop and sing the song with her.

"It did sound better . . . sort of," she said when they'd finished. But you know what, good or not, it doesn't matter. We're going to sing it to Grandpa tomorrow after school."

By the time they got home from school the next day, they were told Grandpa had died in his sleep a few minutes earlier.

Hannah walked over to his bed and threw her arms around him and sobbed. "Oh, Grandpa, come back!" She sat at his side and cried. Josh stood in the doorway and watched.

"Let's sing for him, Josh."

"He's dead."

"I know he's dead, but I'm sure he can still hear us."

"Not if he's dead, he can't."

"Maybe he can, though. Can't we just sing, just in case?"

She seemed so intent on doing it that he shrugged and stood next to her at the side of the bed, looking down at their grandfather's still body.

They did their best, but Hannah was crying during most of the song, and Josh felt foolish, singing to a dead man even if he was his grandfather.

But they got through it.

Hannah gave Grandpa a big hug and then rested her head on the bed and cried.

Even though somewhat awkwardly, Josh patted her on the back, and said, "It's okay."

An hour later, two men from the funeral home came and took the body away.

Grandma, because she needed something to do, stripped the sheets and bedding and began doing the wash.

Dad closed up the station and came home. When he walked in, he went to Grandma and said, "Well, we knew it was coming. We just didn't know when. In a way, it's a relief to know he's out of his pain."

She nodded.

Dad gave everyone a brief hug, hung around for a few minutes, and then stood up. "I've got to go back. I've got an oil change and lube job on the lift, and the guy is coming back for his car in twenty minutes."

Nobody objected, so he got up and left.

Josh and Hannah were given the option of not working that night, but they couldn't see why hanging around would do any good, so they decided it would be work as usual.

"You think this means we'll be getting out of this place and going back home?" Hannah asked Josh during a lull in business.

"Maybe so."

"I hope so. If we go soon, you'll get to play basketball again."

"Yeah, I've been thinking about that."

Three days later the funeral was held at the church. A lot of non-member townspeople came, so it gave the speakers a chance to talk about the plan of salvation. They listened, but nobody asked to learn more about the Church.

The day after the funeral, Dad had a chance to read the recently revised will. In it he was given the station and the joint-ownership of the house.

"How much can you sell the station for?" Hannah asked her dad.

"Well, the station itself isn't worth much. But if a person were to put some money into it and fix it up, and like if we had one of those big tall signs that can be seen from the Interstate, and if we carried a national brand of gas, like Conoco, tourists would be more likely to come to us. And then we'd start to make some real money."

"Be sure to give those ideas to whoever you sell the station to," Hannah said. "We are going to move back home, aren't we?"

"This could be a way to provide for you and Josh's college education."

"So you're thinking of us staying here?" she asked.

"I am."

"Why?"

Dad sighed. "Because I don't have any other choice. I called my old boss, and he said he's got no openings for me."

And so they stayed in Muddy Gap, Wyoming.

Dad got a loan to fix up the station. Over the next few months Josh and Hannah helped paint the station, inside and out, and their dad hired a contractor to completely redo the restrooms and build a new canopy over the pumps.

For a brief time it looked like Hannah was going to have some friends. A girl who sat next to her in class invited her to her birthday party. Josh took her and then drove back to the station.

Twenty minutes later Hannah called him. "Can you come get me?"

"Already?"

"Yeah, right away."

"Yeah, sure. I'll be right there."

As soon as he pulled up to the house, she hurried out and got into the truck.

He drove away from the house. "What happened?"

"They found out I was a Mormon. It pretty much freaked her mom and dad out. They asked me to leave." She sniffed.

"Are you crying?"

"No, I'm not." She wiped her nose with her shirt sleeve.

"Good."

"Take me home. Let me change, and I'll keep you company at the station."

"Sorry it didn't work out."

"It's okay. It doesn't matter."

They never talked about it again.

That spring Hannah and Josh prepared a patch of ground near the front of the station that had previously grown tall weeds. They planted flowers from a nursery, and, every night after that, they watered the flowers. Their dad didn't say much about it. It must have seemed a waste of water to him, but a few local customers, mostly women, commented on how much they liked the little garden.

Over the next few weeks Dad ordered and put up a tall sign that motorists could see from the Interstate.

Business began to pick up.

Josh and Hannah still worked nights, but now instead of closing up at ten, the station stayed open until eleven. Almost every night Josh gave an impromptu five-minute speech, but now, for Hannah's sake, he also read out loud one page a night from the Book of Mormon.

Billy still came around. He would have come every night, but they limited him to two times a week. He made improvements on his car, too, fixing the passenger side door so it could be opened and closed. Hannah also gave him some advice on what to wear. Gone were the baggy pants and black sweatshirts. Hannah got him to cut his hair so it didn't look so out of control. She urged him to shower more often and explained that he needed to wear deodorant.

"Are you my girl?" he asked one night.

"No, I'm your coach. I'm getting you prepared to be with some other girl."

"I wish you were my girl," he said.

"If I were, then we might break up sometime. This way we'll never break up. So actually it's good I'm not your girl."

In mid-July, work began on resurfacing a ten-mile stretch of Interstate, forcing all traffic to be diverted onto a frontage road that ran parallel to the Interstate. Traffic was painfully slow. Their gas station lost business because it was suddenly much more complicated to get to the station, and many tourists, after stop-and-go traffic slowing them down, had only one thought on their mind—to speed away as fast as they could.

On fast Sunday in August, Josh bore his testimony in church. Even though it was a small branch, and there weren't many there, normally it would have been nearly impossible for him to talk without stuttering. But on that Sunday, he spoke clearly and slowly.

When he sat down, Hannah reached for his hand. "Way to go."

"Thanks."

"You've become the way I always knew you'd be. This is the way you'll be on your mission."

"You made it happen." He squeezed her hand.

"I'm very happy today," she whispered. "Are you?"

"I guess so."

"That's a surprise, isn't it? That we'd ever be happy here."

"It is a surprise."

On Wednesday night, Billy came to the station. He seemed very excited as he entered the station. He was carrying a six-pack of beer. "Look at what I got!" he said proudly. "We can have a party right here, just the three of us. Isn't that great?"

"We don't drink," Hannah said.

"Me, either, actually. At least until now, but that's because nobody would ever buy me any beer, but now that my car is fixed up, and I look better, people in school will actually talk to me. So this guy said he could get me a six-pack. I feel like I'm part of the school now. Like I fit in more now than I did. And you guys are the ones who made it happen. So let's celebrate tonight!"

"We can't drink this," Hannah said.

"Why not?"

"It's against what our church teaches."

"What church is that?"

"The Church of Jesus Christ of Latter-day Saints," Josh said.

"Is it a good church?"

"It's a very good church," Hannah said.

"It must be if you guys go there. You've done a lot for me."

Hannah said, "One thing you've proved to me is that you can make changes in your life, and that's what you have to do in our church. You've got to keep changing all the time." She looked at Josh as she said it.

"Sounds good," Billy said. "Well, if you won't drink with me, Hannah, at least go around the block with me, okay?"

She nodded. "Okay, but not if you've been drinking."

"I haven't had anything to drink. All I got was this one six-pack, and you can see I haven't opened even one can."

"All right, I'll go with you."

He grabbed one of the cans. "I'm not going to drink this, but I want to put it in my cup holder, just in case anyone from school at a stop sign pulls up and looks in, I want them to see the beer right there with me, so they'll know I'm just like they are."

"But you're not going to open it, right?" Josh asked.

"No, just drive around with it, that's all. And we'll be back in a flash."

"All right, but don't be long," Josh said.

He watched as Billy with great flair opened the passenger side front door for Hannah and then, still holding the can of beer in his hand, went around and got in. A few seconds later they were gone.

It was a warm night, so Josh and Hannah had moved the chairs outside to take advantage of the breeze. There was the smell of freshly mowed hay in the air, and the sound of crickets.

Josh went to the restroom and filled a large watering can and carried it out to the garden.

He was watering the flowers when he heard the screeching of tires and a loud crashing sound coming from the vicinity of the Interstate.

He climbed a little hill by the station where he would have a clear view of the area.

There had been an accident. A semi-truck was jackknifed across the access road, and the back part of a car stuck out from under the truck.

The car was the same color as Billy's.

Josh jumped in his car and raced to the scene of the accident.

chapter
eight

Madison

for Madison, the best thing about going home was seeing her mom and dad. After her flight landed, she practically ran through the terminal. On the escalator heading down to the baggage area, she saw them waiting for her. At the bottom, she ran and threw her arms around her mom.

"Oh, Madison, you're home!" her mom cried out. "You're finally home! We've missed you so much," her mom gave her a hug and held on.

At first her dad held back, staring at her in disbelief. "Well, you don't look at all like you used to."

"I'm the same, Dad. Just a little different shape, that's all." She went to him and threw her arms around him.

"Okay, yes! This really is my sweet Madison," he said with a big smile.

It felt so good to be home, to be in her room, to go to her ward with her family again. While in California, there was no way for her to get to church. Instead, on Sundays, she had read her scriptures and spent time writing in her journal. It had been a way to balance all the emphasis on learning how to improve her body.

Her Young Women leaders were very complimentary about her new appearance, but she knew why they weren't as enthusiastic as Marianna and the Teen Radiance staff had been about the importance of looking good. Her Laurel adviser, Pamela Andrews, spoke often of developing an inner beauty, and Madison wondered if Pamela was worried about Madison's focus.

One thing that was fun was going with her folks to a family reunion, held just before school started. One of her cousins, a boy her age named Brady, gawked at her. "Have you done something to your hair?" he asked.

"Yeah," she said with a smile, amused that he probably thought that changing a hairstyle was the only thing a girl could do to change her appearance.

"It looks good," he said.

"Thanks."

On the first day of school, she got up early, did her hair and makeup, and put on some of the clothes she had bought in California. She didn't quite know how to feel. She was excited but also a little scared. She wondered how the kids at school would react to the new her.

It turned out to be an amazing experience just to walk down the hall before her first class. Having spent her school years being ignored, it was exciting to notice boys who were talking to each other stop in mid-sentence to look at her as she walked by. It was what she had always dreamed of happening.

Kenny Dikstra did a double take as she passed his locker and then caught up with her.

"Excuse me, are you new here?" he asked.

"Why, yes, yes, I am," she said with a Southern accent.

"Need any help finding your way around?"

"Why, how terribly thoughtful of you."

"My name is Kenny Dikstra," he said.

"I'm Melissa," she said, with a thick drawl.

"What a pretty name."

"Oh, do you think so?" she asked, batting her eyes.

"I lettered in three sports last year," he said, sounding like a little boy trying to impress a grown-up.

"My, you must have been so busy."

"Well, it's something I enjoy. This fall I'll be the starting quarterback for the football team."

"I've heard that a quarterback is the most important player on a football team. But of course, I've never paid much attention."

"I hate to brag, but that's true."

"You must be a very good athlete then."

"I am, for sure."

"Well, I'm flattered to enjoy such attention from a football legend." She touched his hand.

"Would you like to eat lunch with me and a few guys in the team and the cheerleaders?"

"Oh, my, would that be possible for someone as new as myself? That must be a great honor. I'm sure you don't let just anyone do that."

"You belong with us. I can see that already."

"You're much too kind," she said softly. "You know what? My friends call me Sweet Melissa."

"Would you mind if I called you that too?" he asked.

She leaned into him and batted her eyes again. "If you'd like, Kenny. But, actually, a little later on, I will have a big surprise for you."

He got a big smile on his face. "A big surprise? What is it?"

"You'll find out. Bye-bye."

"Madison, is that you?" Emma Jean asked when she saw her in the hall.

She laughed. "Yes. Hi, Emma Jean."

"You look so good!"

"I've learned a few makeup tricks. I'll show you if you want."

"I'd give anything to look like you."

"Good, we'll get together some time, okay?"

The news that she was not new went first from the girls to the guys, who had never paid much attention to her before anyway. So by the time Madison approached Kenny's table for lunch, he got up with a silly grin on his face. "Hey, Madison, you fooled me!"

She put the Southern accent on thick. "Why, Kenny. I'm sure I have no idea what you are referring to."

He shook his head. "I can't believe how hot you look now."

She laughed and dropped the accent. "Why, thank you. That means a lot, coming from someone as shallow as you."

"You think I'm shallow?"

"Of course I do. It's your defining characteristic. You still want me at your table?"

"Oh, yeah, I do. We all do."

Madison glanced at the girls at the table and noticed how threatened they looked. That gave her great satisfaction. "I *will* sit with you then."

After that, Kenny and Madison began seeing each other. She liked him most of the time, but sometimes, just to keep him off balance and unsure of his chances with her, she teased him unmercifully. She enjoyed seeing him grovel for her approval.

Her parents weren't thrilled that he wasn't LDS, but Madison assured them that she and Kenny were just friends.

After they'd been seeing each other for a couple of weeks, he pulled his car into Madison's driveway and honked.

"Is that Kenny?" her dad said.

"Yes."

"You're not going to go out there unless he comes to the door," her dad said.

"I agree with you."

Her father wasn't expecting that. "You do?"

Madison went into the kitchen and got some baby carrots and celery sticks out of the refrigerator, put them on a plate, and sat down to read a fashion magazine.

Kenny honked a couple of more times and then finally came to the door and rang the bell.

"Dad, would you get that?" Madison asked.

Her father opened the door. "It's Kenny," he called out to her.

Madison came into the front hallway. "Hi, Kenny."

"Are you ready?"

"Yes."

Once they were in the car, he asked, "Didn't you hear me honking?"

"Oh, was that you? I thought it was some little kid."

"You knew it was me."

"You're right, I did. Do you usually pull in the driveway and honk for other girls?"

"Well, yeah."

"It won't work with me. You'll have to come to the door. I'm not Chinese takeout, Kenny."

A few days later, they added kissing to what they did when they were together. She liked feeling that she had power over him and that he seemed so needful.

But as the days passed, the kissing took over, and she began to feel that he didn't really care about her as a person.

If that had been all she was experiencing, she could have quit what she was allowing him to do. But at the same time she began to feel that her own body was betraying her, sending a message she shouldn't want. She began to like what they were doing. And that troubled her.

The football season continued. Every week Kenny and his teammates were victorious over another school, and there were lots of pep rallies and parties to attend.

She kept meaning to meet with Emma Jean and teach her some of the tricks she'd learned during her stay at Teen Radiance, but Kenny kept interfering with that.

Finally, on a Friday night when the team had a road game at the other end of the state, she invited Emma Jean over to her house.

Emma Jean showed up with her fifteen-year-old brother, Toby.

"Toby, you want a makeover too?" Madison teased.

He blushed. "No."

Emma Jean explained. "He didn't have anything else to do, so I thought it would be all right if he came. He'll be happy to watch TV."

"Sure, no problem."

Madison spent three hours working with Emma Jean, showing her some of the techniques she had learned about makeup and hairstyling. Then they went through Madison's closet, and Emma Jean picked out some of Madison's old clothes to keep for herself.

"I can't believe you're giving this away," Emma Jean said.

"Well, I was given a lot of clothes when I was in California."

By eleven o'clock, Madison had finished the makeover. They went into the living room where Toby was watching TV. "Toby, turn around and look at your sister," Madison said.

As Toby turned around and saw Emma Jean, his mouth dropped open.

"You look real good," he said.

Emma Jean smiled. "Thanks. Madison taught me how to fix myself up so I can do it anytime I want."

Toby stood up and walked over to Madison. "Thank you for being Emma Jean's friend."

"I'm glad to be her friend."

Toby had a habit of looking at the floor when he talked to someone. "Someone like you doesn't have to even talk to people like us," Toby said softly.

"Hey, I like you guys, Okay? And, Toby, you know what? How many guys would sit around while two girls did makeup and hair? You're a real gem, and that's the truth."

His face broke into a big grin. "Thanks."

That night after they left, Madison had a chance to think about how things were going with her and Kenny. When they were together, all he wanted to do was make out. Each time, against her better judgment, she let it continue until she felt uncomfortable with what he was doing, and then she'd tell him to stop. But the limits of what she allowed were eroding. What would have sent out alarm bells in her head a week earlier became Kenny's starting place the next time they were together.

She began to worry about where this was going.

A couple of nights later, after they had kissed in his car for a few minutes, he whispered in her ear. "I think we should consider taking our relationship to a new level."

"A new level?"

"Yes, I think we're both ready."

"You mean you want us to sleep together?" she asked.

"Yes."

She shook her head. "I don't do that, Kenny."

"Why not? You know I care about you, don't you?"

"Do you, Kenny, or is that just what you tell girls to get your way?"

"No. I really care about you."

That night she felt guilty for never telling him about her commitment to the standards of the Church.

On Monday, in school, Emma Jean said to Madison, "I just wanted to thank you for being so nice to Toby. It's all he's talked about since then." She paused. "He's had kind of a hard time since our dad left. To tell you the truth, I've been worried about him. All he does is stay in his room and play video games. Sometimes I can't even get him to talk to me. When I ask him how he's doing, he always says he's okay, but I know this is really hard on him."

"I'll come sit with you guys sometime at lunch," Madison said.

"No, that's all right. You don't need to . . . you probably need to be with your other friends."

Two weeks later, on a Friday night, Kenny's team won the state championship football title.

The newspaper headline the next day read: "Dikstra Dominates Title Game."

On Saturday night there was a team victory party in a cabin a few miles from town. Kenny picked Madison up at nine o'clock. As soon as they were in the car, he kissed her. "That's how much I missed you," he said.

"I missed you too, Kenny. You played a great game."

Half an hour later, when they pulled up to the cabin, he turned off the ignition, pulled her to him, and kissed her again. "What about tonight?" he asked.

"What *about* tonight?"

"You remember what we talked about last time—about taking our relationship to a new level?"

She shook her head. "Like I said before, I don't do that."

He smiled. "It'd be a great way to celebrate winning the state title."

"A great way for you maybe, but not for me."

"You think I only want this for me?" he asked.

"Tell me the truth. If things happened exactly the way you want, at some point you'd be thinking, *Dikstra scores again!* Right?"

"It's not just about me. I'm thinking about you."

"If that's true, then respect my wishes and stop pressuring me."

"You know what? If you're not ready, that's okay. Don't worry about it. In fact, take all the time you want. Let's just go inside and have a great time."

As they headed toward the large two-story cabin, he put his arm around her waist and pulled her close to him. "You know what? Once you've had a few beers tonight, it might help you relax, so you might end up feeling different about this."

"You know I don't drink."

"I know, but this is a special occasion. It's not every day we win at state. Just a couple of beers, that's all."

"And then what? Look, I'm not going to drink with you, and I'm not going to sleep with you."

He gave her his best, innocent, little boy look. "Whatever. Let's just have a good time."

Madison was surprised to see Emma Jean at the party. She was wearing one of the outfits Madison had given her and had done her hair the way Madison had taught her.

"You look great tonight!" Madison said.

"Thanks. This is my first party like this."

"I hope you're not drinking."

131

"I am, but everyone else is, too."

"Just be careful, okay?"

"I'm always careful."

As the night progressed, Kenny became more and more frustrated he couldn't get Madison to drink. "Hey, it's not going to kill you to have one beer to celebrate our victory."

"And it's not going to kill you to quit pressuring me, either."

Later, out on the cabin porch, he kissed her a couple of times and then whispered, "You want to go upstairs? There's a room where we can be alone."

"How many times do I have to tell you? I'm not that kind of girl!"

He began pacing back and forth, running his hand through his hair. "So how long are you thinking this is going to take? Like a week or two? I'm not pushing for it, you understand. I just need to know if . . ." His voice faded away.

"If what? If it's worth your time to wait? Or if you should give up on me and put the moves on some other girl?"

"You know I'm not like that."

"Why do you want this so much?" she asked. "So you can brag to the team?"

"I'd never do that."

"You brag about everything else."

"Just in sports. Look, I just need to know how long you're going to make me wait, okay?"

"Actually, the truth is I'm set on not doing anything until I get married."

He laughed. "Seriously, how long do you think it will be?"

"I just told you."

Never one to be discouraged by overwhelming odds, he put his arm around her. "How about we just go upstairs and see how it goes?"

She pushed him away. "Stop it, Kenny!"

While they were arguing, two girls came out the door, heading for their car.

"Can I get a ride with you guys?" Madison asked, following after them.

A minute later she was on her way home.

On Sunday she talked to her bishop. In her conversation with him, she shared her concerns over how her standards seemed to be slipping whenever she was with Kenny. She wasn't surprised when the bishop counseled her to quit seeing Kenny. That was something she already knew she needed to do, but she had enjoyed the attention and the acceptance, and she was struggling over giving that up.

On Monday morning, just before her eleven o'clock class, she heard some girls talking about Kenny and Emma Jean. She went over and listened to what they were saying.

"I heard Emma Jean practically seduced him."

"When was this?" Madison asked.

"Saturday night after everyone left."

As the girls told what Emma Jean and Kenny had done, they made it sound like Emma Jean had been sexually forward.

"I know Emma Jean," Madison said. "I can't believe she'd do that."

"It must be true. Kenny told all the guys on the team this morning."

Madison went to Kenny's class, opened the door, and said to the teacher, "Excuse me. Kenny has a phone call from the football coach at USC. Would it be okay if he takes it?"

The teacher nodded. "Kenny, this could be good news. You'd better go take the call."

Kenny came out into the hall. "I can't believe USC might want me to play ball for them."

"They don't. I made it all up."

He stopped walking. "What?"

She turned to face him. "What happened between you and Emma Jean after l left?" she demanded.

"Nothing much. After everyone else left, I got bored, so we kissed a few times, and then she fell asleep. I watched the video of the game again until I fell asleep. The next thing I know, it's morning, and the phone rings. Carlene answers it and finds out her folks are coming up. She freaks out and yells for us to help pick up the beer cans and leave before her folks show up. We help clean the place up and then I took Emma Jean home."

"So, who started the rumors about you and her?"

"Well, I was with some guys on the team, and they'd heard she and I had stayed all night at the cabin, so . . ."

"So you made up a bunch of lies?"

"No, not really."

"Then where did the stories about you and her come from?"

"The guys wanted to know what happened. I told them nothing had happened, and even if something had happened, I would never tell them. So Mike goes, 'Well, if she did this to you, smile.' So I didn't see any harm in it, so I smiled. And then he asked me some other questions and I smiled some more. I didn't *say* anything."

"You knew everyone on the team would tell their friends, though, right?"

"Not really. I thought they'd know I wasn't being serious."

"And if it did get out, that was okay? I can't believe you were willing to ruin Emma Jean's reputation."

"Hey, look on the bright side. Maybe now she'll be more popular with guys."

"How can you be so cruel? People say what a big football hero you are, but you're no hero of mine."

"Okay, I messed up. But there's nothing I can do about it now."

"At the victory rally, you could tell everyone that the rumors aren't true. You wouldn't even have to say Emma Jean's name. At least that would be something."

"I'm not going to do that. This is a time for our team and the school to celebrate."

"You have nothing of value to celebrate, Kenny."

He was scowling now. "Don't make such a big deal out of it, okay?

In a few days nobody will even remember this. Time always makes things better."

"Emma Jean will carry this for the rest of her life."

"Ah, it'll all blow over. In a few days nobody will even remember." He paused. "Look, this is partly your fault, too. If you hadn't walked out on me, this never would have happened."

She looked at him. She couldn't believe how selfish he was. Instead of having any concern for Emma Jean, he was entirely into himself, and Madison couldn't believe his opinion of her had ever mattered. Looking at his cocky grin, she regretted the time she had spent with him. She shook her head. "I don't ever want to see you again, Kenny."

"Where are you going?"

"To find Emma Jean."

She found Emma Jean in the back of the library. She was the only one there. She was staring at the floor, but Madison could tell from her eyes that she'd been crying. "Nothing happened," she said quietly, shaking her head.

"I know. I talked to Kenny. He and the football team made up the whole thing."

"I didn't know anything about it until my second period class. I walked in, and some of the guys on the team looked over at me and started laughing. I didn't know what it was all about, but after class a guy came up to me and asked if I'd do to him what I'd done for Kenny. I didn't know what he meant, so I asked him, and he told me what Kenny said I'd done. I felt sick to my stomach and ran in here, and now I'm afraid to even go out into the hall."

"I'm so sorry."

"I just want to go home," she said.

"You want me to give you a ride?" Madison asked.

"Yes, please. I've got to get out of here."

Madison noticed a few smirks directed at Emma Jean as they walked down the hall and out into the school parking lot.

"Have you talked to Toby about this?" she asked Emma Jean.

"Yes. I told him that none of the things people are saying are true."

"What did he say?"

"Nothing much."

After they arrived at Emma Jean's house, Madison stopped the car. "Do you want me to stay with you?" she asked.

"No, I'll be all right."

"I broke up with Kenny because of what he said about you."

"Are you sure you want to do that?"

"Yeah, I'm sure. It wasn't just that. There were lots of other things, too."

Emma Jean opened the car door. "Well, thanks for everything."

Madison watched Emma Jean walk into her house and then returned to school.

During lunch she went through the cafeteria line and sat down at a table with a girl from one of her classes. As she was eating her lunch, she watched as Toby walked up to where Kenny and his friends were sitting. Kenny didn't even look at him, until Toby blurted out,

"Emma Jean is my sister," Toby said to Kenny. "She just left school crying."

Kenny turned to look at him. "So?"

"Why are you telling lies about her?" Toby asked. His face was twitching with anger and fear.

Kenny glanced at the friends at his table and grinned. "Who says they're lies?"

"Emma Jean is not that kind of girl."

Kenny winked at his friends. "All girls are that kind of girl . . . if you get them in the right situation."

"You mean alone with you, right, Kenny?" one of the guys said.

"Well . . . I hate to brag," Kenny swaggered.

"You lied about my sister," Toby said.

Kenny turned to Toby. "That's a pretty serious charge, kid. You want to take this outside?"

Toby looked like he might cry, but his jaw was clenched tight. "Yes, I do."

Kenny stood up, but instead of moving away from the table he reached for a bowl of pudding on his tray, turned it over, and plopped it on the top of Toby's head, removed the dish and rubbed the pudding into his hair. Everyone at his table laughed.

Madison got up from her seat and walked over to Toby. She put her hand on his arm. "Toby, come on, let's go. You don't need to do this," Madison said.

Toby shook her off and tried to hit Kenny, but Kenny caught his fist in mid-air, turned him around, and marched him out of the cafeteria.

"Leave him alone, Kenny!" Madison yelled as she followed the two of them out into the hall.

"No," Kenny said. "He started this. This is between him and me."

Kenny was holding Toby by the back of his neck as he pushed him down the hall. "You know what, dork? I need to teach you a lesson." With a cruel smile on his face, Kenny opened an empty locker and shoved Toby inside, then closed it and braced his hand on the locker so Toby couldn't get out. "How's that, Pudding Head? You're not so tough now, are you?"

"Let him out!" Madison shouted.

"I will in a while, after I've taught him a lesson. What's his name?"

"Toby."

"Hey, Toby, I'll let you out if you promise never to bother me again."

"I'm not promising anything," he said. "You lied about Emma Jean."

Kenny paused. "Okay, look, even if that's true, there's nothing I can do about it now."

"She says she's never coming back to school."

"Okay, so she's the rumor of the day, but don't worry, it'll all blow over. The thing is, you're starting to make me mad. Say you'll leave me alone, or you'll be in there all day."

"I'm not promising anything. I don't care if I die."

That worried Kenny. He opened the locker and let him out. Kenny shoved him. "Go wash your hair, Toby—it's a mess. And don't ever come around bothering me again."

Toby ran down the hall to the restroom.

Madison stood outside the restroom waiting for Toby to come out. "Toby, please come out and talk to me."

"No, go away," he said. He sounded as though he was crying.

She waited until finally she had to go to a class to take a test.

After her class, Madison went to the victory rally. She would have sat with Toby, but he never showed up.

At the rally, because Kenny was the team captain, he introduced everyone on the team. When he finished the introductions, he had a chance to talk about their season. "Every game was tough, especially after we'd won five games in a row. Every team was out to get us, but that only made us work harder. I can't say enough about these guys. It's easy to look good with an offensive line like we had that opened up holes you could drive a truck through."

He paused, then said, "Now let's hear it for the most successful coach in the state! Coach Grogan!"

Everyone stood, yelling and applauding.

Coach Grogan praised the team and talked about their season. Just before finishing, he officially presented Kenny the championship game ball.

After the rally was over, Madison went to her locker to get her things.

Kenny's locker was down the hall a few feet, and he was standing there, talking with some girls who were surrounding him.

For a moment, he didn't see Toby, who had approached him and was standing there, glaring at him.

"You again? Look, you want me to put you in the locker again? If I do it this time, I swear I'll leave you there all night."

Suddenly Toby pulled a pistol from his jacket pocket and pointed it at Kenny. The girls screamed and moved away, leaving Kenny standing alone.

"I want you to take back all the lies you've been telling about Emma

Jean," Toby said. He was glaring at Kenny, and Madison could see the muscles in his jaw flexing.

"Where'd you get the gun?" Kenny asked.

"Never mind. Take back the lies!"

"Come on, don't do something stupid. I never said anything about Emma Jean."

"You must have said something."

"Ask anyone on the team. They'll tell you."

As soon as they saw the gun, some students ran for the exits, but others just moved out of the way, waiting to see what would happen.

"What are they saying?" Kenny asked.

"They're saying that she . . ." Toby couldn't say it.

"You'll have to tell me, or I won't know what you're talking about."

Toby was near tears. He gestured with the gun. "You know what they're saying! Tell me the truth, or I'll shoot you."

Madison stood frozen in place. She didn't want to spook Toby.

Kenny sighed. "Okay, Toby, you win. I'll tell you the truth."

"Say it loud enough so that everyone can hear."

A teacher on the perimeter of the crowd was moving quietly through the students toward Toby, trying to get students to leave the school.

Kenny turned to the crowd. "Okay, everyone, listen up! Can you all hear me? If you can hear me, raise your hands."

As Toby turned to glance at the upraised hands, Kenny threw the game ball as hard as he could. It hit Toby in the face, knocking him down. As he fell, he fired the gun into the ceiling.

"Go! Go!" the teacher yelled to the students, who began running toward the exits.

Toby got up from the floor, then, almost in slow motion, turned the gun toward himself.

Oh, no, he's going to kill himself, Madison thought.

Madison held up her cell phone. "Toby, Emma Jean is on my cell. She wants to talk to you!" she shouted.

Toby turned to her as she came toward him. She showed him her cell phone. "Here. You'd better talk to her."

He took the cell phone. "Hello?"

Out of the corner of her eyes, Madison saw the teacher physically pushing students down the hall, toward the exit.

Toby handed back her phone. "There's nobody on the line."

She stepped between him and Kenny. "Toby, I'm your friend, okay? Don't do this, please. There are other things we can do both for you and for Emma Jean. Please give me the gun, okay?"

He shook his head. "I don't care if I live or die."

"I know, but hurting yourself is not the answer. I'd miss you too much. I love you."

"You don't love me."

"As a friend I do."

"Nobody loves me."

"I do, though. You're like my brother, okay?"

Slowly, Toby held out the gun to her, then, like a balloon with a slow leak, sank to the floor and lowered his head and covered his face with his hands and rocked back and forth.

Madison placed the gun on the floor a few feet from Toby and then knelt next to him and put her arm around his shoulders. "It's okay now, Toby. Everything is going to be all right. It's okay . . . it's okay . . . it's okay."

She noticed everyone staring at them. Suddenly she was angry with all of them. She called out to them, "Why do we make people feel so bad about themselves? It's not right. All of us are responsible for what happened here. Can't you see that? We're all responsible."

Because the gun was on the floor, it was no threat to anyone, but Kenny ran over and grabbed it and held it in the air. "It's okay, everyone! I've got the gun! It's perfectly safe now!"

One of the teachers rushed in and took the gun, and Kenny's friends slapped him on the back and congratulated him for his heroic actions.

Madison held Toby in her arms and talked quietly to him until the police came and took him away.

That night on the local news, Kenny was, once again, a media hero. When asked if he knew what caused Toby to pull a gun on him, Kenny said, "I don't know. I was just standing at my locker when he freaked out. I'm just glad I was able to get the gun away from him before someone got hurt."

From that day on, Madison gave up trying to be friends with the most popular kids in school. Instead she was content to eat lunch with Emma Jean, and she inquired frequently about how Toby was doing in the Juvenile Detention Center. Emma Jean said he was depressed and that she didn't know exactly what was going to happen to him.

"But thanks for caring about him. If it hadn't been for you, he might have . . . killed himself."

Madison had a sudden feeling that she ought to say something to Emma Jean about the Church. At first, she tried to ignore the prompting, but it wouldn't go away. Her heart was pounding, like it sometimes did in fast and testimony meeting when she knew she needed to bear her testimony, and she finally blurted, "Can I tell you something about what I believe?"

"About what?"

"About my religion."

Emma Jean looked surprised. "Yeah, I guess so."

Madison ended up inviting her to listen to the missionaries and was blown away when Emma Jean said she would and that her mother would also probably be interested.

Two sister missionaries taught Emma Jean and her mom, and Madison sat in on every lesson. The sister missionaries were impressive. They weren't pushy but really knew how to use the scriptures and express themselves, and Madison was fascinated by the way they taught. She found herself learning things she hadn't thought of. Besides, the sisters were kind and radiated love. And when they bore their testimonies,

Madison felt the Spirit. She looked forward to the discussions and found herself wishing she were more like Sister Lowe and Sister Bennion.

It was at the baptism of Emma Jean and her mom that Madison decided she wanted to serve a mission someday.

nine

Josh

billy was pronounced dead at the scene of the accident, but Hannah hung on and was life-flighted to the hospital in Rapid City, South Dakota.

Josh and his folks spent the night waiting.

At about three in the morning, Josh cheered up. "I just thought of something! She's not going to die."

"How do you know?" his mom asked.

"When Grandpa gave her a blessing, he promised her she'd get married and have children, so that means she's not going to die."

"Well, that would be wonderful. We'll just hope and pray that's what happens."

Josh fell asleep sitting up in the chair for a few hours.

Just before sunrise, the ER doctor came out and wearily told them, "I'm sorry, but we couldn't save her."

Josh stood up. "What does that mean?"

"She died a few minutes ago."

"No! You're wrong. You'd better go back and check. She's not going to die! You must have taken a bad reading or something, but she's not dead."

"I know this is a shock for you, but—" the doctor began.

"No, let me see her. I'll prove to you she's not dead. She's just sleeping, that's all. Just sleeping."

The doctor glanced at his mom and dad, and then turned back to Josh. "All right, you can come with me."

A minute later, Josh was standing by Hannah's bed. "Hannah? Wake up! Please wake up! The doctors think you're dead, so you need to wake up so they'll know. Please, Hannah. Let them know you're okay. Hannah, please, please, don't do this to me."

Tears obscured his vision. "Hannah, please wake up. Please. I need to tell you something. I need to let you know how sorry I am I let you go with Billy. Please wake up, Hannah. I can't go on without you. Don't leave me here all alone," he wailed.

"She can't hear you," the doctor said quietly.

"No, you're wrong about that! She can hear me. I know she can. My grandfather heard us, and he was dead. I'm sure Hannah will, too, because she's not dead."

The surgeon turned on the monitors hooked to Hannah. He pointed to one of the machines. "I'm sorry, but that flat line means she's dead," he said.

With tears rolling down his cheeks, Josh pleaded, "But she's my sister."

"I know. I'm terribly sorry. We did everything we could. Her injuries were just too massive."

Josh stood there and sobbed. The surgeon patted him on the shoulder and slipped away.

After a few minutes, his mom and dad came into the room, which was in the emergency receiving area of the hospital. The three of them stood in a circle and held each other as they tried to accept the idea that Hannah was really gone.

They stayed for an hour, but then a nurse came in and asked them if they would mind stepping outside. There had been a bus accident, and patients were on their way to the hospital. The staff would need the room where Hannah had died.

Josh's parents had to fill out some papers and decide where they wanted to have her buried. They decided they would have her buried at the cemetery in Muddy Gap. Josh wanted her to go back to Iowa where she'd had friends and had been happy, but his dad said it would cost too much, and his mom said it didn't matter—she was with Father in Heaven.

They didn't make it home until noon. A little before three that afternoon, there was a knock at the door. Josh was asleep on the couch, and he woke up and went to the door. Two highway patrol officers were on the porch.

"Is this the Baxters'?" one of them asked.

"Uh-huh."

The officer looked at his clipboard. "Are you Josh?"

"Yes."

"We would like to talk to you and your parents about the accident," the other officer said. "If this isn't a good time, we can come back later."

"No, that's okay. Come in. I'll get my folks up. We didn't get home from the hospital until late."

The couch he slept on had a sheet and a pillow on it, so the officers sat on the couch where Hannah usually slept. To Josh, having them sit there was just very wrong. "You can't sit there," he said, pulling the sheet and pillow off his couch and laying them on the dining room table. "Sit here, and I'll go get my mom and dad."

He gently knocked on their bedroom door. There was no answer, so he opened the door. His mom was asleep in bed but his dad was gone.

"Mom?" he said.

"Yes?"

"There are two men from the highway patrol. They want to talk to us about Hannah's accident."

She sat up in bed. Her eyes were red and puffy. "Tell them I'll be just a minute."

"Okay."

"You'd better go get your dad, too. He's at the station."

"Okay."

Josh told the men his mom would soon be up and that he was going to get his dad at the station.

When he pulled into the station, his dad was just finishing up processing the credit card of a man and his family driving a late model Suburban.

As they drove away, Josh entered the station.

"Those folks are from North Carolina. They always buy Conoco products. That's why they stopped here. So that means the sign is working."

"Dad, there're two men from the highway patrol at our house. They want to talk to us about Hannah's accident."

He nodded his head. "The sign has nearly paid for itself."

His dad took two steps, then stopped, lowered his head, and closed his eyes. Josh had never seen his dad cry, but it looked like that was what he was going to do. When he looked up at Josh, his eyes were red. "This is pretty rough, isn't it?" His voice cracked as he said, "You know what I've been thinking? If we hadn't moved here, Hannah would still be alive."

"You did what you thought best," Josh said. It was the best he could come up with.

Back at the house, the two officers were very polite and expressed their sorrow at their loss.

Officer Gardner, the older of the two, glanced down at the clipboard he'd brought in with him. "There is just one additional thing we need to determine, and we're hoping you can help us."

"Yes, of course," Josh's mother said.

"An open can of beer was found in the car. We are wondering what you can tell us about that."

"Hannah didn't drink," Josh's mom said.

Officer Gardner looked over at Josh. "Can you tell us anything that will help us understand what happened?"

"I'm not sure what you want."

"I'm sorry for not making myself clear. First of all, how often did this William Garff come to the station?"

"Once or twice a week."

"Was that to get gas or to be with Hannah?"

Josh felt guilty he'd never told his folks about Billy. "Well, I guess he mostly came to see Hannah."

"Had she ever left with him before?"

"Yes, about once a week. He always wanted her to go for a ride with him. But they were gone for only about five minutes. They'd drive into town and then turn around and come right back."

"Why didn't you tell us this was going on?" his dad asked Josh.

"Nothing was going on. She did it more for his sake; you know, to give him more self-confidence around girls. She felt sorry for him."

"Did he usually bring beer with him?" Officer Gardner asked.

"No, just the last time. He had a six-pack with him. I guess he thought we'd help him drink it, but we told him we didn't drink. He was okay with that. He asked Hannah to ride into town with him. They were only going to be gone a few minutes."

"You let Hannah run off in a car with a boy who wanted her to drink?" his mom asked.

"They always came right back."

"If you'd told us this was going on, your sister would still be alive today," his mom accused.

That was the thought that had been haunting him since the accident.

"We trusted you to take care of Hannah, not let her run off with anybody who came along," his mom continued.

"It wasn't the way you think it was."

"She's dead, isn't she?" his mom shot back.

Josh couldn't stay there any longer. "I need to go."

"Do you have any more questions?" his dad asked the officers.

"No, that's all. The open can of beer makes the accident alcohol-related."

"Dad, I'll take over at the station until closing," Josh said. "You need to be here with mom."

He kept the station open until eleven, then turned off all the lights and locked the door and sat in the dark and closed his eyes. "Hannah, I let you down. I wish I had been the one who died." He broke down.

He stayed there in the dark until two in the morning, and then he went home. Inside the house, with only a dim light to guide him, he grabbed the blanket and pillow he used at night.

He lay down, looking at the couch where Hannah had slept. He had grown accustomed to seeing her blanket and pillow there, and now it too was gone.

He got up and set her blanket and pillow on the other couch, then sat down on her couch and touched her blanket lightly. He pulled it to himself and held onto it as if it were her before gently laying it back in place. He returned to his couch and lay down and stared at Hannah's couch until he finally fell asleep.

◆　　◆　　◆

"Life goes on," was what his mom always said when asked how they were doing. Whenever Josh heard her say it, it made him mad. Life did not seem to be "going on" for him. What he felt his mom meant was that they quit talking about Hannah's death. Instead they focused on superficialities. They talked about the weather and other things that make no difference.

If his mom felt life was going on, then maybe it was for her, but it wasn't for him. Not a day went by when he didn't grieve over Hannah's death.

After their initial shock had worn off, his mom and dad tried to assure him they didn't blame him for Hannah's death, but it was hard for him to believe that.

To stay away from them, he worked long hours at the station.

His senior year had begun, but he had no interest in school. He had no friends. He went to his classes and then he went to work. He tried to arrange it so he worked every Sunday instead of going to church, but his dad would only let him work every other Sunday.

All he wanted to do was to graduate and leave town and never come back.

He didn't believe that college was a possibility for him since it was so expensive, but he did put away everything he earned on the slim chance he could someday go to college.

In December his dad came to him, looking sheepish and apologetic. "I know you've been saving most of the money you've earned working for me. What were you thinking of doing with it?"

"I haven't thought much about it. Maybe use it to go to college."

"That'd be good. Also, you could use it for your mission."

"I'm not going on a mission," he said.

"Really? Why not?"

"It's a waste of time."

"For some I'm sure it is."

"I'm not going."

His dad looked down at his shoes as if he were ashamed of what was coming next.

Josh knew what was coming. "Do you need some money?" Josh asked.

"Well, yes, I guess I do, but I'll pay you back. Every penny of it."

"What do you need it for?"

"Well, you know, we have no insurance and very little savings."

"I know."

"Hannah's medical expenses and the funeral cost about six thousand dollars." He sighed. "We're just barely making it as it is, and having a funeral for a daughter isn't something we budgeted for." He shook his head. "I've made a few payments here and there, but if I don't start paying it off, it will affect my credit rating, and that could make it harder to take loans to improve the station to where we can get the kind of business we need to make a good living. So I'm hoping you can help me out."

Josh was embarrassed that his dad had to come to him to ask for a loan. "You can have it all, Dad. And you don't have to pay it back. I probably won't ever need it anyway."

"No, I'll pay it back, just not right away."

"I'll write you a check for it right now," Josh said, grabbing his checkbook.

He didn't really expect his dad would ever pay it back, but that was okay because he didn't have any use for the money. He expected to work the rest of his life at the station, sleeping on the couch in the living room, never leaving town because if he left it would be like he was trying to forget Hannah.

For weeks Josh managed to avoid any real contact with anyone. He worked long hours alone at night at the gas station, sometimes staying open until well past midnight, not because he was supposed to, but just to avoid having to go home.

Sometimes his mom and dad asked him how he was doing.

"I'm okay," he would always say. If they tried to press him for details, he would say, "Look, I said I'm doing okay. And I am. So quit bugging me all the time."

He liked being alone at the station late at night when there was no business.

Sometimes, late at night, with the station closed, he would sit in the dark and think about Hannah. He remembered how much she had hated Muddy Gap when they first moved there, but how she had suddenly changed her attitude. Josh admired her for how she had learned to love their grandfather and how she had tried to get Josh to come out of his shell. Hannah had become so good, he even wondered if she hadn't had some premonition of her death and was trying to do everything she could to be ready when the time came.

Josh also spent some of those dark hours talking to Hannah. Sometimes he had the feeling she was listening to him, and he told her over and over again how sorry he was he'd ever let her go for a ride with Billy. He also told her their folks held him responsible for her death and that he couldn't talk to them anymore.

A few weeks after the accident, as he was talking to Hannah one night, he had a sudden feeling that what he was doing wasn't right.

She's not here, he thought. *She's dead and she's never coming back.*

Losing even that one fragile link to her made him feel even more isolated and alone.

He didn't pray anymore. He'd quit after Hannah died. He blamed God for letting her be in Billy's car at the exact instant the semi-truck was in the area. Fifteen seconds either way, and there would have been no accident.

Couldn't God with all his powers add or subtract fifteen seconds? he thought. *The trucker could have dropped the tip he was going to give his waitress when he left a truck stop after getting something to eat hours earlier. Reaching down to pick it up would have made the difference. Billy could have had trouble getting his car to start. Hannah could have needed to use the restroom before they left. Any fifteen-second difference could have prevented the accident.*

He didn't read scriptures anymore, either, but he did have Hannah's blue, paperback copy of the Book of Mormon. He didn't read it, but sometimes, late at night, he would hold it in his hand because just knowing she had thumbed through its pages helped him feel close to her.

One night in February, long after he'd closed up the station, and after sitting in the dark for a long time, the thought came to him that what he was doing wasn't doing him or anyone else any good. The first thing he saw when he turned on the light was Hannah's Book of Mormon. He opened it and started leafing through the pages, hoping to find any marks she might have made on it.

His eyes fell on these words in Mormon chapter 8, verse 5:

Behold, my father hath made this record, and he hath written the intent thereof. And behold, I would write it also if I had room upon the plates, but I have not; and ore I have none, for I am alone. My father hath been slain in battle, and all my kinsfolk, and I have not friends nor whither to go; and how long the Lord will suffer that I may live I know not.

He read the verse again. *Moroni was worse off than me,* he thought.

That was enough to get him reading. From then on, every night when he was alone, he would read in the Book of Mormon.

And then one night, as he was reading, he remembered how Hannah had encouraged him to give talks for her when they were in the station all alone at night.

From then on, he read out loud when he read the book. Sometimes he felt that she was listening in, but he never told anyone about that.

Within a few days, he realized that he was looking forward to reading each night. But even so, he couldn't see how it would make any difference in his life. He still greatly mourned the death of his sister. He thought a lot about her energetic enthusiasm for things and her laughter and the kindness she had taught Josh to have toward Grandpa. She really had been not only his *best* friend but his *only* friend.

Even with reading, his grief was like a dark cloud that overwhelmed him even during the few minutes of happiness that sprang up occasionally. And that continued until mid-March, when a blizzard swept across northeastern Wyoming and the western Dakotas.

School was cancelled, so Josh slept in until noon, then got up, grabbed something to eat, and went in to help out at the station. He used the tow truck with a blade on it to clear the snow away from the gas pumps and the entrances to the station.

His father was kept busy putting on chains, so Josh took over pumping gas.

At times the wind was blowing so hard it was a complete whiteout, and they could barely see across the street.

For a time in the afternoon, the Interstate was closed completely, but even then they were kept busy with locals stocking up on gas, getting chains put on, or tourists buying snow tires.

By eight that night, conditions had improved, and the Interstate was opened up again.

His dad went home at eight-thirty. "Don't stay open too late tonight. You've worked hard enough for one day."

"Okay. I'll close up at ten-thirty."

His dad started on his way out and then stopped and turned to look at Josh. "You're as good a son as a man could ever have."

He shook it off. "Too bad I killed my sister, though, right?"

"You didn't kill her."

"It happened because of me," Josh said.

"You didn't know what was going to happen."

He didn't want to talk about it. "You'd better get home, Dad."

"Are you okay?"

"Yeah, I'm fine."

"All right then, I'll see you when you get home."

After his dad left, Josh went outside to use the pickup to take one more swipe with the blade to plow away more snow. The wind had died down, but it was snowing even harder.

As he got out of his pickup, he saw a car making its way to the station. The tires were spinning, and it was going so slow it was barely able to bust through the bank of drifted snow that was piled up in the approach to the pumps.

It was a brand new Cadillac with Kansas plates. A woman driver got out of the car and hurried through the falling snow into the station.

"I need studded snow tires," she said. "Can you do that here?"

"Let me check if we still have your size. We've had quite a run on 'em today."

Josh went outside, knelt down, and brushed enough snow away from the tire to read the size, and then came back in. "Yeah, we can do that for you."

"Thank you." She handed him her keys. "Do you have anything to eat here?"

"There's some frozen pizza you can heat up."

She scowled. "I see. Well, I guess that will have to do."

She was in her mid-forties, tall, with brown hair mingled with gray and sad eyes. She had a numbness to her movements that he'd seen before on drivers who had traveled a long time without stopping.

"Where'd you come from today?" he asked.

"What day is it?"

"Friday."

"I left Kansas City Thursday afternoon. I've been on the road since then."

"I take it this isn't your vacation then, right?"

She laughed tiredly. "This is no vacation."

It didn't seem to him she wanted to fill him in on the details, so he let it go.

"Let me figure out how much this will cost you."

She shook her head. "I don't need an estimate. Just go ahead and put them on."

He pulled her car into the bay with the hydraulic lift and began to work.

A few minutes later she opened the door. "I had a slice of the pizza, but I guess I'm not very hungry. Do you want the rest?"

"Yeah, sure, just leave it on the counter. I'll eat it after I'm done."

She put on her coat and stepped inside the shop where he was working. Even though they were inside, it was still cold.

"I'm on my way to Sheridan. Have you heard anything about the conditions there?"

"I think they're pretty much the same as here, but I don't think you'll have any trouble, especially with studded snow tires. What's so important about getting to Sheridan in this weather?"

"To collect my son."

Josh paused. "Did you say 'collect'?"

"Yes, he's dead. I need to make arrangements to have him flown back home."

He put down his tools and faced her. "Oh, ma'am. I'm so sorry. When did he die?"

"We're not exactly sure. Less than a week ago."

"How did it happen?"

"He was living alone in a small cabin, and when it started to snow, he just walked into the woods without his coat and never came back. I like to think he became disoriented, but there is also the possibility that he did it on purpose. Some cross-country skiers found him two days ago."

"I'm sorry to hear that."

"Thank you. We weren't close. He left home even before he graduated from high school and didn't stay in touch—maybe a card or e-mail
every six months." She paused. "I think he was mad at me for divorcing
his dad."

"Oh."

"His dad was physically abusive to me. And there's only so much of
that a person can take."

Josh didn't even know how to respond. "I suppose." After a long
pause, he added, "My sister died in July."

"I'm very sorry to hear that."

"Her name was Hannah. She's two years younger than me. She was
not only my sister, she was my best friend."

"How are you dealing with it?" the woman asked.

"I try to keep busy enough that I don't have time to think about it."

"I'm sure that's what I will do, too. I work for an investment
company specializing in real estate."

"Sounds important."

"It isn't." She sighed. "I have many regrets."

"That's the way I am, too. Many regrets."

"I'm going back inside where it's warmer."

"Okay."

After finishing with her car, he pulled it out of the garage and filled it
with gas, and then returned inside.

The woman had made herself a cup of coffee and was drinking it.

"I keep wondering if my son is . . . well . . . somewhere. I know he's
dead, and I've never been much of a Bible reader, but still I wonder. Do
you ever think about your sister that way?"

"I'm pretty sure she's okay."

"Why would you think that?"

"Well, for one thing, she was a really good person." He picked up
Hannah's copy of the Book of Mormon. "This is from something I was
reading this week."

He found Alma Chapter 40 and began reading, beginning with verse 11:

Now, concerning the state of the soul between death and the resurrection—Behold, it has been made known unto me by an angel, that the spirits of all men, as soon as they are departed from this mortal body, yea, the spirits of all men, whether they be good or evil, are taken home to that God who gave them life.

And then shall it come to pass, that the spirits of those who are righteous are received into a state of happiness, which is called paradise, a state of rest, a state of peace, where they shall rest from all their troubles and from all care, and sorrow.

The woman lowered her head and closed her eyes. And then the tears came, rolling down her face, splashing on the napkin she'd picked up with the pizza she had microwaved.

Josh thought about giving her a hug, but she was a formidable-looking woman and didn't look like someone accustomed to hugs from anyone.

"You okay?" he asked.

"I'm better. Read me some more of what it says."

He read the rest of Chapter 40, all of Chapter 41. And then he started with Chapter 42.

He noticed she was no longer sobbing but was listening very carefully to every word.

"And thus God bringeth about his great and eternal purposes, which were prepared from the foundation of the world. And thus cometh about the salvation and the redemption of men . . ."

She stopped him. "What book is that?"

"The Book of Mormon."

"Where can I get one?"

He glanced at the book he was holding. It had been Hannah's book, and it had been precious to him because it was hers.

But now it was precious to him because it was the Word of God, and it had given comfort to this woman he didn't really know and would probably never see again.

He folded down the corners of the pages he'd read to her, then handed her the book. "You can have this one."

"Are you sure?"

"I'm sure."

He showed her where he'd left off.

"Do you mind if I finish reading the chapter out loud?" she asked.

"No, go ahead."

She read it out loud. When she got to the last verse, it was as if it were a message for him:

"And now, O my son, ye are called of God to preach my word unto this people. And now, my son, go thy way, declare the word with truth and soberness, that thou mayest bring souls unto repentance, that the great plan of mercy may have claim on them. And may God grant unto you even according to my words."

A few minutes later she thanked him for the book and drove away.

Josh turned off the lights to close up, then standing in the dark said a prayer, asking Heavenly Father to bless the woman in her travels and that everything would work out for her as she arranged for her son's body to be flown back to Kansas City.

"Hannah, are you here?" he asked.

He couldn't feel her nearness like he had just after she'd died, but it didn't matter, he'd be okay.

But then, for one brief second, it was as if he was hearing her sing the way she had once in the shop. *A sunbeam, a sunbeam, Jesus wants me for a sunbeam. A sunbeam, a sunbeam, I'll be a sunbeam for him.*

"Heavenly Father, thank you," Josh whispered.

"Hannah, I just thought you'd like to know, more than anything now, I want to serve a mission," he said softly.

chapter

ten

Mission Postlude

J osh knew he'd grown tremendously on his mission. What he wasn't prepared for was how much things had changed at home. His dad's gas station, after extensive remodeling, was nearly twice as big as before, and now housed a convenience store as well.

With the growth of the business, his dad had also hired some extra help—a retired farmer who wanted to keep busy a few hours a day and a mechanic. The new pay-at-the pump gas pumps made it possible for one person to man the cashier's station and, except for repair work, keep the station going.

Success had been good for his dad. He seemed happy with life now. He had become more outgoing and treated customers like they were old friends, and, in time, that's what they became.

His mom, who before had seemed resigned that nothing good would ever happen to the family, had also come out of her shell. She smiled and laughed more, but she was also more willing to speak her mind when situations arose she didn't approve of.

Three days after returning home, Josh returned to working nights at the station. That first night, after closing up, he turned off all the lights and sat in the semi-darkness, as he had done so often before.

He had to try this just to see if it would work. "Hannah, are you here? Well, I hope you can hear me because I need to talk to you."

He felt a little foolish trying to talk to his sister, who had been gone for so long. He never would have thought of it were it not for the two times since Hannah died when he had felt her presence.

The first time was less than a week after she'd died. He'd been working late at night. After closing up he had sat in the waiting room, trying to decide how he was going to get along without her in his life. For a brief instant he sensed she was in the room with him. He felt strangely happy, and the feeling came over him that she wanted him to know she was all right and that he shouldn't worry about her.

The second time was on his mission. He'd been out less than a month and had been fighting discouragement. He wasn't getting along with his companion, they had nobody to teach, and they weren't working very hard. Sometimes his companion would sleep in until ten or eleven in the morning. There was nothing for Josh to do except to wait. To top it off, he had spoken in church on Sunday and had stumbled over his words, and, in fact, had had to stop and get his composure back before he was able to go on. He had seen some youth in the ward leaning over and whispering to each other, and he knew they were making fun of him.

On that night, his companion had already gone to bed, but Josh sat at the kitchen table, trying to decide if he should call his mission president in the morning and tell him he was going home.

I can't do this. It's just too hard, he thought.

Suddenly it was once again as if Hannah were in the room. In his mind he could hear her saying what she had so often said. *You can do it, Josh. You can do anything. All you've got to do is just keep doing your best. God will take care of everything else.*

And now, after his mission, Josh took a deep breath and quietly said, "I just wanted to thank you for helping me on my mission.

"I really miss you. I wish you were still here. I'd like it if I could feel your presence once in a while. I don't know what the rules are for you, but sometimes I just need somebody to talk to. I don't have anyone like that in my life now. Being home makes me miss you even more.

"Something happened the last night of my mission that I need to tell you about. I'm still not sure what it means. I thought maybe you could help me."

He talked for almost an hour and then locked up and went home. He was disappointed that he hadn't felt Hannah's presence.

A few days later he received a phone call from Sister Richardson. After asking how he was doing, she said, "I called Sister Forsgren last night. I told her about what you experienced during the blessing you gave her."

Josh felt a wave of embarrassment. "What did she say?"

"She was very surprised." Sister Richardson chuckled. "Actually, shocked would be a better description."

"I can understand that. What do you think I should do?"

"Well, you definitely need to talk to her. I have her phone number."

Scared to talk to her and not knowing what to say, Josh waited two weeks before calling Madison.

She answered the phone. "Hello?"

"Hi, this is . . . uh . . . Elder . . . I mean Josh Baxter."

To Josh, Madison's sigh sounded like a groan. "Oh, yes. Sister Richardson said you might call."

"Yes. Well, I did . . . I mean I have . . . That is, I am." He sighed. "Sorry. I'm a little nervous."

"Me, too," Madison admitted. "So, what do we do now?"

"I'm not sure."

"Me, either. Uh . . . I really don't know what to say. I mean, you always gave good talks at zone meetings, but that alone would probably not be enough for me to even consider . . . well . . . you know . . . what you told her."

"I understand. Totally."

"Are you serious about this . . . uh . . . fantasy or whatever you call it?"

"Well, I . . . uh . . . that is . . . I'm not sure. It was just a feeling I had."

"This is awkward, isn't it?" she said.

"Yeah."

"So what do we do, trade e-mails for a while?" she asked.

"Actually, I was wondering if I could come and see you."

"What for?"

"Well, you know, to get better acquainted. And I could meet your folks."

"Why do you think you have to meet my folks?" She sounded very defensive.

"Is there a problem?"

"Well, if you come here, they might think that . . . well, you know."

"You mean that we like each other?" he asked.

"Exactly. I'm glad you understand. How about if we agree to meet at the next mission reunion?"

"I was hoping this could move a little faster than that."

"I'm sure you do," she said.

"The reason is because I can't move on with my life until I find out if what I felt was real . . . or just a strangely active imagination."

"Have you told your mom and dad?" she asked.

"No."

"Me, either. It's too weird," she said.

"We probably should get to know each other first."

"You mean we should, like, know each other's first name before we actually get married?" she practically shouted.

There was a long, painful silence.

Finally, she took a deep breath and, trying to be in control, said, "Look, I've got to be perfectly honest with you. I am very close to asking you to never call me again."

"You know what? I wouldn't blame you one bit if you did."

She sighed. "Well, at least we agree about that."

"You think I don't know how crazy this is? This is the hardest phone call I've ever made. But, crazy or not, I think the best thing would be for us to try and figure out what we want to do. So, for that reason, I'd like to come out and visit you . . . real soon."

"How soon?"

"This weekend?"

After she accepted the idea, they made the arrangements. The plan was for him to arrive Friday in time to have dinner with Madison's family and stay until Monday morning.

Thursday night at eleven, after he got off work at the gas station, he left Muddy Gap, driving his grandfather's old Buick. Half an hour later the engine seized up, and he had to call his dad to come get him.

His dad showed up forty-five minutes later in the tow truck. After checking things out, his dad said, "I'd have to order parts. The earliest I could get this fixed is tomorrow afternoon."

"I need to go now. I'm only going to be there for the weekend."

"Who is it again that you're going to visit?"

"Madison Forsgren. She was a sister missionary on my mission."

"So why are you driving to Duluth, Minnesota, to see her?"

"Just to talk about our missions."

"Couldn't you do that over the phone?"

"I'm going to go see her, Dad, one way or the other."

"Well, I don't know what to tell you." He looked around. "I guess you could take the tow truck. If someone calls, I could borrow Chester's down the road."

"You want me to take a tow truck to visit my . . ."

"Your what?"

He paused. "Nothing. All right, I'll take the tow truck."

His dad called the owner of the only other gas station in town and asked him to come out and tow the Buick back into town.

"Sorry to be such a bother," Josh said.

"No problem. You just be careful, okay?"

They hugged each other and then Josh took off in the tow truck. He drove until two in the morning and then pulled over and slept until eight, then started out again.

He arrived in Duluth, Minnesota, at four in the afternoon. As he pulled up in front of the address Madison had given him, he was immediately intimidated by the size of her family's two-story brick house.

The three-car garage alone was much bigger than the house where Josh and his parents lived. The curved front walk was paved with brick, and the manicured lawn could have come from a golf course. And to top it off, they had what Josh had only seen in movies—bushes trimmed to look like animals.

Josh shook his head. "What am I doing here? This was such a dumb idea," he said to himself.

He walked up to the door and rang the doorbell. He could hear the chimes play the start of some classical melody.

Madison's father came to the door. He looked past Josh to stare at the tow truck. "Can I help you?"

"Is Madison here?"

"Oh, my gosh, has her car broken down again? We've had nothing but trouble with it since we bought it. We just had it in the shop last week."

"I'm not here for that. I'm here to see Madison. We served in the same mission," Josh explained.

"Oh, I see! I'm sorry. The tow truck threw me off." He extended his hand. "I'm Andrew Forsgren."

"Josh Baxter." They shook hands, and Josh was impressed by Madison's father's firm handshake.

"Would you like to come in and wait for Madison? She's not here at the moment. She and her mother are shopping. But they shouldn't be too long. Or you could come back later—whatever you'd like."

"Actually . . . I'm supposed to be staying here this weekend."

"You are? I mean, good. Sorry, I wasn't told. I've been out of town most of the week, so I really don't know what's going on. Please, come in."

Andrew Forsgren led him into a large and impressively decorated living room. "Please sit down. Can I get you anything?"

"No, thanks. But . . . uh . . . would it be possible to use your bathroom?"

"Yes, of course. It's just down the hall."

By the time Josh returned to the living room, Madison's father had fixed them each a glass of tomato juice and a small plate of crackers. "Help yourself."

"Thank you." Josh took a sip of the tomato juice. It tasted like someone had dumped cough syrup into it.

"Sorry, I couldn't find any cheese," Madison's dad said. "It's in the fridge somewhere. After twenty-five years of marriage, I still have no clue where my wife keeps things."

"This is great. Thanks." Even though Josh had gone through a grocery bag full of junk food while he was driving, he ceremoniously picked up a cracker and took a nibble. It had a weird cheese taste to it. "This is really good."

"They're from France. Now, what is it that brings you to town?"

"Well, just to, uh, talk with Madison, you know—about our missions," Josh stammered.

"Well, good for you. Where did you say you're from?"

"Wyoming."

His thick bushy eyebrows raised. "Really, Wyoming? You've come quite a ways then, haven't you?"

"Yeah."

"I was in Casper once on business. Do you live anywhere near there?"

"No, I'm from Muddy Gap."

"I don't believe I've ever heard of . . . Muddy Gap, you say?"

"Not many people have."

"What do you do in Muddy Gap?" Andrew asked, making the name of the place sound like a third-world country.

"I work for my dad. He owns a gas station."

"Well, sure, that explains the tow truck, then."

"Right. I have an old Buick, and I started out in that, but it broke down about half an hour out of town, so my dad suggested I continue on in the tow truck."

"How did he get back to town?"

"He called the man who owns the other station in town and asked him to come with his tow truck and get him."

"Well, so it all worked out. Would you like to move your things into the guest room? Maybe lie down and rest up?"

"No, I'm okay."

"So what are your plans for the fall?" Andrew Forsgren asked.

"I'll keep working for my dad at the gas station."

"I see."

Aware that her dad probably valued higher education, Josh quickly added, "I do plan on going to college. I just need to work a year to save up some money."

"I admire you for being frugal. What would you like to study in college?"

"I'm not sure. What do you do?"

"I'm an attorney. I have my own practice."

Josh glanced around the room. "It must pay well."

"It has, but there are other rewards, too. Helping people defend their rights is a privilege."

"It's probably a lot like running a gas station," Josh said.

Madison's father gave him a confused look. "In what way?"

"Well, people come to you with a problem. You fix it and then you send 'em on their way. That's what we do, too."

"Oh, sure, I see what you mean."

Josh felt intimidated by the house and by the tomato juice and crackers that didn't taste like any he'd ever had and by the fact that Madison's dad was a successful lawyer. "You know what? Maybe I'll take your offer and move my things into the guest room. I need to wash up, too. The tow truck doesn't have air conditioning, so I was sweating a lot this afternoon. Would it be okay if I took a shower?"

"Well, of course. Please, make yourself at home."

"Also, is it okay if I use some of your shampoo? I forgot to bring some."

"You can use anything you can find in there."

To Josh it felt like he'd knocked on some stranger's door and asked to use their shower. In the middle of his shower, there was a loud knock on the bathroom door. He turned off the water. "Yes?"

"Josh, excuse me, this is Madison's mother. My husband should have given you the guest towels. I've got them here with me. I'll put them by the door so you won't have to use our everyday towels. I'm so sorry about that."

"Thank you."

He finished showering, then turned off the water and tried to decide what to do. Clearly, Madison's mother didn't want him to use the towels on the rack, but he also knew he wouldn't feel very comfortable flinging the door open without a towel around him. But if he did that, would she be upset with him because he'd used their everyday towels?

He stepped out of the shower and dripping made his way to the door and listened. There didn't seem to be anyone moving about. He decided that if he opened the door quickly, grabbed the towels, and then shut the door, he could get away with doing it without a towel wrapped around him.

He put his hand on the doorknob.

"Josh, I'm here!" Madison called out through the door.

He jumped back and grabbed one of the everyday towels and quickly wrapped it around him. "Madison?"

"Yes. I'm sorry I wasn't here when you came."

"That's okay. I had a nice talk with your dad."

"What did you two talk about?" she asked, sounding worried.

"Just the usual."

"You didn't tell him about . . . well, us, did you?"

"No."

"Good. Because I still haven't told my folks."

"I understand."

"What are these towels doing here?" she asked.

"They're for me. They're guest towels."

"Are you going to use them?"

"I will if you'll get away from the door so I can grab them. I just got out of the shower."

"Oh, sorry. I'll talk to you later."

He waited a bit, then, still holding one of the family's towels around him, inched open the door, grabbed the guest towels, and quickly closed the door.

After he'd shaved and dressed, he worried about the towel he'd wrapped around him. It was obviously wet. He wondered what Madison's mom would think about him going against her request. He sniffed the towel, trying to see if he could catch a whiff of grease or oil that seemed to permeate his hands after working on a car. He couldn't detect anything, but that didn't mean it wasn't there.

He found a hair dryer and tried to dry the towel so nobody would know he'd used it. But afterwards, as he hung the towel back where it belonged, he felt guilty and wondered if it would be better to just confess what he'd done.

A few minutes later he entered the living room, where Madison was waiting for him.

She stood up, and he walked over to her and held out his hand. As they shook hands, she suppressed a smile. "My folks are outside on the patio. I hope you like northern pike. My dad is grilling some for us."

"Yeah, sure."

"Let's go outside so you can meet my mom."

On the way out, Josh noticed that the screen door needed repairs. He couldn't help but feel superior that her dad was a big-time lawyer and couldn't fix a screen door.

"Mom, this is Elder Baxter . . . uh, Josh. He was my zone leader on my mission."

They shook hands. "It's so nice to meet you, Josh. I'm glad your business brought you here."

Madison's father raised his eyebrows at that but didn't say anything.

"Me, too," Josh said.

"I noticed the truck when we pulled in," Madison said. "You drove that all the way from Wyoming?"

"The car he started out in broke down," Andrew Baxter said. "His dad drove out in their tow truck, and then because they couldn't fix it, let Josh drive the tow truck. But that left his dad stranded for a while. I'm impressed with your father, Josh. That was a very generous thing for him to do."

"Yeah, you're right. I didn't think about it at the time. I was so anxious to get here."

"What business do you have in town?" Madison's mom asked.

Josh glanced at her lawyer dad and decided he wouldn't get very far by avoiding the truth. "I don't have any business in town. Actually, I came here to see Madison."

"Really? Did you two work in the same district on your missions?"

"We were in the same zone for awhile," Josh explained.

"Elder Baxter was my zone leader," Madison added.

"Oh, I see," Madison's mom said.

Josh was intimidated by her dad's steely gaze and decided to come clean.

"Uh, the reason I came is because, well, . . . we're thinking about getting married."

Madison put her hand to her forehead as if she suddenly had a killer headache.

Her dad looked very confused. "Madison, I know I've been out of town a lot lately. Did I miss something in your mission letters? Because, I really don't recall you even talking about Josh."

"I never wrote about him. I never had anything to do with him."

"Then why would you be thinking about marrying him?"

"Uh, I'd better explain," Josh stammered. "I'm thinking about marrying *her,* but she isn't thinking about marrying me. And, to tell you the truth, it's pretty scary for me, too, because, well, the thing is, we don't really even know each other."

Her parents were stunned. "Really?" her mom said, her voice barely above a whisper, but her smile remained clamped in place.

"Madison, do you have anything to say?" her dad asked.

Her face was bright red. "It's not like we're actually going to get married. It's just that, well, Elder Baxter, I mean Josh, gave me a blessing the last night of our mission. He claims that during the blessing he had a feeling that we were going to get married."

Josh noticed the phrase, *He claims . . . She talks like her dad. Maybe she'll become a lawyer. I bet that's been their daddy-daughter plan since she was just a little girl. So what am I doing here? Oh, sure, I could fix their screen door, I could work on her car, I could get 'em some decent tomato juice and crackers, but other than that, I could never fit in with these people. It was a huge mistake even coming here.*

Josh was very uncomfortable. Her parents were struggling to behave graciously, but they were obviously confused. "Well, that must have been a big surprise," her mom said.

"Are you two sure you didn't know each other?" her dad asked.

"We didn't break mission rules, if that's what you're thinking," Madison said. "We shook hands a few times, but that's all. I never did or said anything to encourage him." She turned to Josh. "Did I?"

"No, you never did. And I never thought about you . . . that way."

"In what way didn't you think of me?" she asked with an edge to her voice.

Josh was confused. "What?"

"It's a simple question, Josh," she said. "When you say you didn't think about me *that way,* I'm not sure I believe that."

"Why wouldn't you believe it?"

"Because, in order to say you didn't think about me that way implies you did think about me. Because you have defined the way you didn't think about me, which requires thought about the way in which you claim you didn't think about me."

Josh shook his head. "I have no idea what you just said."

She raised her hands to end the entire discussion. "Never mind, I can see this is over your head."

"It's not over my head. You just aren't making any sense. What I meant was I never gave any thought to us getting married."

"What *did* you think about me?" Madison asked.

"When?" he asked.

"What do you mean by *when?* Were you spending a lot of time thinking about me on your mission?"

"No, are you crazy? I never thought about you."

"You had to have thought about me, Josh! These things don't come out of nowhere!"

He paused. "Well, okay, on our last night together—"

"Your last night together?" her dad asked.

Madison spit out each word. "What Josh was trying to say is that on our last night in the mission field, at the mission home, with President and Sister Richardson, and the others who were going home the next day."

Josh shrugged. "That's what I said, isn't it? Well, anyway, on our last night in the mission field, I remember looking at you and thinking that you were really good-looking."

"You had no right to think about me that way while we were both still on our missions."

I can be a lawyer, too, he thought. He pointed his finger at her. "Do you deny that you are good-looking?"

"People do not say *good-looking* in this day and age."

"Well, they do where I come from. My dad likes to sing this song to my mom. He cleared his throat and sang with a cowboy twang. 'Hey, good lookin', what you got cookin'? How's about cookin' somethin' up with me?'"

His singing was followed by a stunned silence.

"Oh, I'm sorry, Josh. I forgot you're from Muddy Gap, Wyoming," she said mockingly. "That explains a lot, doesn't it?"

170

"I'm proud to be from there. It's a great place to raise a family."

"None of my children will be raised there," Madison snapped back.

In an act of desperation, her mom called out, "You know what? I think we're ready to eat now!"

A few minutes later Andrew Forsgren handed Josh a full glass of tomato juice. "There you go."

"Thanks." Josh grabbed the glass and downed it in one gulp, following it up with a glass of water to get the wretched taste out of his mouth.

He noticed them all staring at him.

"That was really good," he said lamely.

"Would you like some more?" Andrew Forsgren asked.

"No! Please. That was more than enough. Thank you very much."

"We like it," Andrew said.

"I hate that tomato juice," Madison muttered.

Josh turned to face her. "Well, maybe you just haven't given the juice a fair chance," Josh said. "Like you haven't given Muddy Gap a chance."

"This pike is so delicious!" her mother exclaimed, taking a tiny taste. "Andrew, you've really outdone yourself. You're becoming such a great cook on your new grill."

"We got the grill just a few weeks ago," Andrew explained to Josh.

"Where did you get it?" Josh asked.

"Home Depot."

Josh jumped on something else to talk about other than him and Madison. "A lot of times we do our shopping in Rapid City, South Dakota. They have a Home Depot there."

Madison stared glumly at the food on her plate.

"We also like to shop at Home Depot!" her mother said, much too enthusiastically.

"I know what you mean! It's great. Why, just a few weeks ago, my dad and I bought a snowblower. It was on sale."

They dutifully made their way through the food. But, finally, mercifully, the meal was over.

"I hope you've saved room for dessert," Madison's mother said.

"What do you have for us tonight?" Andrew Forsgren asked.

"Coconut Flan."

Whatever flan is, I bet it's from France, Josh thought. "Oh, great, flan!" he said.

"Do you even know what flan is?" Madison asked cynically.

"Are you kidding? Of course I do."

"What's it made from?" she challenged.

"Uh . . . coconut."

"Not all flans are made from coconut," Madison said condescendingly.

"I know. Mostly coconut flans are made from, well, coconut."

Madison sighed, placed her elbow on the table, and rested her head in her hand.

"Madison?" her dad said.

"Yes?"

"Be nice to Josh. He's traveled a long ways in a non-air-conditioned tow truck that probably gets very bad gas mileage."

She sighed, looked up, and said, "You're right. I can do better than this. Sorry, Josh."

After the flan, Madison's mother said, "Why don't you two go into the living room and talk. We'll clean up here."

Madison nodded. "All right. Let's go."

Once they reached the living room, she plopped down on the couch and rested her head on the backrest. "Don't sit next to me, okay? I still think of you as my zone leader."

He sat on what looked like a miniature couch.

She was staring at the ceiling. She touched her stomach lightly. "I think I'm getting an ulcer."

"Nice chair," he said.

"It's not a chair," she said. "It's a loveseat."

"Why do they call it a loveseat?"

"I don't know. They just do."

Another awkward few moments went by.

"It's not big enough for two people," he said.

"So?"

"So why would they call it a loveseat if it only seats one?"

"Do we have to talk about this?" she asked.

"No, not at all. We can talk about whatever you'd like."

"Makes you wonder how arranged marriages ever happen, doesn't it?" she asked.

"Yeah, it does."

"I'm sorry for being so hard to get along with. I'm usually not this way."

"No problem."

"I can do better than this." She moved to another couch, one closer to him. "While you're here, would you like to see Duluth?"

"Just you and me?" he teased. "Isn't that against mission rules?"

"If you want, I'll bring my honorable release letter and read it every ten minutes."

"No, that's okay."

"Let's go, then," she stood up.

"Right now?"

"What else are we going to do?"

"Before we go, can I ask you a question?" he asked.

She got a panicky look on her face. "I guess it depends on the question."

He smiled. "Don't worry. It's not *that* question. It's about the towels in the bathroom."

"What about them?"

"I used one of the towels on the rack when I opened the door to get the guest towels. But your mom said for me not to use your regular towels. So is she going to be mad?"

"No, she won't. I promise."

"If we go into the bathroom, I can point out which towel it was. In case she wants to wash it before anyone in the family uses it. Also, maybe you could do me a favor and smell the towel for me."

She stared at him. "Excuse me?"

"Sometimes, after I get home from work, my mom says I smell of oil and grease, even after I've taken a shower. So I just wanted to find out if that's a problem."

"Just forget about it, okay? Nobody cares. That's just a guest bathroom anyway. We all have our own bathrooms upstairs in our rooms."

"Oh, okay. Thanks."

After Madison told her parents where they were going, they left. She drove her car, a new Mitsubishi.

"My mom and dad met at BYU. They became good friends first before they got serious. I always thought that's the way it would be for me."

"It can be that way for us. We can become friends first."

"I know, but we live so far from each other. Since I found out you were coming, I've tried to figure out what you think this trip is about. Like, do you expect me to leave with you on Monday, on our way to the nearest temple?"

He laughed. "No, of course not!"

"Then what do you think is going to come from this weekend?"

"I was hoping that by the time I leave we could be calling each other by our first names."

She smiled. "I think we can manage that . . . uh . . . Josh, right?"

"Right, and you're Madison."

"Your coming here is already a great success then, isn't it?"

"Definitely. And also, I hoped that maybe we could start to become friends."

"Becoming friends sounds good to me."

They drove for a minute without speaking.

"Where are we going?" he finally asked.

"It's called Lake Walk. In town it goes along the shores of Lake Superior. It's my favorite place to jog when the weather's nice."

She pointed to Duluth's most imposing feature. "That's the aerial lift bridge. When a ship is going through the waterway between the harbor and the lake, it lifts up."

A few minutes later she parked the car near the jogging path, across from several hotels, and a short time later they started walking. The path was a busy place. Joggers and people on bicycles streamed past them in both directions as they walked.

A nearly bald man with a large belly, wearing purple shorts and an orange T-shirt, was jogging toward them, alongside a woman who was pushing a baby carriage. They were almost a block away when they first saw them. A boy perhaps ten years old ran alongside his dad.

"Do you like kids?" Josh asked.

"Why do you want to know? Is this like a job interview? Do you need to see a resumé from me or anything?"

"I didn't mean it that way."

"Sorry. I overreacted—again. This is kind of a stressful situation, isn't it?"

"Tell me about it," he said. "While I was waiting for you to come home, your dad gave me the third degree."

She laughed. "Sorry. That's just the way he is." Then she added, "Look, I'm usually a very nice person. In seventh grade, I even got the Good Neighbor Award from my school. I've still got it in a drawer somewhere if you want to see it."

"That's okay. I'm sure it was well-deserved."

She pointed to an area with shops and hotels. "There are some great places to eat over there. You want some dessert?"

"We already had dessert."

"I know, but we've walked it off."

"Okay."

A few minutes later they were seated at a table for two in a busy restaurant. On the walls were signs from old gas stations. She looked around. "Does this make you feel at home?" she asked.

"Yeah, actually, it does."

The waitress brought their desserts. They each took a bite. "This is great," he said. "How is yours?"

"Really good," she said. "Taste for a taste?"

He frowned. "Do we know each other well enough for that?"

"What's the matter? Are you afraid of my germs?"

He suppressed a grin. "Well . . . to tell you the truth, I don't even know your germs."

"I can't believe this. You're willing to marry me but not to share a dessert with me?"

He smiled. "I suppose it would be over the top to ask for immunization records, right?"

She leaned over and, with a spoon, suddenly stole some of his apple pie, and put it in her mouth. "Oh, my gosh, that is so good!"

"Yes, it *was* a good pie, but don't worry. I can always order another one."

"I didn't take *that* much."

"No, just half the pie and most of the ice cream. Yeah, you really held back. Anyone can see that."

She held up her hands as though surrendering. "Go ahead, take your best shot. I'm a giving person. If someone wants some of my pie, I'm willing to let them have it."

"Is that how you got your Good Neighbor Award?"

"Yeah, something like that."

"Okay, I'll try some of your dessert. What's it called again?"

"Pastiera Napoletana."

He moved the pie closer to him and carefully studied it.

"Is something wrong?" she asked.

He looked up with a serious look on his face. "How far, would you say, can a germ travel, in, like, two minutes?"

She started laughing.

Using his knife, he made a circular arc from where she'd been eating. "I'm thinking it's probably safe to say it's uncontaminated from your germs beyond this circle."

"Really, well, guess what? I feel a sneeze coming on." She inhaled as if about to sneeze.

"Must work faster!" he announced, pretending to be giving orders to himself. He jabbed his spoon into her dessert, far away from where she'd eaten, put the spoon into his mouth, then pulled his pie away from the table. "Sneeze away!"

They started laughing.

"That was fun," she said, dropping her defensive attitude.

"Yeah, it was," he agreed, really looking at her face for the first time since he had arrived.

She returned his gaze for a moment but then looked away when a small combo, consisting of piano, drums, and bass, began to play in one corner of the restaurant. A couple got up from one of the nearby tables, moved to an open area in front of the band, and began to dance.

Madison glanced at Josh. "You want to dance?" she asked.

He cleared his throat. "Actually, I don't know how to dance."

"Well, I'm sure you know the basics. Come on, it'll be fun. If we dance a lot, we'll work off the calories, and then we'll be able to order another dessert."

He thought about it and shrugged. "Okay, let's do it."

When they got to the area where the other couple was dancing cheek to cheek, he panicked. "Do we have to do *that?*"

"No, but you will need to put your hand on my waist and hold this hand."

He did as he was directed. "And then what?"

"Watch my feet. One . . . two . . . three . . . four. Okay that's it. Now you do it."

He pulled away from her and repeated her movements.

"Now do it holding me. I'll do it, too, and that's called dancing."

After a couple of songs, he began to feel more comfortable.

"Should we be as close to each other as that couple?" he asked.

"No, they're probably married."

"Oh, yeah, sure, probably so."

"But, actually, you can come just a little closer," she said.

As he moved in, he felt her pull back. "Not that close," she said. "There, that's about right."

"I like dancing."

She smiled. "Yes, I can see you do."

"We could probably do this even without the music," he said.

"Without the music, we'd have no excuse."

"You're right."

After a moment, she leaned toward him. "You want to know a secret? I like it, too, Josh."

"You do?"

"Yeah. I'll explain why sometime."

"Now?"

"No, not now. Let's just dance."

After a few more dances, they returned to their table.

"You really didn't know how to dance, did you?" she asked.

"No."

"Didn't you ever take a girl to a high school prom?"

"No, I worked nights for my dad. And there weren't any members of the church in my high school."

"That's the way it was for me here. I felt alone a lot of the time in high school. Also, I'm an only child. I should know this, but I don't—do you have any brothers or sisters?"

"I had a younger sister, but she died not too long after we moved to Wyoming."

"Oh, I'm sorry. How did she die?"

"Car accident."

"What was her name?"

"Hannah."

"Were you two close?"

"We were very close. I'll tell you about it sometime."

"Now?"

"No, not now. Let's dance some more."

alone, together

They danced a few more times and then returned to Madison's house.

◆　　　◆　　　◆

On Saturday, Madison took Josh to the zoo. They ate lunch on a patio overlooking the monkey display, and Josh embarrassed Madison by doing his best impression of an orangutan eating a banana. She tried to look disgusted, but couldn't help laughing at the way he looked as he stuffed it in his mouth and rolled his eyes with pleasure.

In the afternoon they played miniature golf and then had dinner at a Chinese restaurant, and Josh found out Madison was both a better putter and more skilled at using chopsticks than he was.

They ended up that evening, sitting at the kitchen table, going through photo albums, beginning with pictures of Madison as a baby, and then page by page, pictures of her as she grew older.

At some point she showed Josh a picture of five teenage girls at a water park. They were all wearing swimsuits.

"Wow! Who's that?" he asked, pointing to one of the girls.

"Who do you think it is?"

"I don't know, but she's gorgeous."

Madison waited for a moment before she said, "That's me."

Before he stopped to think, Josh blurted, "You're kidding! That's you?"

"Uh-huh."

"What happened to you? I mean. . . ." he suddenly realized he was in trouble and tried to cover himself. " . . . I mean . . . you look so . . . *different.*"

"Really? In what way?"

"I don't know . . . just . . . different."

"You mean, thinner?" she asked.

"Well, maybe. But, I don't know, your face and your hair are . . . it hardly looks like you."

She showed him a picture of her taken a year before the group picture had been taken and explained, "The summer before my senior year I won an eight-week makeover in California."

Josh switched back and forth between the two photos, and then turned to look at her.

"You don't even look the same now as you did after the makeover."

"Do you wish I did?" she asked.

"No, not really. You're plenty good-looking now."

"I learned a few tricks of the trade that summer—ways to do my makeup and hair, and I worked out—a lot. But working out constantly and dieting to excess are no longer the most compelling things in my life." She closed the album and said, "By the time I left California, I was happy with the way I looked, but I'd also decided that the people who are caught up in that kind of life aren't necessarily happy. I'd pretty much decided that being good is more important than looking good. And on my mission, I learned that if your number one goal is to help others, you can't focus all your energies on yourself. And now I have a good job as a social worker working with disadvantaged youth. I think I'm going to find that very fulfilling, especially when I can actually make a difference."

"So you like your job?" he asked.

"Yes, I do. Very much."

"Good. I like my job, too, working with my dad. I didn't used to, but now I do."

"So we're both very happy doing what we're doing," she said.

"Yes, we are."

"Even though we live very far apart," she added.

At that point, her father walked into the kitchen.

"Looking at some family albums, are you? Josh, are you having any trouble staying awake?"

"No, not at all. I like looking at family pictures."

"Well, then. Madison, why don't you show Josh the DVD of our family vacations? I'm sure he'd enjoy that, too."

Five minutes later, Josh and Madison were sitting on a couch in the

TV room, watching at first snapshots of family vacations. But then, once Madison was in high school, it became all video.

Madison's father elected to stay with them and give a play-by-play explanation. "This video is from when we went to Hawaii for ten days. It was just after Madison graduated from high school."

"Dad, I think that's more information than Josh wants or needs," Madison said.

"You're right. I should go and leave you two alone. You will show him our European trip, though, won't you?"

"Yes, I promise."

Her dad got up but continued talking. "After Madison graduated from BYU, and just before she left on her mission, we went to Europe for a month. That was our best vacation. Of course, it cost plenty, but we knew this would probably be our last family vacation with just the three of us."

At first Josh enjoyed seeing the family vacation DVD, but once it got to Scotland, he got sleepy, seeing one bleak Scottish castle after another.

"Josh, wake up."

He sat up. "What?"

"You need to go to bed."

He stood up. "You're right. Sorry for falling asleep."

"It's okay. Videos of other people's family vacations are boring. Actually, I fell asleep, too."

"Okay, then, I'll see you in the morning."

"We have church at nine. Do you need a wake-up call?"

"Maybe."

"If you're not up by eight, I'll knock on your door."

"Okay. Good night."

"Good night."

He had taken two steps when she called him back. "Josh?"

"Yes."

"Thanks for everything. I had a good time today."

He returned to her with the thought of giving her a hug, but once he was standing close to her, all he did was reach to shake her hand.

She smiled. "No music," she said, explaining why they wouldn't be giving each other a hug.

He nodded. "Right, we need music. Lots of music. Good night," he said and then turned to leave.

"Good night, Josh."

Ten minutes later, Josh was ready for bed, but by then he wasn't sleepy. He made a tour of the guest bedroom, pausing to look at the books on the built-in mahogany bookcase. Apparently someone in the family enjoyed scholarly European history books. A series of books, all bound in black leather, took up nearly one shelf. Another section dealt with American history, and another with the history of the Supreme Court.

Josh picked one book at random, opened it up somewhere in the middle, and began reading. After one page he realized he had no idea what he had just read. He put the book back on the shelf.

He pictured his family's bookshelf back in Wyoming. It was made of cinder blocks and boards and contained mostly paperback western novels. His dad especially liked Louis L'Amour books. Also, there was a road atlas and back issues of the *Ensign* magazine.

Josh thought about Madison's parents and the house they lived in as he looked around the elegant room.

I don't belong here, he thought. *I should never have come. What made me think that someone like Madison would have any interest in me? I work nights at a gas station in Muddy Gap, Wyoming. That just about says it all.*

Well, it won't last much longer. I'll go to church with the family, eat lunch with them, and then be on my way. And that will be the end of it.

He got into bed and tried to go to sleep.

But he couldn't.

Knowing that Madison was sleeping upstairs in her room kept him awake. He remembered how it felt, dancing and holding her close to him.

He remembered what she had said when they said good night: *Thanks for everything. I had a good time today.* Did she mean it?

He pictured her in her bed, sleeping, with one hand under her head. *What is going on?* he thought. It was as though he had some kind of radar so he could know every motion she made three rooms away.

At first he felt guilty that he kept thinking about Madison in her room, but after a while he realized that what he was thinking was not inappropriate.

It's something else, he thought. *It's like . . . it's like . . .* He struggled for an explanation. *It's like what my mom told me once, how when just after I was born, when they brought me home from the hospital, how she could key in on my every movement during the night, always checking to make sure I was still breathing.*

That's what it's like. But I have no idea what it means.

Just before falling asleep, he wondered what his sister, Hannah, would think about Madison—if she would approve, or if she would say Madison was too refined for a Wyoming cowboy like him. *I wish I knew.*

For her part, Madison also had trouble falling asleep. She kept thinking about Josh.

He's not what I want in the guy I end up marrying. He only has a high school education, and he doesn't seem motivated to even start college. I'm not going to end up living in some Podunk town in Wyoming, married to a guy who works at a gas station. That's not why I spent four years in college. I love to learn. I want to take graduate classes at night after work. And I like my job.

He's a cute guy, and fun to be around, so it's too bad he doesn't fit in with my plans. After he leaves, that will be the end of it.

And yet even with all that, one thing kept playing through her mind—the memory of what it had been like, dancing with Josh.

She remembered high school and how it had been being in Kenny Dikstra's arms, trying to anticipate where his hand would wander next and what she would do to stop him.

With Kenny, everything he did was part of a game plan. And even at BYU, even with guys who'd been on missions, I always felt like I had to be on guard, careful not to get myself into a situation that could cause problems. So why was it that when Josh and I were dancing, being close to him seemed so natural and good? For the first time in my life, I can see how good it could be to be married to someone I loved and trusted.

Strangely enough, for someone who usually worried about every detail of even the smallest aspect of her life, she fell asleep unexplainably happy.

◆ ◆ ◆

At eight-fifteen the next morning, Madison knocked on Josh's door.

"Come in," Josh said sleepily.

Madison opened the door to see Josh still in bed.

"You're not up yet?"

Josh sat up in bed and looked around. "No, I guess I'm not."

"Then why did you tell me to come in?"

"I didn't think about it. My mom is always knocking on my door to get me up, and I always tell her to come in."

"I'm not your mom."

"I know. Sorry."

"You'd better get going. Church starts in forty-five minutes, and it's a fifteen-minute drive."

"Give me ten minutes, and I'll be ready to go."

"Do you want me to fix you anything for breakfast?"

"No, I'll be okay."

"I can make you some toast."

"Okay."

"What would you like on it?"

"Peanut butter?"

"Nobody eats much peanut butter around here. But maybe we have some. I'll check."

"Just as long as it's not from France."

"Anything else?"

"No, just close the door."

"Okay, see you in fifteen minutes."

By the time Josh was ready, Madison's folks had already left for church, so they took her car. He ate the toast with peanut butter and some milk while she drove.

"Thanks for fixing me something to eat," he said as he wiped his hands on the napkin she'd included.

"You're welcome. How did you sleep?"

"Great. How about you?"

"The same."

By the time they arrived at the meetinghouse, her parents were boxed in on one of the large pews, so Madison and Josh ended up sitting on the side in the second row.

They had the row to themselves. Without any forethought, they ended up sitting close enough that their shoulders and arms were touching. They both sang loud enough to realize they sounded good together.

After the sacrament, the youth speaker spoke for five minutes, and then the ward choir sang a hymn. The final speaker was a member of the high council.

Josh had a hard time staying awake. Once, when his eyes were closed, Madison jabbed him in the side. He woke up to see her grinning at him. "Don't fall asleep on me, Josh," she whispered.

"Sorry."

"It's okay. My dad falls asleep all the time at church."

During Sunday School class, they each made one comment, which the teacher seemed to appreciate.

In the opening exercises of priesthood meeting, Madison's father was asked to introduce his visitor. "This is Josh Baxter. He and Madison served in the same mission. He's visiting with us this weekend."

"Where are you from, Josh?" the counselor in the bishopric who was conducting asked.

"Wyoming."

"We're glad to have you with us, Josh."

In elders quorum, Josh looked around for other single guys who might give him competition for Madison. He didn't see anyone that would make him worry.

On the way home after church, Madison pulled into a park and stopped the car. "I was hoping we could talk," she said. "It's easier away from my folks."

"Okay."

"How was church for you today?" she asked.

"Good."

"It was good for me. Would you like to know the most remarkable thing about it for me?"

"Sure."

"It felt so natural being with you," she said.

"That's the way I felt, too," he said.

"Not exciting, right? Just very comfortable. You want to take a walk for a few minutes?"

"Yeah."

They began walking. They were the only ones on the path wearing church clothes.

As they strolled, Madison said, "This has been really strange. I didn't know what to expect when we agreed you would come for the weekend. I was really nervous, and we didn't get off to a very good start, did we?"

Josh agreed. "Meeting your father was pretty intimidating."

She laughed. "I know. He still intimidates me."

She continued, "Being with you yesterday is not how I pictured what it would be like being with someone I might end up marrying. I thought it would be like the Fourth of July. Not like this. This is more like two people sitting around a fireplace reading a book while a blizzard rages outside. You know you're safe, you know you're going to be okay, and that's all that matters."

He reached for her hand. She smiled, and suddenly they were holding hands.

"Like this," she said. "It feels comfortable."

"Yeah, it does."

"Let's just let it be that for a while, okay? I don't want to even talk about where we'd live if we got married because whenever I do think about that, it just seems impossible for either of us to change our situation. Let's not ruin this by pushing too fast. Is that okay with you?"

"Yeah, sure."

"Good. I like you more now than I would have thought possible in such a short time. So that's pretty good, isn't it? What would you think if I came and visited you in Wyoming in a week or two?"

"Yeah, sure, good idea," he said.

"All right, we'll work it out."

A few minutes later she stopped walking. "Let's go home and eat lunch."

After lunch, Josh went out to the tow truck and got some tools.

"I'd like to fix your screen door before I go, if that would be all right with you guys," he said to Madison's mom.

"Really?" Madison's mom asked. "That would be wonderful!"

One thing led to another. After fixing the screen door, he had a look at Madison's car and made a few adjustments so it'd start easier.

"Anything else you need?" he asked.

"No, but thank you so much," her mom said.

"It's something I can do. Well, I'd better be going. Thanks for your hospitality this weekend. It's been great."

Her dad came over to shake hands. "We've enjoyed having you with us, Josh. Come back anytime."

"Thank you. Maybe I will."

"I'll walk you out," Madison said.

The two of them ended up standing by the tow truck.

"Well," he said, "thanks a lot. I know this was kind of awkward for both of us, but I don't think any harm was done."

"No, it was all good."

They stared at each other, not sure if they were going to hug or not.

"Well, I should go. I need to get back to work at the station. My dad's been covering for me. Thanks again." He turned to get into the truck.

"Josh?" she said.

"Yes."

"We could dance," she said.

"No music."

"I'll sing to you."

He put his arms around her, and they hugged.

"You're not singing," he said a moment later as they continued to hold each other.

"You're not dancing," she countered.

"I like you a lot, Madison."

"I like you a lot, too, Josh."

He pulled away from her, got into the truck, and started it up. Then he waved, gave two blasts of his air horn, and drove off.

chapter
eleven

i might be getting married," Josh told his folks the day after getting back home from Duluth.

"Really? Who to?" his dad asked.

"Madison, the girl I went to see."

"Do you two know each other well enough to get married?" his mom asked.

"No, we don't, but . . ."

"But, what?" his mom asked.

"When I was giving her a blessing our last night on our mission, I had a feeling she was the girl I would eventually marry."

His dad stroked his chin thoughtfully. "Well, the way I see it, a car can look good on the lot, but it's always best to take it out for a test drive."

"What on earth are you talking about?" his mom asked.

"I'm just saying, they ought to get to know each other before they do something crazy like get married."

"I invited her to come out and visit us. Is that okay?" Josh said.

"Oh, yeah! That's what I'm talking about!" his dad said. "We'll take a good look at her and see what she can do."

"This girl is *not* a car, and I will not having you two talking about her like she is!" his mom insisted.

"I'm just trying to teach Josh here a lesson, that's all. If that's a crime, I plead guilty."

Two weeks later, Madison flew into Rapid City, South Dakota, the nearest major airport to Muddy Gap. Josh waited for her in the baggage area. There were big smiles on their faces as they hurried to each other. *Are we going to shake hands or hug?* Josh wondered. *I'll leave it up to her. I'll keep my hands ready for a hug and then try to figure out what she'll be comfortable with.*

With ten feet to go, it still wasn't clear. But then at five feet, she held out her arms as if she expected a hug.

I'm going in for the hug! he thought.

At three feet and closing fast, she suddenly drew her hands back, but by then he had already committed himself, so he put his arms around her.

Her hands remained in midair, as if trying to avoid as much contact as possible. But a second later, she shrugged, gave up, and also wrapped her arms around him.

When they broke the hug, they were both blushing. "Well," she said, "that was a surprise."

"I know. For me, too."

He feared she'd make them talk about the underlying reasons for them hugging each other. To avoid that, he asked, "So, how was your flight?"

"Good, real good. And yours?"

"Actually, I drove here."

She blushed. "I knew that. Sorry. I'm a little nervous right now."

"Yeah, me, too."

It seemed to take forever for her bags to show up, and they stood awkwardly at the baggage carousel, not knowing what to say to each other. Three very active children who'd been cooped up in the plane were running around chasing each other and laughing. The mom and dad seemed too exhausted to do anything to quiet them down.

"I like children," Madison said. It was the answer to a question he'd asked when he visited her family, a question that had at that time made her mad.

"Ours will be better behaved," he said.

She smiled faintly. "I'm sure every couple says that before they actually have any."

"Should I have said that about . . . uh . . . *our* children?"

"I'm sure you meant it hypothetically."

He nodded. "Yes, I did. Very hypothetically."

The baggage carousel began rotating. Passengers fanned out around it, waiting for their luggage to show up. "Oh, my mom and dad told me to say hi," Madison said.

"Tell them thanks."

"I will."

He looked at her and smiled. "I'm glad you came."

"Me, too. Oh, that's mine," she said pointing to a black bag with a pink ribbon tied on its handle.

He grabbed her bag. "Well, let's go. It's kind of hot out, so be prepared for a shock."

"When you're from Duluth, you're happy for a hot day."

As he pulled the old Buick out of the airport and onto the highway, he said, "Welcome to the Black Hills of South Dakota. I was wondering if you'd like to see a few of the sites while you're here. We're only about half an hour from Mount Rushmore."

"Sure, that sounds fun."

On their way to Mount Rushmore, they stopped at a place that took old-fashioned western photos. He chose to dress up like a gunfighter. She picked the outfit of a bar girl. When they came out of the dressing rooms and saw each other, they both started to laugh.

"Let's send a copy to President and Sister Richardson!" she said.

"Perfect! They'll get a big kick out of it."

They spent the rest of the day enjoying the attractions at Mount Rushmore. It helped to play the part of tourists; it removed any pressure of talking about themselves.

On the way home, while they enjoyed an ice cream cone, Josh tried to prepare Madison for what she was about to experience.

"My mom and dad are not much like your folks."

"I wouldn't expect them to be."

"And the place we live, well, it's a very small house."

"That's okay."

"They're good people, though."

"They must be. Look at their son."

They didn't arrive in Muddy Gap until a little before five-thirty. As they pulled up to the house, his mom and dad came out to greet them.

"This is Madison," Josh said, as he opened the car door for her.

He was surprised that his mom hugged Madison. "Oh, we're so happy to have you. How was your flight?"

"Fine, thank you."

His dad shook her hand. "Has Josh been treating you right?"

"Yes, he has. Very much so. We've had a great time today."

"Well, good. I'm glad to hear it."

The four of them went inside.

"Let me show you where you'll be staying," Josh's mom said.

While Josh was on his mission, his grandmother had died, and his dad had remodeled her bedroom, a topic his dad loved to talk about. "See that paneling? I got it free. One of the motels in town did some remodeling, and they said I could have all the paneling for free if I'd take it off the walls."

"It looks very nice," Madison said warmly.

To Josh the paneling still smelled of cigarette smoke from years of tourists, but his parents said they couldn't smell a thing.

After his dad had exhausted the topic of remodeling the bedroom, he turned to something else he was proud of. "But that's nothing compared to what we've done on the station. Did you see the Conoco sign coming into town?"

"Josh showed me. It really stands out."

"Guess how high it is."

"Oh, wow, I have no idea. I know it's really high."

"Go ahead and guess," he pressed.

"Fifteen feet?"

His dad chortled. "No, you're not even close. Guess again."

"Twenty feet?" she suggested.

"No, you're way off."

"Well, it couldn't be as high as thirty feet, could it?"

His dad laughed. "More. It's thirty-five feet high. Plus it's on a hill. So, really, if you take in the hill, it's like it's eighty feet high."

"That is amazing! Who did you get to install it?"

His dad beamed. "Nobody! We did it all ourselves! The whole thing! The welding, digging the foundation, pouring the concrete, setting it up. The whole thing."

"Wow, that *is* impressive!" Madison said.

Josh hated it when his dad started talking like that, but he never knew how to get him to stop. He stood there, uncomfortably listening to his dad brag.

"True, but the best thing is what it's done for business. Business is up two hundred and fifty per cent over what it was when we first came here."

"You should be proud of what you've accomplished," Madison said.

"I am. And, let me tell you, I couldn't have done it without Josh, here. He's a gem, that boy, a real gem."

Josh was grateful that his mom came back into the guest bedroom just then.

"Dinner is ready. Madison, I hope my husband hasn't been boring you too much. Once he gets started, it's hard to get him stopped."

"No. I've really enjoyed talking to him."

For Josh, having Madison eat dinner with his parents was another uncomfortable experience. He had grown up just a little embarrassed by his mom and dad—the way his dad used every conversation to try to get people to compliment him on his accomplishments and how his mom seemed content to be in the background. It was the same way in her church callings. She was always the one who got the work done but never called attention to herself.

What impressed him about Madison was how comfortable she seemed to be with his folks, how willing to listen and to give compliments, not only to her dad, who craved them, but also to her mom.

"Mrs. Baxter, this coleslaw is so good!" Madison said.

"Really, you like it? It's very easy," his mom said.

"Could I have the recipe?" Madison asked.

Josh couldn't believe it. To him, it was just ordinary old coleslaw, but Madison made it sound as though it was something special.

"Of course, you just take—"

"Do you have some paper? If I don't write it down, I'll never remember it."

After getting the recipe, Madison said, "I'm going to make it for my folks when I get home. I know they'll love it."

Madison insisted on helping clear the table after dinner. That made it almost required for Josh to help out, too, but after carrying plates and silverware into the kitchen, he knew his work was done simply because his mom never let anyone except herself load the dishwasher.

He stood in the doorway between the kitchen and living room and watched in amazement as Madison loaded the dishwasher without a word of advice from his mom.

"You load the dishwasher the same way I do," his mom said. "Everything toward the center."

"I think it's the best way."

"I agree. Josh just throws things in."

"My dad does the same thing," Madison said, laughing easily.

After everything was cleaned up, they all went into the living room.

His dad glanced at the clock hanging on the wall next to the front door, then went to the window. "You want to see something?" he asked Madison, gesturing to her to come to him.

"What is it?" she asked, walking over to stand beside him.

He pulled the lace curtain to one side. "In two minutes the lights to the sign are going to turn on. It's on a timer, you know. I can change it whenever I want."

"Dad . . ." Josh protested. "Madison isn't interested—"

Just then the floodlights came on, illuminating the tall sign.

"There! Isn't that something?" his dad said proudly.

"It's awesome! Nobody's going to miss that sign!" Madison chimed in.

"It's been worth every penny."

At nine o'clock his dad excused himself, went and changed into his work clothes, and returned to the living room. "Josh, I'll go spell the help and close up. You and Madison can just stay here and relax."

"Oh, do you need to go to work, Josh?" Madison asked.

"No," his dad said. "I'll go. I like to close and make sure everything's buttoned up."

"How late are you open?" Madison asked.

"Just until twelve. We're only closed six hours a day. I figure anyone driving after midnight needs to pull over and sleep. I don't want to be responsible for someone falling asleep at the wheel."

"I'm sure that could be a problem driving in Wyoming," Madison teased.

"Are you saying our state is boring?" Josh said.

Madison gave him an innocent look. "Not at all."

His dad put on his Conoco baseball cap. "Josh, what would you and Madison think about working tomorrow night? She needs to see what we do."

Josh was about to protest when Madison said, "Oh, I'd love that!"

"All right, then!" his dad said.

His dad left, and a few minutes later his mom excused herself for the night, and they were left alone, sitting on opposite ends of the couch.

"I like your mom and dad," Madison said.

"I think you'd like anybody's mom and dad," he said with a smile.

"They're good people."

"Yeah, I guess so. Thanks for being so good with them."

"Does your family have photo albums?" she asked.

"No, but we do have a box with pictures."

He went to the closet and pulled out an old shoebox stuffed with snapshots and carried it to where Madison was sitting. "Have at it," he said.

The first picture she pulled out was a picture of Hannah. It was on top because after she died, Josh often looked at her picture at night after his folks had gone to bed. He didn't want them to know how tough it was for him to deal with her being gone.

"Who's this?" Madison asked.

"My sister, Hannah. That was taken about six months before she died."

"Oh, that's right. You told me about her. How old was she when this picture was taken?"

"Just fourteen."

"I'm sorry. She was a beautiful girl."

He nodded. "I guess so. She was my best friend. Without her I couldn't have made it after we moved here."

"Why *did* you move here?"

"My grandfather was very sick. He needed my dad to run the station. He had me working every night until we closed, and Hannah hated being home because there was nothing for her to do. And the house really smelled bad. So every night she came with me to the station."

"You still miss her, don't you?"

"I'll *always* miss her." He paused. "She was the reason I went on a mission, and, once, when I was having a really hard time, I had the feeling she was actually with me, encouraging me not to quit."

"I wish I'd known her."

"I wish you had, too. I think she'd have really liked you."

"And there weren't any other brothers or sisters?" Madison asked.

"Nope. Just Hannah and me."

"You were lucky to have had her. I've always felt bad that I was an only child, and I envied kids who had large families."

"With Hannah gone, I guess that's something we have in common, then," Josh said.

"What's that?"

"We're sort of alone, together, aren't we?"

Photograph by photograph, Madison went through the entire box. When they came to the layer that had pictures of him when he was young, she said, "Oh, Josh, you were so cute when you were a little boy!"

"Are you sure? I always thought I was kind of funny-looking," he said.

"No you weren't. I would love to have a little boy like you someday."

"I know I was a handful. I was always taking things apart and trying to put them back together again. My mom had to hide things so I couldn't get at them."

"You were just curious, that's all."

It took them until midnight to get through the box.

"Thank you for letting me see these," she said.

"I'm sure they were boring to you."

"Hey, I loved it."

"We don't have any vacation pictures because we never went on a real vacation."

"That's okay." She stood up and stretched. "Well, I'm tired. I'll see you in the morning, okay?"

"Yeah." He paused, then asked. "Do you want to have a prayer together?"

"You and me?"

"If you want to," he said.

"That would be like family prayer," she said.

"Yes, I guess it would."

"But we're not a family."

"I know. It's up to you."

"I guess we could do it. Here, right?"

"If that's okay."

They knelt down together in front of the couch. "Will you offer it?" he asked.

"I'd be happy to."

Even though their shoulders were barely touching, there was a feeling of closeness, and even comfort, in the simple act of praying together.

She expressed gratitude for many blessings, beginning with the Savior's atonement and the plan of happiness, but after praying for the missionaries and expressing gratitude that they both had been able to serve missions, she focused on the purpose for her trip. "Please bless us that it will be clear to both of us what we need to do." She paused. "That is . . . help us to know what we should do."

While she was praying, Josh remembered their mission experiences together. In their zone, "Sister Forsgren" had been known as a very effective missionary, and the one time he had sat in on a discussion she taught, he had been blown away by her skill—that and the easy way she related to her investigators. As she prayed, he was reminded of how spiritual and articulate she was.

After closing the prayer, they looked at each other.

And smiled.

Is this where we kiss each other? he thought. *After family prayer? How weird would that be?*

As he moved a fraction of an inch toward her, she suddenly stood up.

"Is it okay if I use the bathroom first?" she asked.

"Yes, of course."

"Good night, then," she said.

"Good night."

After she was done in the bathroom, he got ready for bed and then went into his room.

But he couldn't sleep. There were too many things on his mind.

He wondered again what Hannah would think of Madison, and he did what he had so often done following her death. He took her blanket, which he kept in his closet, and a blanket from his bed, and went in the living room. He carefully laid out her blanket on the couch where she had slept, and his on the other couch, and then he sat down and thought about Hannah.

It had always worked before, but this time the only feeling he had was that this was foolish. *What am I doing here? What if Madison comes out of her room and finds me like this? She'll think I'm crazy.*

He removed both blankets and took them into his room, folded her blanket up and placed it in his closet, laid his on his bed in case it got cold during the night, turned off the light, and went to bed. A few minutes later he was asleep.

◆　　◆　　◆

After breakfast the next day, Josh and Madison climbed the small, barely vegetated mountain near Muddy Gap. It was rumored that the Sundance Kid once holed up near the top of the mountain.

When they sat on a boulder to rest he noticed how comfortable they seemed to be sitting close to each other, with their shoulders touching. And as they started down the path, their hands were precariously close, so he reached for hers, and they held hands until they got back to the car.

After lunch, he asked if she would help him do some work at the station.

"Sure. What are we going to do?" she asked.

"Work on the flower garden."

"How fun."

"It was Hannah's idea to even have a garden. I like to take care of it. It's sort of my way of honoring her."

While they worked, Josh's dad could not resist the temptation to brag about improvements he'd made on the station. Through it all, Madison was an eager listener and asked lots of questions.

Josh and Madison weeded, picked dead blossoms from some of the flowers, cultivated the soil, and watered the patch. When they were done, they both agreed it looked much better.

"You two need to go back to the house and take a nap," his dad said. "At least that's what I do when I'm going to work late at night."

They ended up sitting in the shade of the house, drinking lemonade and talking, but neither was sleepy enough to take a nap.

After dinner, they watched a movie, and at eight o'clock they drove to the station.

His dad went through in detail all the things she would need to remember if she were a new employee. "Dad, I'll be here with her. She doesn't have to know everything. It'll be fine."

"This is a lot more complicated than it looks, believe me."

"I'm sure it is," Madison said. "It would take me a long time before I'd ever learn to do all the things you do here every day."

"Well, you'd do it, though. I'm sure of that. Oh, by the way, I got a big surprise for you both, but it's got to wait until tomorrow before I tell you about it."

"I love surprises," Madison said.

"Well, that's great. Me, too. See you guys in the morning." With that, his dad left.

Madison and Josh kept busy with customers until about ten-thirty, and then business dropped off.

To take advantage of a cool breeze, they sat on a couple of stools just outside the station.

At eleven-thirty, Josh turned off the sign and the outside lights. It took ten minutes to fill out the deposit slip, and then they drove to the bank and dropped it in the night depository.

They were on their way home when he turned to her. "Would you mind going back to the station with me for a few minutes?" he asked.

"Did you forget something?"

"No. I just want to tell you something."

He parked the car and led her into the station, and then with only the lights from the pop machine illuminating the room, he closed the door.

"You're not going to try something funny, are you?" Madison teased.

"No," he laughed. "You're safe with me."

Josh's dad had kept two of the old, vinyl-covered chairs from Grandpa's original station, but they had been reupholstered. Josh and Madison sat on them as he continued.

"Sometimes Hannah and I would lock up, but we wouldn't go home. We'd stay here and talk."

"What would you talk about?"

"Lots of things. How much we didn't like living here. How hard it was having our home turned into a hospital, how nobody paid any attention to us at school. Our folks were so busy taking care of my grandfather. We talked about a lot of things."

Madison was listening, but when she didn't say anything, Josh continued.

"I grew up being made fun of because of stuttering, so even after I grew out of it, I never wanted to say anything. At night Hannah would bug me into giving talks for her." He laughed. "It sounds weird, but she would tell me I had a great future and that I needed to quit feeling sorry for myself and get off my rear and do something with my life. Even after she died, she was the one who got me to go on a mission because of the things she used to tell me."

Josh paused for a moment, then said, "There's something else I need to tell you. In a way, I feel responsible for her death."

"Why would you feel that?"

He told her about Billy and then added, "If I hadn't let him take her for a ride, she would still be alive today."

She reached for Josh's hand and said, "Things happen, Josh, things we have no control over. That was one of those things."

"I'd like to believe that, and one thing that makes me think so is that she turned into such a good girl. I've wondered if she didn't know she wasn't going to live all that long."

They sat in the dark and watched the occasional car and big semi-trucks as they moved silently along the Interstate.

After a while, Madison said, "Growing up wasn't easy for me, either.

For most of high school I had no real friends. There were no other LDS kids in my school. Everyone partied on the weekends. I was overweight and overlooked."

"We have a lot in common then. After we moved here, I didn't have any friends either."

"After my summer makeover experience, though, I became popular. Guys thought I was, well, hot, and I started dating the quarterback of the football team. I sort of lost my bearings for a while. One time at a party he tried to talk me into sleeping with him, but I wouldn't go for that, so I left the party. He turned his attention to a friend of mine, her name is Emma Jean. The next day at school, he made up stories that she'd done some things with him that are really bad. It devastated her."

She told him about Toby bringing a gun to school and trying to force Kenny into admitting the stories about his sister weren't true.

"It turned out all right, except Toby spent some time in juvenile detention. After that I decided I didn't want to be popular anymore. I ate lunch with Emma Jean from then on. What was really neat was that after a while she and her mother ended up taking the missionary discussions and were baptized. That's when I decided I wanted to serve a mission."

Their conversation drifted to the future.

"What are your plans?" she asked.

"I need to work here until I save enough for school."

"How long will that take?" she asked.

"Well, at least a year. Do you want to know what worries me? That I'll never leave here."

"How do you feel about that?" she asked.

"Well, this is a steady income." He sighed. "The thing is, I've never been to college. I have no idea how I'd do."

"You'd do fine."

"I just don't feel like I'm college material."

She shook her head. "How are you going to find out unless you try?"

He shrugged. "I don't know."

She sat forward on her chair and turned to face him. "Josh, do you want to know what I see when I look at you? I see someone who Heavenly Father loves. There's something about you. I can't put my finger on it, but it's there. You're someone who God wants to be an example to others. I don't see how you can do that unless you get some schooling or training of some kind."

He shook his head. "I wish I felt that way. Maybe it's because I stuttered when I was growing up, and people my age made fun of me, but it's hard for me to see myself being much good to anyone."

"But you were a strong leader on your mission."

"That was because Heavenly Father helped me. When I was a zone leader, before every talk, I would go to some place where I could be alone and ask Father in Heaven to please help me. I would always say, 'I can't do this without you.'"

"And Heavenly Father *did* help you, didn't he?"

"Yes, every time." He sighed. "But I'm not on a mission now. I'm on my own." He stood up and walked over to the cooler. "You want something to drink?"

"Just water."

"Okay." He opened the case and took out a couple of bottles of water and brought them back to where they were seated. He twisted the cap on one and handed it to Madison, then sat back down.

"If you could pick one scripture that means a lot to you, what would it be?" he asked.

"Alma 32. Where Alma is preaching the gospel to a group of poor people. When they ask him what they should do, since they aren't even allowed to worship in the synagogues, he teaches them about faith and assures them they are important to God. I love him for doing that. In high school I had my fill of popular people who treated everyone else like they were worthless. That's why I majored in social work; that's why I went on a mission."

"Good scripture," he said. "That is one of my favorite chapters in the Book of Mormon, too."

"What would you pick?" she asked.

He cleared his throat. "Alma 26, verses 11 and 12." He quoted it from memory. "'I do not boast in my own strength, nor in my own wisdom; but behold, my joy is full, yea, my heart is brim with joy, and I will rejoice in my God. Yea, I know that I am nothing; as to my strength I am weak; therefore I will not boast of myself, but I will boast of my God, for in his strength I can do all things.'"

"That's the way you were on your mission, isn't it? You never boasted of your own strength."

"There's not much there to boast of." He sighed. "And now I'm off my mission and left on my own."

"I think Heavenly Father will always want to help you."

"You do?"

"Josh, listen to me. You can do anything you set your mind to do."

Josh's mouth dropped open and he stared at her.

"What?" she asked.

"That's just what Hannah used to say to me."

"I know," she said.

"How do you know?"

"It's like she's here with us," she said.

He stood up and began pacing the floor. "No, she can't be here! If she was, don't you think I'd know it?" Suddenly he felt embarrassed and sat down. "Sorry. You probably think I'm crazy."

"No, not at all. I know you loved your sister. And I think that's great."

"Hannah helped me so much," he said. "She believed in me. I don't know why, but she did."

"I believe in you, too, Josh."

"How can you say that? With your college degree, your job, and parents who gave you every opportunity when you were growing up, how can you say you believe in me? Look around you. This is my life."

"You don't have to do this your whole life. You can go to college just like everybody else does. Can't you? You're not stuck here, are you?"

"Not really."

It was late so they got into the Buick and started home. "You're probably sorry you even came here now, aren't you?" he asked.

"I came here to get to know you better. I think we're accomplishing that, don't you?"

"Maybe so."

A short time later they pulled in front of the house. "I can't understand why someone like you would have anything to do with me," he said. "You are so beautiful. And I know you probably don't appreciate me saying that, but sometimes I look at you, and I wish I could stop time so I could spend the rest of my life looking at that one picture. And just that would be enough to last me my whole life. It's not just because of some dumb makeover either. It's who you are. You're beautiful because you're a good person. You care about others. You radiate the gospel. You look for the good in everyone you meet."

"Thank you. Can I tell you what I see when I look at you?"

"I guess so."

"In high school, I went with a guy who was conceited, self-centered, and egotistical. He was willing to destroy others just to make himself look good. After high school he went on to become a national football celebrity. His junior year he was runner-up for the Heisman Trophy. And now he's on an NFL team as a back-up quarterback. All he'll ever think about is himself—his career, his standing among other quarterbacks. I think he's on his second marriage now. He likes tall, gorgeous Hollywood types."

Josh wasn't sure where she was going with this.

She reached for his hand. "And then there's you. The first time I saw you was at a zone conference. You'd given a talk, and it was a good talk, but it wasn't very long. And instead of making yourself look good, you talked about other missionaries and the good things they had recently done. Not a word about yourself, even though before you'd been called to be a zone leader, you'd led the mission in baptisms two months in a row. And then after the meeting, while everyone else was in a hurry to get in line for food, there you were, sitting with a new elder, someone who was having a tough time. I watched you. You let him talk, and you weren't in any hurry, and I stood in line with my companion and noticed how after a while he started to smile, and it was like you'd given him enough hope to keep going. That's what I knew about you before we'd even met. That was the day you became one of my heroes."

"I didn't think anyone noticed."

"No, of course not. You never think anyone notices you, but how can we help it? You're a disciple of Jesus Christ. That's who you are. You can't hide it."

"That's what I want to be," he said. "Well, it's getting late," he said, glancing at his watch.

He went around the car and opened the door for her.

A minute later, as they stood next to each other on the porch, she suddenly got a big grin on her face. "My, gosh! Is that music I hear?"

He chuckled. "Yes, definitely! I hear it too. It's dance music."

He held her in his arms.

She sighed. "That does feel good."

"I know. It really does."

She spoke softly. "I don't know how this is going to work out, you know . . . about us, but one thing you should know, I have always respected and admired you for the kind of person you are."

"Thank you. I feel the same way about you."

They said goodnight at the door. "I'll be in, in a minute," he said. "If you want to get ready for bed first."

"Thanks. I'll see you in the morning."

He opened the door for her and then returned to the Buick and listened to the radio and thought about what Madison had said. A few minutes later he saw the bathroom light go off, and he went inside and got ready for bed.

Josh was hoping to sleep in late, but his dad woke him up at six the next morning.

"Josh, get up. I've got a big surprise for you and Madison today! But we have to get going so I can get back and open up the station. Go see if you can wake Madison up. I'd kind of like to leave in about ten minutes."

Fifteen minutes later, Josh and Madison, just barely awake, slipped into the rear seat of his dad's pickup.

"Where are we going?" Josh asked.

"It's a big surprise!" his dad said, excitedly.

Josh and Madison leaned against each other and drifted in and out of sleep. Josh's dad talked non-stop the entire time.

After an hour and a half, they pulled into a small town. "Well, here we are!"

"Where are we?" Josh asked.

"Edgemont, South Dakota. You know why they call it Edgemont? Because it's at the edge of the Black Hills. Edge of the mountain. Edgemont. Get it? Actually, this road we're on is one of the main ways to get into the Black Hills. You want to know how many people go to the Black Hills every year? A lot, believe me. I bet it's over a million."

They pulled into a vacant, weed-strewn lot near the edge of town. "What do you two think about this, huh?"

"About what?" Josh asked.

"Wouldn't this be a great location for a gas station and convenience store?"

"Yeah, I guess so," Josh said.

"It's only about twenty miles to Highway 85, so with a big sign at the junction, you could get traffic from both highways."

"You're thinking about building another station?" Madison asked.

"That's right, but, and here's the surprise. Josh, this could be your station! It would give you and Madison a steady income, so you could get married, and settle down right here in Edgemont. It's like a dream come true, right?"

Madison had a deer-in-the-headlights look in her eyes. "Oh," she said.

"See that ridge up there! We could put up, like a fifty-foot-tall sign that could be seen for miles. And since there's no real place to eat in town, we could throw in a Subway sandwich shop, so it'd be a one-stop shop for the million or so tourists that are on this road every year."

"There are other ways to get into the Black Hills, though, aren't there?" Madison asked. "So probably not every tourist goes through Edgemont."

"Well, that's probably true, but I bet most of them do. I mean, if you just look at the road. It's not in that good of shape, so it must get a lot of traffic, right?" Josh's dad said.

Madison looked at Josh as though she wanted him to explain the logic behind his dad's statement, but Josh could only shrug his shoulders.

"Well, let's get out and look around!" his dad said.

While Josh and Madison stood there politely, his dad enthusiastically laid out the details of the station. After ten minutes, he turned to Madison. "Can you make cinnamon rolls?"

"What? Uh, no, not really. I made a pie once, though."

"Well, no matter. Think about this. You could bake maybe two or three dozen cinnamon rolls every morning and pretty much just name your price. I bet you could sell 'em all every day. So what I'm saying is, this could be a little extra income for you. You know, to put up drapes or whatever for your home."

"I never would have thought of that idea," she said quietly.

"Hey, that's why I'm here. You know what? The good thing about this deal is that you're not just buying a lot. It's everything you see that's within the fences. That's over half an acre. See over there by that tree? You two could build a nice home there. It'd work out real good. Of course, I know that sometimes it takes forever to get anything built, especially out here, so far from any big town, but another thing you might consider buying a manufactured home. It's like a trailer, you know, but it's big and comes in two halves, so you just join the two halves, and you got your-self a real nice place. So there's a lot to think about." He looked at his watch. "Well, I know you two would like to walk around the place, but the thing is, I got to get back to open up the station."

His dad took two steps toward the pickup and then turned back to face them. "Oh, by the way, I told the owner of this property I'd give him an answer, one way or the other, by tonight at five. So if you two want to put your heads together and tell me what you think, well, we'll get this thing finalized and on its way!"

On the drive back to Muddy Gap, Madison sat as far away as she could from Josh. She turned her back to him, curled up, and pretended to sleep.

A hour and a half later, Josh's dad dropped them off at home and then took off to open up the station. As they watched him drive off, Madison slowly raised her hand to her forehead.

"You okay?" Josh asked.

"Just a headache, that's all."

"You want some aspirin?"

"I don't know. I can't decide if I even want to go inside."

"Why wouldn't you want to go inside?"

"You think your mom might have some practical hints about nursing my first baby?"

"We can hike up the mountain again," Josh offered.

"Yeah, whatever."

A few minutes later they parked his car and started up the trail, this time walking very slowly.

"Look, I didn't know my dad was going to do this," Josh said.

"I know that, but do I really look like someone who would enjoy making cinnamon rolls every morning for truckers and tourists?"

"Not really."

"This is like a bad dream. Stuck in Edgemont forever. But it's no problem for you, right? Because if you can be happy in Muddy Gap, Wyoming, you can pretty much be happy anywhere."

"You know what? I think sarcasm is lost on me. Why don't you just tell me what you're thinking."

"Does your dad know that I haven't even decided if I want to marry you? He makes it sound like a done deal. I do get a choice in this, right?"

"My dad's like that. He's very enthusiastic."

She looked at her watch. "My plane leaves in a few hours. I wouldn't say we were any closer to deciding to get married than we were before I came. If anything, I might be further away from that."

"That's okay. We're in no hurry."

"Really? Then why does your dad need a decision by five o'clock today? And if I drag my feet, will you go ahead anyway with the Edgemont deal? You might as well. You don't actually need me for this. I'm sure you can find some local girl, just out of high school, who'd love to marry you and make cinnamon rolls every morning, and work alongside you every day, pumping gas and doing lube jobs."

"You're getting clever on me again. Just say what you think."

"I'm thinking, what is going on here? This whole thing seems more like a business deal than two people trying to decide if they love each other enough to get married. I can't do this, Josh! At least not this way. I'm not ready to make any kind of decision today."

"That's okay. I'll tell my dad we need some more time."

"Time? It's way more than time." She turned to face him. "I want to fall in love with the guy I marry. Is that asking too much? I want to be friends first and then gradually fall in love. I want to see him every day, not just one weekend a month. That's what I want. But that's not what you want, is it? You want to get this taken care of as fast as possible. Why? So you can make your mom and dad happy? But what about you? Don't you have any hopes or dreams about what you want to do with your life?"

"That will come in time, but, until then, what would be wrong for us to help my dad out in Edgemont?"

"Josh, the truth is I'm not going to fit in very well with your dad's idea of the kind of wife you need."

"Look, go easy on my dad, okay? I know that it's easy to find fault with him. I used to do that, too. But now I feel different. When we moved here, we had nothing. He's worked hard to make the station profitable. And now he's a successful businessman, and that's not easy to do. So if you're expecting me to bad-mouth him, or just walk away from how he makes his living, I can't do it."

"I wasn't being critical of your dad. But, at the same time, I will not let him or you or anybody else pressure me into deciding to get married when I'm not ready. And, believe me, I am definitely not ready to marry you."

They continued in silence to the top of the mountain. She left him and moved to the edge of a cliff and looked out at the rolling hills that seemed to go on forever.

She turned to face him. "It must be so easy for you. You feel like God wants you to marry me, so what else do you need? You were probably ready the day we left the mission. If it'd been up to you, we'd have been married a week later, right? How convenient. It saves the trouble of actually getting to know each other."

Josh shook his head. "It's not like that." He walked toward her but stopped a couple of feet from her. "Let me tell you something. If that hadn't happened when I gave you a blessing, I would never have contacted you because you're more wonderful than anyone I could dare hope for."

She smiled faintly. "If you think I'm wonderful, that's just another indication of how little we know each other."

"It's obvious to anyone how amazing you are."

"Thanks, I guess." She sighed. "Can you take me to the airport now? I might be able to get an earlier flight."

"Sure. If that's what you want."

She paused and with a soft voice said, "I'm embarrassed to say this, but before I leave, could you hold me in your arms one last time?"

"Yes."

She broke into tears as they held each other close.

"I'm so sorry," she said through her tears.

"Me, too," he said, stroking her hair.

After returning to the house and picking up her things and thanking Josh's mom for her hospitality, they took off for the airport in Rapid City.

Madison spent most of the time in the car on her cell phone, trying to arrange an earlier flight. By the time they arrived at the airport, it was only twenty minutes until the earlier flight departed.

"You can just drop me off at the curb," she said.

"Are you sure?"

"Yes."

He stopped the car and got out to get her luggage from the back. "Well, I guess this is it."

She leaned into him, kissed him on the cheek, and backed away. "Thank you very much. Call me some time."

"Right."

She took a deep breath, turned, and walked quickly into the terminal.

It's over, Josh thought.

chapter

twelve

f orget about the property at Edgemont, at least as far as Madison and I are concerned," Josh said when he showed up for his shift at the station after dropping Madison off at the airport.

"Why's that?" his dad asked.

"She doesn't want any part of me, or the way we live here."

"Did she say that?" his dad asked.

"Yeah, pretty much."

"What else did she say?"

Josh shrugged. "Who ever understands what a woman says?"

His dad shook his head. "I can't argue with you on that one."

"Last night I noticed we were running low on 10–30 oil," Josh said. "Could you order some tomorrow?"

"Sure. Let me write that down," his dad said, pulling out a pad he kept in his pocket. "Too bad about Madison. She's a really nice girl."

"Yeah, she is."

"So what are you going to do, just give up?"

"I don't see what else I can do."

"Well, maybe so, but let me tell you something. If there's anything I've learned since coming here, it's to never give up on your dreams. Are you ever going to contact her again?"

"No."

"See, I think that's a mistake. Your mom turned me down three times before she finally agreed to marry me."

Josh was tired of getting advice from his dad about this. "Dad, you've put in a long day. Why don't you go home? We'll talk about this later. I'll take over here."

"The least you can do is call her once in awhile, just to see how she's doing. That's what a friend would do. The least you can do is be her friend."

"I'll think about it, okay?"

"Just remember this. It's not the size of the dog in the fight. It's the size of the fight in the dog." He paused. "What that means is never give up."

"I know that, Dad."

"Your mom will really be disappointed."

"I suppose she will."

"But that's life, right? Well, I'll be going now."

Josh needed something to keep his mind off Madison, so when there weren't any customers, he worked hard, putting tools back where they belonged and wiping up months of accumulated gunk from under the lift. But by eleven o'clock that night, there wasn't anything else to do.

It was at times like this, when he was discouraged, that he missed Hannah the most. And so, after closing up for the night, he stayed in the waiting room with the lights out. "Hannah, can you hear me?"

He felt ashamed to be doing this again. "Look, I know this is crazy, okay? But who else am I going to talk to when I feel like this?"

No answer.

"Fine, then, don't help me, see if I care! I can get along without Madison, and I can get along without you. I don't need anybody." He slammed the door, locked it, hurried to his car, and drove away.

◆　　◆　　◆

Two days after Madison arrived back in Duluth, her mom said to her, "Explain to me again why you broke up with Josh?"

Madison sighed. It wasn't something she wanted to go over again. "Well, first of all, we were never really *going* together. He visited here, and I went there, but that's it. It's no big deal."

"He seemed like such a nice young man."

"I suppose he is, but so what? If he thinks I'm going to just drop everything, marry him, and spend the rest of my life getting up early to make cinnamon rolls for bloated, red-neck customers at some stupid gas station in the middle of nowhere, then he's dead wrong! I have a life here. I have friends. I have a job I like. I'm not willing to give up any of that for some Wyoming cowboy."

"You would be willing to give those things up if you loved him."

"Well, yes, that's right, Mother, I would. Thanks for bringing that up. Another excellent point. The fact is I *don't* love him. In fact, I hardly even know him, and I don't see how that is ever going to change with us seeing each other every six months or so. And let me add, he doesn't love me, either. Oh, sure, he feels some sort of obligation to get married in the temple to somebody. But other than me being temple worthy, I think anybody would do. If he could go to Home Depot and pick himself up a wife, he'd do it. Especially if he could get a good deal. And while he was there, he might get himself a snowblower, too. I would just hope that his new bride and the snowblower wouldn't both end up in the back of his pickup on the way home."

Madison's mom was looking at her skeptically.

"What?" Madison demanded.

After a long pause, her mom said, "You seem to have strong feelings about this."

"Strong feelings? Why, yes, I do! When I was with him in Wyoming it felt like my whole identity was being sucked out of me, and that if I stayed there any longer, I was going to turn into a cinnamon roll-making, wife-robot, popping out one kid after another, making little knickknacks for the tourists and thinking my life was heaven if I could even go shopping once a month."

"I've never seen you so angry over a boy," her mom observed.

"He is not a boy! Although I guess I should thank you for reminding me that he is actually two years younger than me! And that, yes, I do not have any other prospects! And, yes, the biological clock is ticking! I am quite aware of that, Mother! And let me point out that I am also aware that you desperately want grandchildren from me and whatever *boy*, as you call it, I choose to end up with. But let me assure you that that person is not Josh. So let's both just move on with our life, shall we?"

"Madison, I'm your mother."

"I know that."

"I love you with all my heart. More than anything, I want you to be happy."

Madison let out a big sigh and closed her eyes. After she gained a little control, she said, "You're right. I'm sorry for being such a witch. Sorry."

"Let me ask you one more question, and then I'll let it go. What if for some reason Heavenly Father would be pleased if you and Josh got married?"

Madison lowered her head, considering the question for a long time, then quietly said, "Then, if that were the case, I would, once again, be a big disappointment to Father in Heaven. I can't do this out of faith, Mom. I just can't. Sometimes I wish I could, but I can't. I wouldn't be able to respect myself if I just gave in, married the boy, and moved to Wyoming for the rest of my life."

Her mom patted her on the shoulder. "It's okay. Things will work out."

"Yes, they will, but without Josh. I'll tell you what, Mom, if it'll make you feel any better, I'll go online and see what's available for someone like me. For you I will shop for a husband. Now are you happy?"

Her mother sighed and shook her head.

◆　◆　◆

A week later, when Josh showed up to work that night, his dad asked him to help fix a leak in the men's restroom. As far as Josh could tell, his only function was to hand tools to his dad, who was lying on the floor underneath the sink, with his legs sticking out the door.

"What are your plans, Josh?"

"You mean for tonight? I thought I'd hose out the shop."

"I'm not talking about tonight. I'm talking about your life."

"I haven't thought about it much."

"See, that's a mistake. You want to know how I know it's a mistake? Because that's what I did. I expect more from you than that."

"Things turned out okay for you."

"We're not talking about me. Oh, I need a Phillips screwdriver."

Josh handed him the screwdriver.

"Okay, let's try this," his dad said. "Suppose we had the ultimate satellite system in our home. Two hundred channels. You can watch anything you want. What kind of program would you choose?"

"Let me think about it."

"Sure, take your time. Stupid rusted piece of junk! While you're thinking, how about you go into the shop and get me some WD-40?"

Josh ran the errand and returned a few minutes later.

"Okay, I decided what I'd watch if we had satellite," Josh said. "I like programs where they show how machinery works. Like sometimes when I'm fixing something, I start to think about who it was that designed this. I mean, it must be satisfying to start from scratch with an idea and keep working on it until someday you end up with something you can hold in your hand, and it does everything you wanted it to. That's got to be a great feeling, you know what I'm saying?"

His dad smiled. "More often than not, when I'm working on an engine, I end up thinking *What idiot designed this pile of junk?* But I guess it's the same thing. Well, that's great. You'd be good at that."

"I don't even know what a person would study for that kind of a job."

"I don't, either, but I bet you could find that out. You're such a whiz with that online stuff you do."

"I'll look into it," Josh said.

"That's all I need to know. There's something else. Right after

217

Hannah died, I borrowed some money from you. Well, I'm in a position to pay you back."

"You don't need to, Dad. You helped me on my mission."

"No, this is different. The money's there. In fact, it's been earning interest for a long time. I didn't tell you about it before because I was afraid you'd go buy a new pickup with it. You can do whatever you want with it, but I'd be pleased if it went into you getting a college education. That's what I never had."

"I'll think about it."

"You can do anything you set your mind to, Josh."

He shook his head and sighed. "Anytime anyone says that to me, I think about Hannah because she always used to say that to me when we were working here nights." He sighed. "I miss her so much, Dad, even now."

"Me, too, Josh. Not a day goes by when I'm not thinking about her. I'd give anything to have her back with us again. But, one thing for sure, we'll see her again someday."

"I know."

"Until then, we just have to do the best we can."

"Yeah, that's right."

His dad squirmed out from under the sink and slowly got to his feet. "Well, let's test it out, see if it's any better."

They turned on the water and waited. It wasn't leaking anymore.

◆　　◆　　◆

It was a Saturday night and Madison was home alone. Her folks had gone to the annual dinner-dance her dad's law firm sponsored every year.

Earlier in the week, anticipating being alone while her parents were at the party, Madison had tried to get some young adults from the stake to come over to watch movies, but, although several initially expressed interest, one by one for various reasons, they all bailed.

At seven-thirty, Madison sat down in front of the TV with a big bowl of popcorn and a pitcher of ice water. She finished one movie and was about to start another when she caught a glimpse of herself in the mirror. She looked the way someone would look if she had to schedule at-home activities to keep from being reminded she had no friends.

"I'm sick and tired of this. I'm going to do something about it." She walked to her dad's study, sat down at his desk, and soon was at an Internet site designed to help LDS singles find each other.

She paid for the premium membership, filled out her personality profile, did a search for males from ages 22 to 28, put in her zip code, and got ten profiles—four from Minneapolis; one from Green Bay, Wisconsin; one from Fargo, North Dakota; one from Winnipeg, Canada; two from Chicago, Illinois; and one from Saskatoon, Saskatchewan, Canada. After taking a picture of herself with her digital camera and transferring it to the Web site, she sent an e-mail to them all, and then returned to the living room to watch another movie.

By the time the movie was done, she had received a reply from Viper T. Cranborough. It read: "Madison, you're such a hottie! Believe me, I know. Every night after work I spend a few minutes trying to see what's available. You're the best! As for me, well, I'm a miner. I work at the potash mine at Esterhazy. In case you don't know it, potash is used for fertilizer. So the next time you work on your plants, think of me. Ha! Come visit me and I'll give you a free tour of the mine. I don't travel much, but I am planning on coming to the states in about ten months. But if you want to come before then, hey, I say full speed ahead! You can stay with my mom and three crazy sisters. None of them are LDS, but I think they wouldn't give you a bad time, like they do me, especially if they knew we were thinking about getting married. So let's stay in contact, whataya say?"

Nearly gagging, Madison shut down the computer and began pacing the floor. "A potash miner from Saskatchewan? Is that the best I can do? My gosh, this guy makes being married to Josh look good!"

In her room a few minutes later, she turned off the lights, opened her blinds, and sat on a chair, looking out the window.

In the darkness, in the privacy of her room, with her parents not around to see, she began to cry.

Twenty minutes later, she heard the garage door go up, and soon after, heard the door from the garage into the house open. Madison stood up and dried her eyes and got into bed.

◆　　◆　　◆

In August, Josh signed up for an online calculus class. At first he was intimidated, but he forced himself to work on it an hour a day. After submitting a few lessons, he found he enjoyed the time he spent.

A month later, Josh had some news for his dad. "I've decided I want to be an engineer and work for an automobile manufacturing company."

"Good for you! Who knows, in a few years I might be fixing something you designed!"

Josh smiled. "If I design it, it won't need fixing."

His dad laughed. "I guess we'll see about that, won't we?"

A few days later he mentioned to his mom how well he was doing in his online calculus class. He was not at all prepared for her reaction.

"You spend a lot of time on that math course, don't you? How much do you spend talking to Madison?"

"We e-mail each other once a week."

"If it's only once a week, why bother?"

"We're both busy."

"You talked to her about marrying you, but why should she marry someone who shows no interest in her life? How is she going to know you care about her if you don't pay more attention to her?"

"We don't talk about getting married anymore."

"No, of course not. You pay more attention to math problems than you do her. To me, that's not right. And while we're on the subject, why are you still living here? Why aren't you living in Duluth?"

He was stunned. "I thought you liked me being here."

"I'm sure you've heard the General Authorities say the best thing they ever did was marrying their wife. So if the best thing that will happen to you will be getting married to a wonderful woman in the temple, don't you have a responsibility to pour some time and effort into that instead of into some dumb math course?"

"I can't win, can I? No matter what I do."

She put her hand on his arm. "Let me put it so you can understand. No matter what your dad may say, you've got to get out of this place. You've got to get away from the station. You've got to move on. You've got to grow up. You've got to put some time and money into that girl before she finds someone else and it's too late."

"All I came in here for was to tell you that I'm getting an A in my math class."

"That's good, but in ten years how much difference is that going to make?"

Josh was relieved to go back to work that night where he was his own boss.

But, even so, he began to think about what his mom had said.

◆   ◆   ◆

A week later, on a Sunday afternoon, while Madison was taking a nap, she heard the phone ring. Since the phone was seldom for her, she let her mom answer it.

Ten minutes later, her mom knocked on her door.

"Yes?"

Her mom opened the door. "It's Josh."

"Was he the one who called a few minutes ago?"

"Yes. We've been talking. We had a wonderful conversation."

Her mom handed her the phone. "Ask him about his calculus class," she whispered.

Josh and Madison talked for an hour.

Before they hung up, Josh asked, "Is it okay if I call you tomorrow night?"

"I guess, if you want."

"I do."

"Why?"

"So we can get to know each other better."

"Oh, okay."

They talked every night after that but never about their relationship or future. That subject was off limits.

◆   ◆   ◆

December 28

At work that night there were very few customers at the station, and the lull gave Josh some time to think.

By the time he closed up, he had decided what he needed to do.

On the way home, he drove to the cemetery where Hannah was buried.

It was snowing, and the wind was blowing. He pulled his parka hood over his head, zipped up, and made his way through the drifts to Hannah's gravestone. Then to get out of the wind he sat down with his back resting against the granite grave marker.

"Hannah, I need to talk to you."

He looked around to make sure nobody was watching him. Then he laughed. In the cold and dark, there was little chance of that.

"You know, having you and Grandpa die so close together was hard on me, and I guess I'm still trying to make sense out of it, but it did teach me one thing. None of us knows how much time we have, so we all have to live the best way we can. And, also, if I want to be happy, then I can't just sit around and wait for happiness to come to me. I need to create my own happiness by moving toward those things that will make me happy."

He turned and began to slowly trace along each letter of her name with his gloved finger.

"I've decided I want to be an engineer and design cars."

He sighed. "The second thing I've decided is that I'm going to move to Duluth, Minnesota, and start college there. And that brings me to the third thing I've decided, and that is that being with Madison is something I need to do. I know there's no guarantee she'll want me, but I need to move toward what I believe will make me happy. Well, that means I'm leaving Wyoming, maybe for good. I just thought you ought to know."

He sighed. "Hannah, I still love you, but the thing is, I can't talk to you anymore. It was okay for me to do that in the beginning, right after you died, but now, the thing is, I need to be talking to Heavenly Father to get the help I need. So that's what I'm going to do from now on. I might ask Him to pass on a message or two to you, but I'm not going to be talking to you. But I want you to know that I love you and I always will, and I'm grateful for what you taught me. You're the best sister a guy could ever have."

He stood up, put his gloved fingers to his lips, and touched the headstone. "I'll see you around, okay? Take care."

He hurried through the blowing snow back to his car.

◆　　◆　　◆

December 29

At two-thirty in the morning, Andrew Forsgren woke up after hearing a crashing noise downstairs. He got out of bed and slowly went down the stairs to check it out.

As soon as he stepped into the hall, he smelled smoke. From the top of the stairs, he could tell there was a light on in the kitchen. Cautiously, he made his way down the stairs, and as he entered the kitchen, he saw Madison with her back to him, scraping at some darkened blobs on a cookie sheet.

"Madison, what are you doing?"

She turned to him and glared. "What does it look like I'm doing? I'm burning cinnamon rolls. Is there a law against that, Counselor?"

With a great deal of effort she managed to pry one of the burnt cinnamon rolls loose.

"What does this mean?" her dad asked.

She scraped at another stuck roll with her spatula. "It means I give up! That's what it means."

"Don't be so hard on yourself. Not everyone is good at making cinnamon rolls."

She dropped her hands to her side and began to cry. "That's not what I'm giving up!"

"What are you giving up?"

She began banging the tray on the rim of the trash can to try to knock some of the burned rolls off.

"I'm giving up my season ticket to the symphony!" She grabbed a roll and pried it off the tray and threw it into the trash can.

"I'm giving up my aerobics class!" Another cinnamon roll ended up in the garbage.

"I'm giving up my bedroom, my wireless connection, my calling as a young single adult representative." Three more cinnamon rolls ended up in the can.

"Do you know why? Because I'm moving to Wyoming, that's why. Oh, yes, that's what I'm going to do! Stupid? Yes. Illogical? Of course. Demeaning to me as a woman? Definitely! I am going to get a dead-end job in a dead-end town in Wyoming! I'm giving up my career, my education, my self-respect, my freedom, and for what?"

"For Josh?"

"Yes, that's right, for Josh! For some guy two years younger than me who's never been to college and who has no goals except to sell more hubcaps."

"So . . . you're going to move to Wyoming?"

"That's right! At least that's what I think now, but you know what? Come morning, maybe my sanity will return, and I'll change my mind.

So if he calls, which he won't, you are not to tell him anything because I will change my mind if I ever become rational again! Do you understand me?"

Her dad sighed and looked at the clock on the wall. "So, you're okay, then, right?"

Madison rolled her eyes. "Never better, Dad. Go back to sleep. I'm sure you have a busy day tomorrow."

That made him feel guilty. "It's okay. I can stay up. If you want, I can even help you burn the rolls."

She smiled tiredly and went to him and put her arms around his neck and laid her head on his shoulder. "No, that's okay, I'm okay. You go back to bed. I just needed to vent, that's all."

◆　　◆　　◆

December 31

After staying the night in a motel at Albert Lea, Minnesota, Josh woke up at six in the morning, showered, took advantage of the complimentary continental breakfast, and piled into his car.

As soon as he pulled out onto the snow-packed highway, he used his cell phone to call Madison's home phone.

Madison's mom answered it. Once she realized it was Josh, she said, "Hold on, I'll get Madison. She's still asleep."

"No, wait! Actually, I wanted to talk to you. I'm on my way to Duluth. Do you know if Madison has any plans for New Year's Eve?"

"Not that she's mentioned to me."

"Okay, that's good. I should be there by noon. Don't tell her I'm coming, though, okay? I want it to be a surprise."

"Will you stay with us while you're here?"

"If that's all right with you and your husband."

"We'd love to have you."

"Thanks. I'll tell you more when I get there."

At eleven that morning, Madison was still sleeping. Because she didn't have to go to work, she'd stayed up late the night before on a chat line, talking to Viper Cranborough from Saskatoon. He had explained in fascinating detail how to gut a deer. What was more alarming was that she'd found it somewhat interesting—in a perverse kind of way.

Her mom burst into the room and opened the plantation shutters. She seemed strangely happy. "Time to get up!"

"What time is it?"

"It's time to get up!"

"Why?"

"It just is. This is the last day of the year! No use wasting it. Oh, you will be taking a shower this morning, won't you?"

"What?"

"I just asked if you would be taking a shower."

"Why would you ask that? Is there some problem with my personal hygiene lately that has escaped my attention?"

"It's the last day of the year! Let's start it clean. That's all I'm saying."

"Okay, I'll take a shower! Anything else I need to do along those lines?"

"Well, whatever you usually do to get ready for church."

"Why?"

"Well, for one reason, there's the stake New Year's Eve dance tonight."

"Nobody my age is going to be there."

"You never know. What dress are you going to wear?"

"Mother! I don't even know if I'm going."

"This is New Year's Eve! You have to go! It's a tradition."

Her dad peeked in through the door. "Is she going to take a shower?"

"I believe she is."

Her dad smiled. "Good."

"Oh! Will you two please get out of my room so I can get ready?"

The first thing Madison did after her parents left the room was to smell one of her armpits. She couldn't detect anything out of the ordinary. But just to be safe she went to the linen closet and got a bar of her dad's Irish Spring soap for her shower.

After thinking about her folks' strange behavior, she could only come up with one answer. *It's senility. It's finally set in for both of them,* she thought.

By quarter to twelve that morning she finally made it into the kitchen.

"You're not going to eat now, are you?" her mom said.

"Yes, of course. I haven't eaten anything all day."

"Wait a while, give your stomach a chance to be completely empty," her dad suggested.

"What is going on here? I'm hungry and I want to eat."

Her dad leaned forward and sniffed. "What is that smell? Did you use my Irish Spring soap for your shower?" he asked.

"Yes, why?"

"You don't smell feminine," he said. "Go take another shower."

"I will not take another shower! I will eat! And I will not go to the dance! There, I think that pretty much covers all the vital issues of the day. Now if you'll excuse me." She approached the refrigerator.

"Don't open the fridge!" her dad called out, holding up a hand.

"What is *wrong* with you two?" Madison demanded.

Madison opened the refrigerator door. There, on a tray, were crackers, a pitcher of tomato juice, and some cheese, all from France.

And then the doorbell rang.

"It's for you," her dad said.

As Madison headed for the front door, she called back to them, "Even if I don't move to Wyoming, I'm still getting my own apartment!"

She opened the door, and there stood Josh. Behind him in the driveway was his car.

"Happy New Year," he said with a tentative grin.

She couldn't help it. She started laughing. "Well, this explains why my mom and dad have been acting so weird. They knew you were coming, didn't they?"

"Yeah, I called this morning and told them, but I asked them to keep it a secret."

"I should have guessed when I saw the cheese and crackers in the fridge."

"French crackers?" he asked, grimacing.

"Yes, and French tomato juice. Let's go into the kitchen. I know my mom and dad are excited to have you here."

"Happy New Year, Josh!" her dad exclaimed. "Here, we know how much you like these," he said, pushing a plate of crackers and cheese and a tall glass of tomato juice toward him.

"Thank you very much, sir," Josh croaked, casting a dreaded eye on the size of the glass.

Madison's mom was beaming. "Hello, Josh," she said. "We're glad to see you again."

At Madison's mom's insistence, they spent the next couple of hours playing every family game they'd ever owned.

Then, after watching part of a football game with Madison's dad, Josh and Madison wandered into the living room and sat down together at the piano. They sang a few hymns before Josh noticed a book of Primary songs. He thumbed through it until he found "Jesus Wants Me for a Sunbeam."

"This has always been a favorite of mine," he said.

They sang it a couple of times.

"That's like us," he said.

"What?"

"'A sunbeam, a sunbeam, Jesus wants me for a sunbeam. A sunbeam, a sunbeam, I'll be a sunbeam for him.' Don't you see? We're two sunbeams for the price of one."

"I don't get it."

"You got a minute?" he asked.

"I've got plenty of minutes."

"I need to tell you a story."

"Is this a story about your sister?" she asked.

"Yeah, it is."

"I love Josh and Hannah stories."

Josh told the story about how Hannah had insisted they sing the Primary song for their grandfather.

"I'm not sure how I'm feeling about you, Josh, but Hannah is another story. I love her more all the time."

"I'm glad to hear that. She would have loved you."

At eight-thirty they left with her parents for the New Year's Eve dance at the stake center.

The music started at quarter to nine, but very few were even there. Josh and Madison didn't mind.

"Hey, we've got music," Madison said with a silly grin.

"Yes, we do." They began to dance close.

"You smell good," Josh said.

She smiled. "Do you think so? It's Irish Spring. My dad thinks I smell like a linebacker for the Green Bay Packers." She closed her eyes and rested her head on his shoulder.

"You still awake?" he asked a minute or two later.

"Sorry. I'd forgotten how good it feels to be in your arms. It's very nice."

"Good."

The song ended, and still holding hands, they strolled to the sidelines to sit down. "So what's going on in your life these days?" he asked.

"I know how to gut a deer," she said.

"Really?"

"If you think about it, it's really an art."

"You've been in contact with that guy from Saskatoon again, haven't you?"

"Yeah, Viper. He's a charmer, all right."

"I have a confession to make," he said. "I've never actually gutted a deer."

"I suspected as much," she said.

"I ran over a squirrel once, though. Does that count?"

She suppressed a smile. "No, sorry."

Just before twelve, they were all given noisemakers. "We need to decide if we're going to kiss at the stroke of midnight," Josh said.

"I don't know. What do you think?"

"Well, as you know, it's a tradition, and I for one believe in observing traditions," he said, grinning.

"Really? I wasn't aware of that."

"Oh, yes, kissing at midnight on New Year's Eve. Now *there's* a great tradition!"

"If it's only a tradition, then it probably wouldn't mean anything," she said, teasingly.

"Yeah, true, but you know what? It could be a lot of fun."

She playfully punched him. "You are such a guy."

"Ten . . . nine . . ."

"We very much need a decision here!" he called out.

"Eight . . ."

"I don't know! Don't rush me! I can't decide!"

"Seven . . ."

"Ask me how long I'm staying here," he said.

"Six . . . five."

"How long?"

"A long time. I've got my own apartment. I start at the U of M in January."

"Two . . . one . . . Happy New Year!"

As the band played and while some couples hugged and kissed, Madison stood there gaping at Josh, her mouth open and her eyes wide.

"You're moving here?" she shouted, over the noise of the crowd and the music.

"Right. I'm going to be majoring in mechanical engineering," he hollered back.

"There are other places you could study mechanical engineering. So why are you moving here?" Madison said, over the sound of the celebration.

"Hey! Why do you think? To be near you. Think about it. We'll see each other every day. We'll go dancing. We'll take long walks along the lake," Josh said loudly, just as the music ended.

Madison lowered her voice. "Long walks along Lake Superior in January? Are you crazy? Nobody around here does that."

He shrugged. "Whatever. But that's not all we'll do. We'll go to the symphony. We'll join the ward choir. And, if you really want to, we'll even gut a deer."

She looked thoughtful. "Forget the deer. I can't believe you'd move here for me. Does that mean you *like* me?"

He was grinning stupidly. "Oh, yeah. It definitely means that."

She was grinning, too. "Well, then, if that's the case, excuse me. I'll be right back."

She went to the stage and spoke to the man who had counted down the number of seconds to midnight. He smiled and picked up the mike as Madison took Josh's hand and escorted him onto the dance floor.

The man with the microphone made an announcement: "Brothers and sisters, it has been pointed out to me that we had our clocks all wrong and that we're just going to have to do this all over again. Well, mainly for Madison's sake, really. But let's start in, shall we? Ten . . ."

"You're under the gun here, Josh! You'd better kiss me, because everybody is watching!"

"Nine . . . eight . . . seven . . ."

He started to laugh.

"Close your mouth! There's not much time!"

"Four . . . three . . . two . . ."

As everyone shouted "Happy New Year!" and sounded their noise-makers again, Josh and Madison kissed for the very first time. But as it turned out, it wasn't the last.

Six months later, they were married in the St. Paul Minnesota Temple.